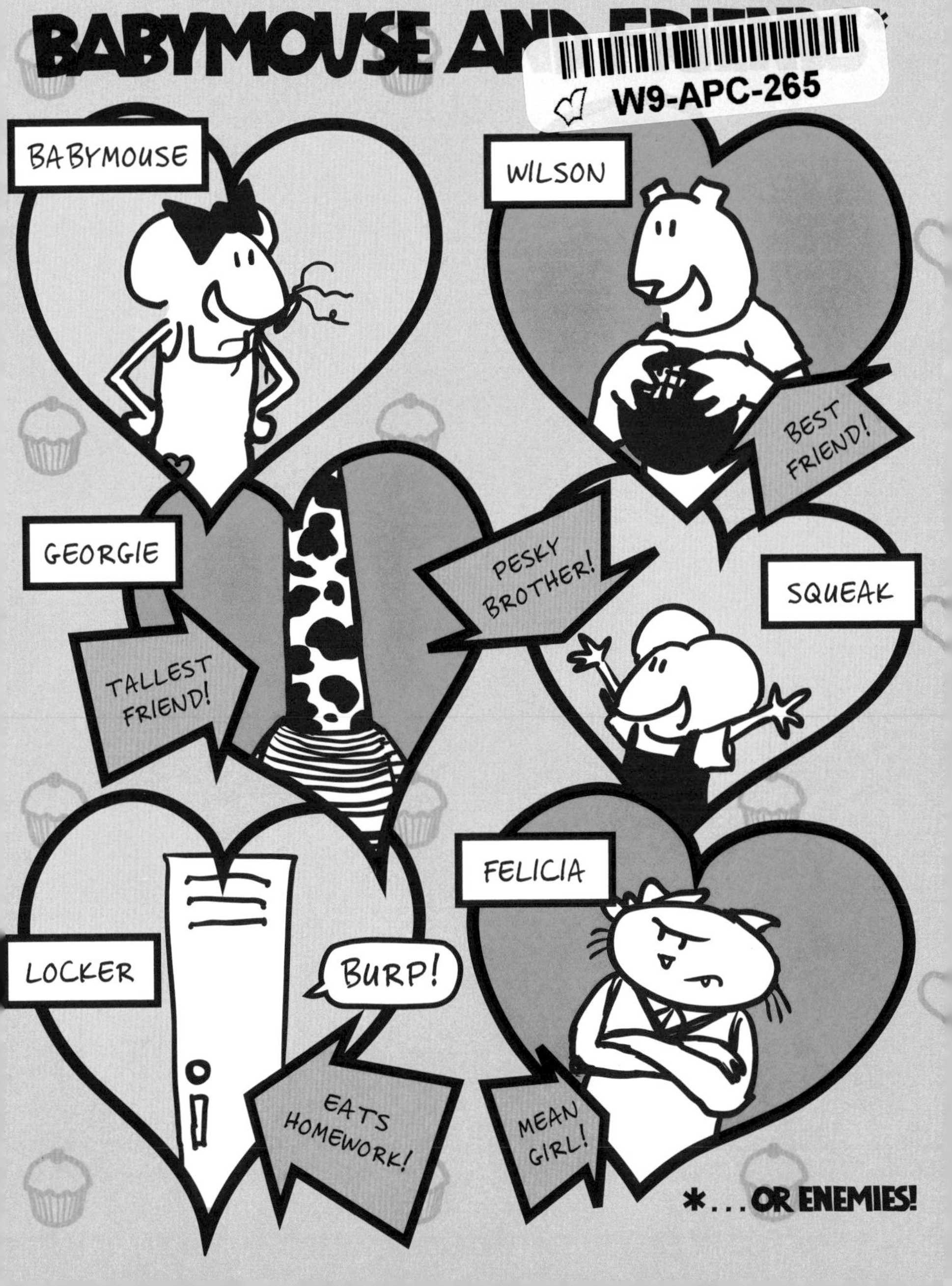
BABYMOUSE AN
BABYMOUSE
WILSON
BEST FRIEND!
GEORGIE
TALLEST FRIEND!
PESKY BROTHER!
SQUEAK
FELICIA
LOCKER
BURP!
EATS HOMEWORK!
MEAN GIRL!
*... OR ENEMIES!

Be sure to read **ALL** the **BABYMOUSE** books:

#1 BABYMOUSE: Queen of the World!
#2 BABYMOUSE: Our Hero
#3 BABYMOUSE: Beach Babe
#4 BABYMOUSE: Rock Star
#5 BABYMOUSE: Heartbreaker
#6 CAMP BABYMOUSE
#7 BABYMOUSE: Skater Girl
#8 BABYMOUSE: Puppy Love
#9 BABYMOUSE: Monster Mash
#10 BABYMOUSE: The Musical
#11 BABYMOUSE: Dragonslayer
#12 BABYMOUSE: Burns Rubber
#13 BABYMOUSE: Cupcake Tycoon
#14 BABYMOUSE: Mad Scientist
#15 A Very BABYMOUSE Christmas
#16 BABYMOUSE for President
#17 Extreme BABYMOUSE
#18 Happy Birthday, BABYMOUSE

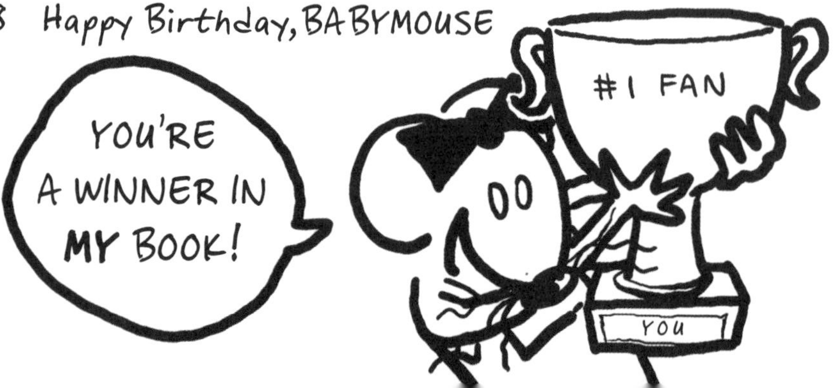
YOU'RE A WINNER IN MY BOOK!
#1 FAN
YOU

BABYMOUSE
SKATER GIRL

WITHDRAWN

BY JENNIFER L. HOLM & MATTHEW HOLM

RANDOM HOUSE 🏠 NEW YORK

YOU'D THINK THEY COULD COME UP WITH SOMETHING MORE INTERESTING TO PUT ON THIS PAGE.

Copyright © 2007 by Jennifer Holm and Matthew Holm.

All rights reserved.
Published in the United States by Random House Children's Books,
a division of Random House LLC, a Penguin Random House Company, New York.

Random House and the colophon are registered trademarks of Random House LLC.

Visit us on the Web!
randomhouse.com/kids
Babymouse.com

Educators and librarians, for a variety of teaching tools, visit us at
RHTeachersLibrarians.com

Library of Congress Cataloging-in-Publication Data
Holm, Jennifer L.
Babymouse : skater girl / Jennifer L. Holm & Matthew Holm.
  p.   cm.
ISBN 978-0-375-83989-4 (trade) — ISBN 978-0-375-93989-1 (lib. bdg.)
I. Graphic novels. I. Holm, Matthew. II. Title. III. Title: Skater girl.
PN6727.H592 B35 2007 741.5'973—dc22 2006050444

MANUFACTURED IN MALAYSIA   25 24 23 22 21 20 19 18 17 16 15 14 13 12 11

HE'S AN OLYMPIC-CLASS LIBRARIAN!
FOR UNCLE TOMMY

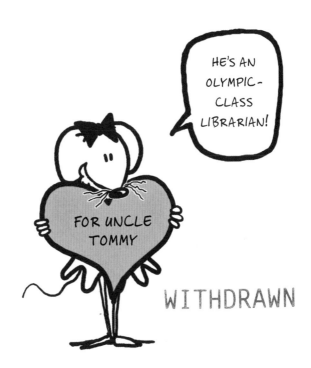

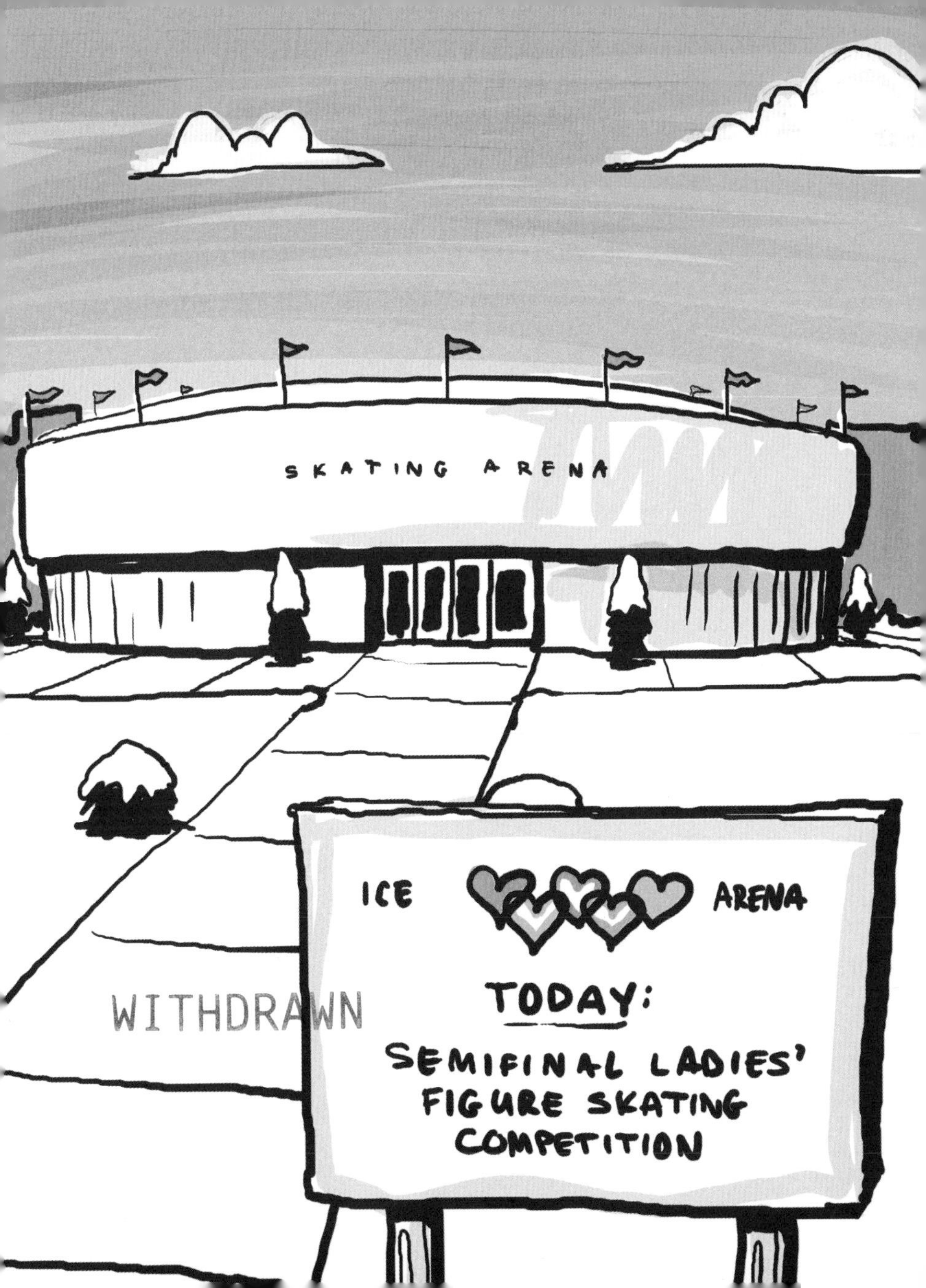
SKATING ARENA
ICE ARENA
TODAY:
SEMIFINAL LADIES' FIGURE SKATING COMPETITION

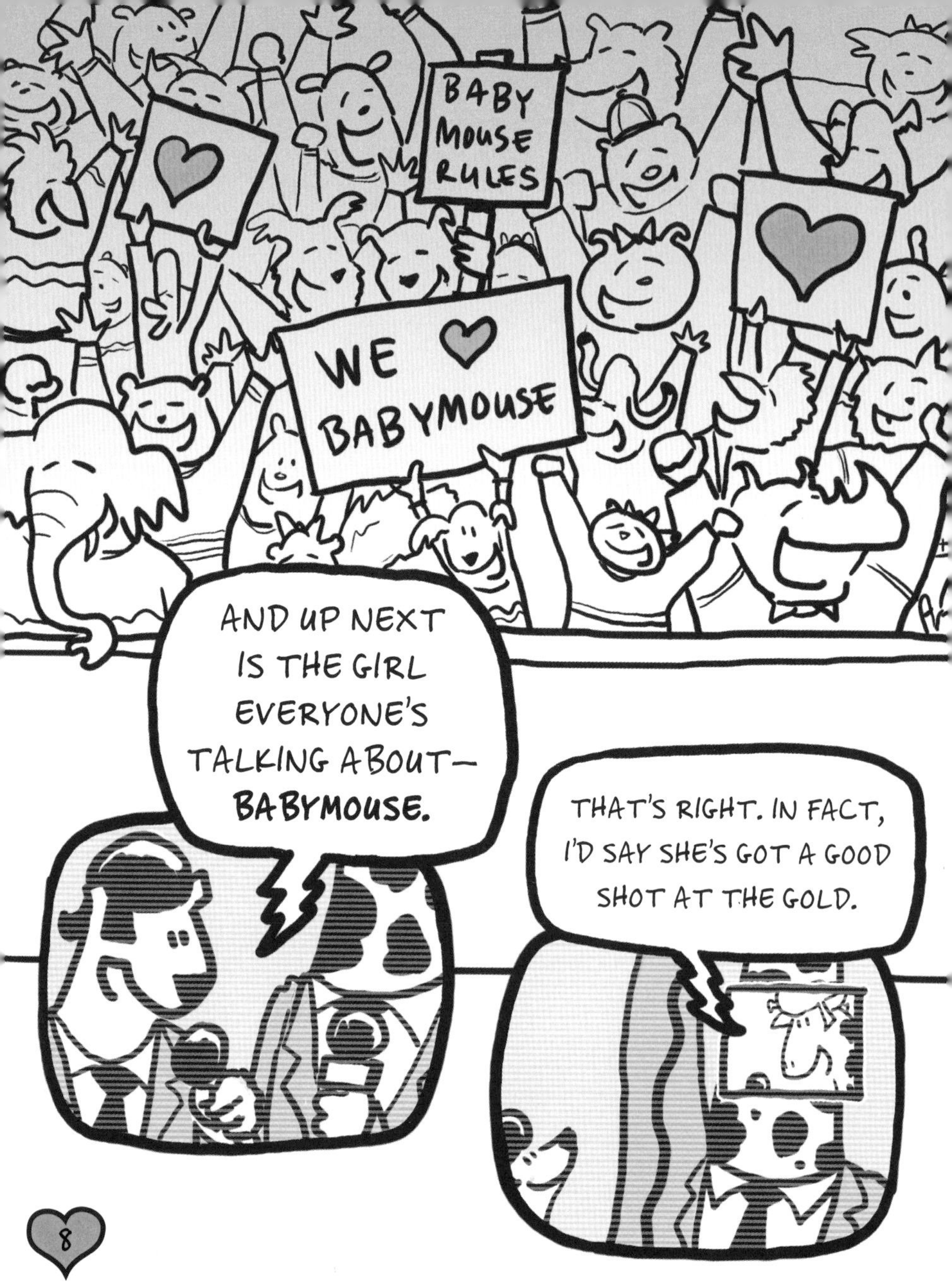
BABY MOUSE RULES
WE ♥ BABYMOUSE
AND UP NEXT IS THE GIRL EVERYONE'S TALKING ABOUT—**BABYMOUSE.**
THAT'S RIGHT. IN FACT, I'D SAY SHE'S GOT A GOOD SHOT AT THE GOLD.

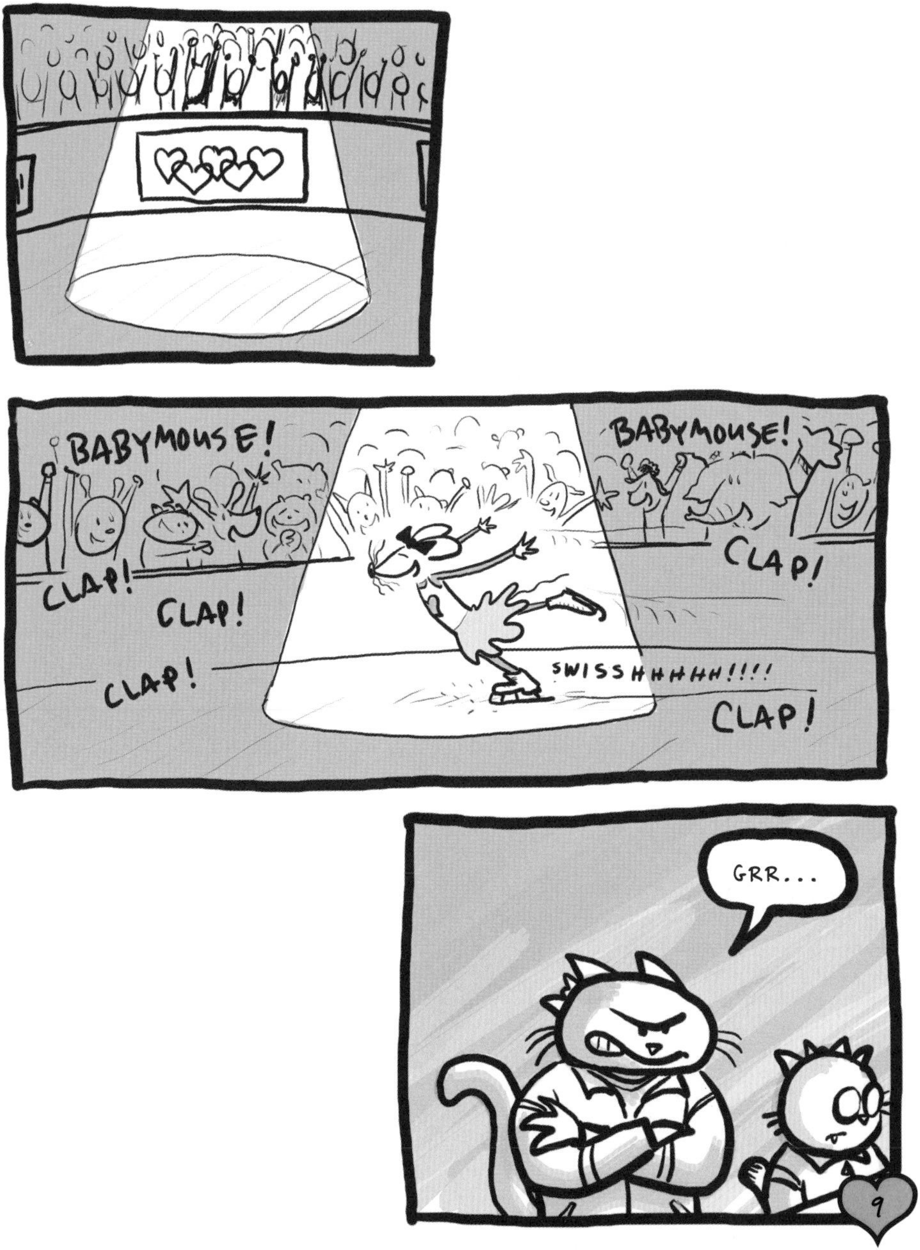
BABYMOUSE!
BABYMOUSE!
CLAP!
CLAP!
CLAP!
CLAP!
SWISSHHHHHH!!!!
CLAP!
GRR...

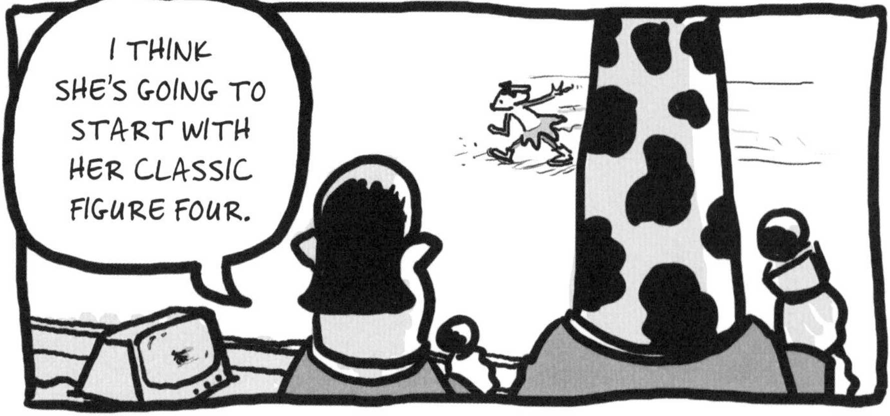
I THINK SHE'S GOING TO START WITH HER CLASSIC FIGURE FOUR.

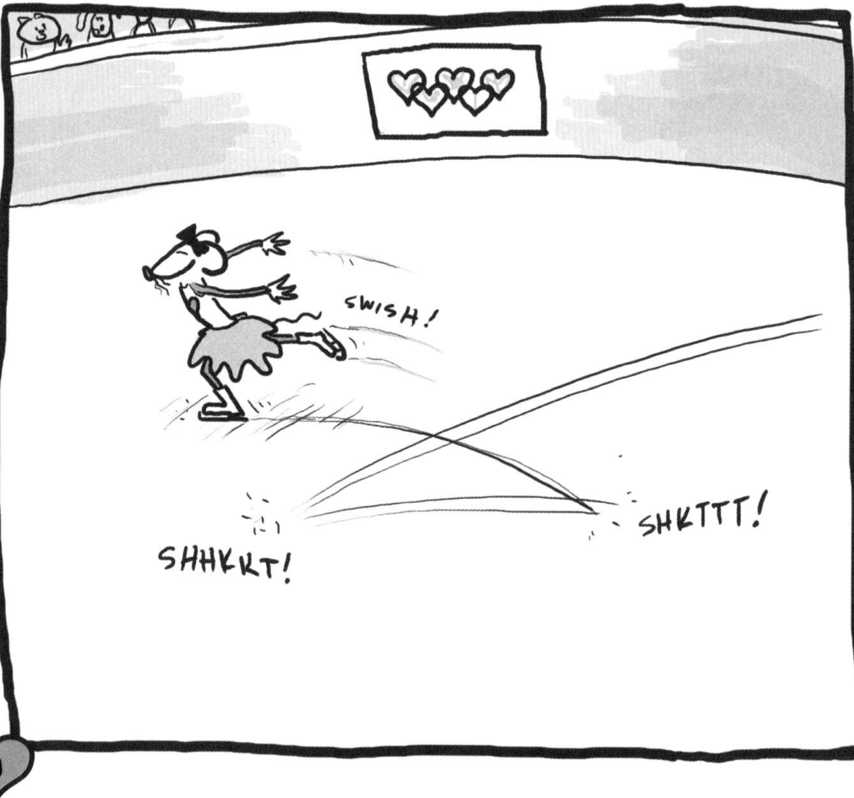
SWISH!
SHKTTT!
SHHKKT!

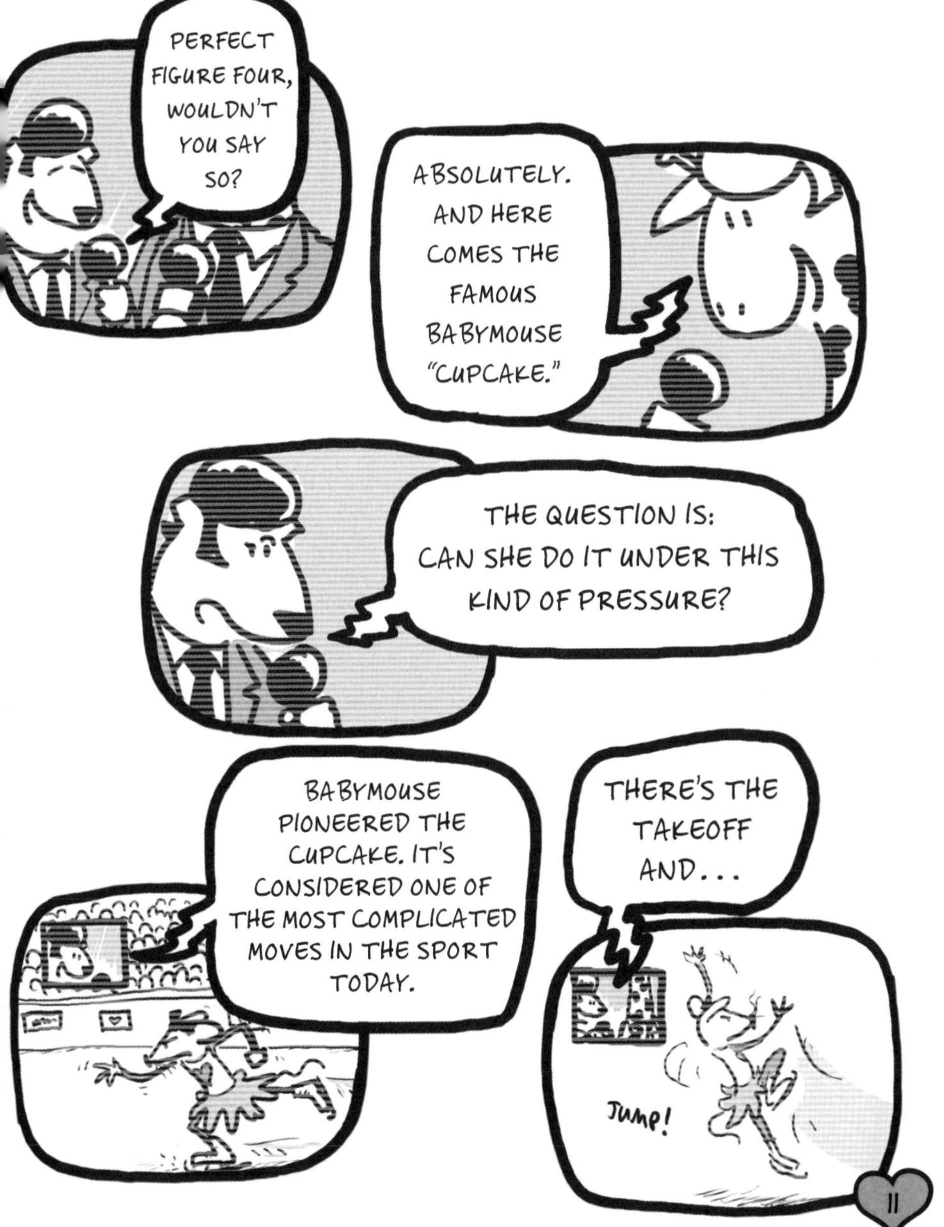
PERFECT FIGURE FOUR, WOULDN'T YOU SAY SO?
ABSOLUTELY. AND HERE COMES THE FAMOUS BABYMOUSE "CUPCAKE."
THE QUESTION IS: CAN SHE DO IT UNDER THIS KIND OF PRESSURE?
BABYMOUSE PIONEERED THE CUPCAKE. IT'S CONSIDERED ONE OF THE MOST COMPLICATED MOVES IN THE SPORT TODAY.
THERE'S THE TAKEOFF AND . . .
JUMP!

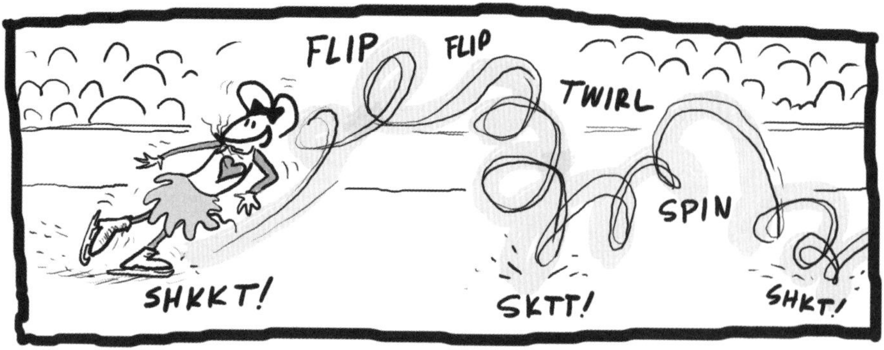
FLIP
FLIP
TWIRL
SPIN
SHKKT!
SKTT!
SHKT!

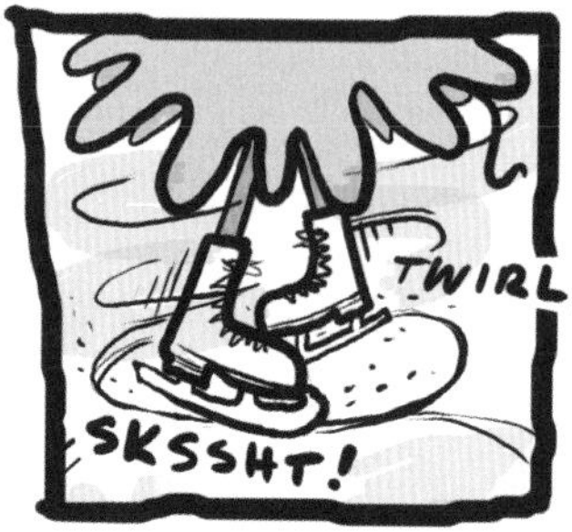
TWIRL!
SKSSHT!

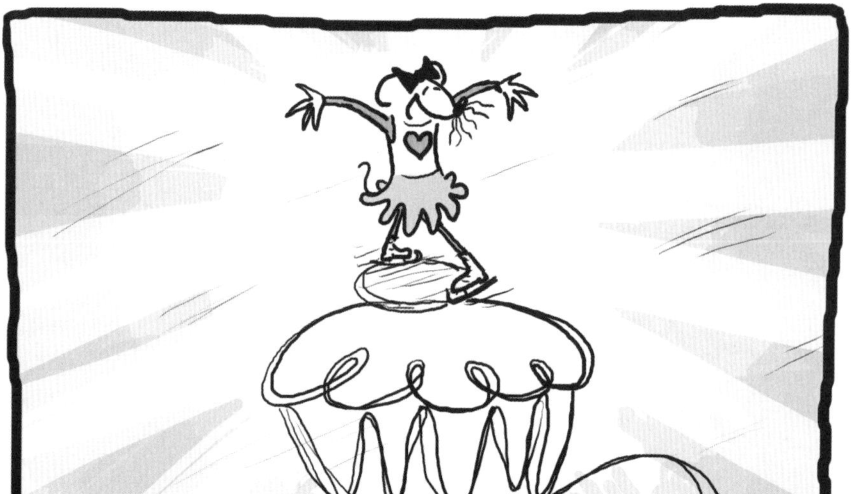

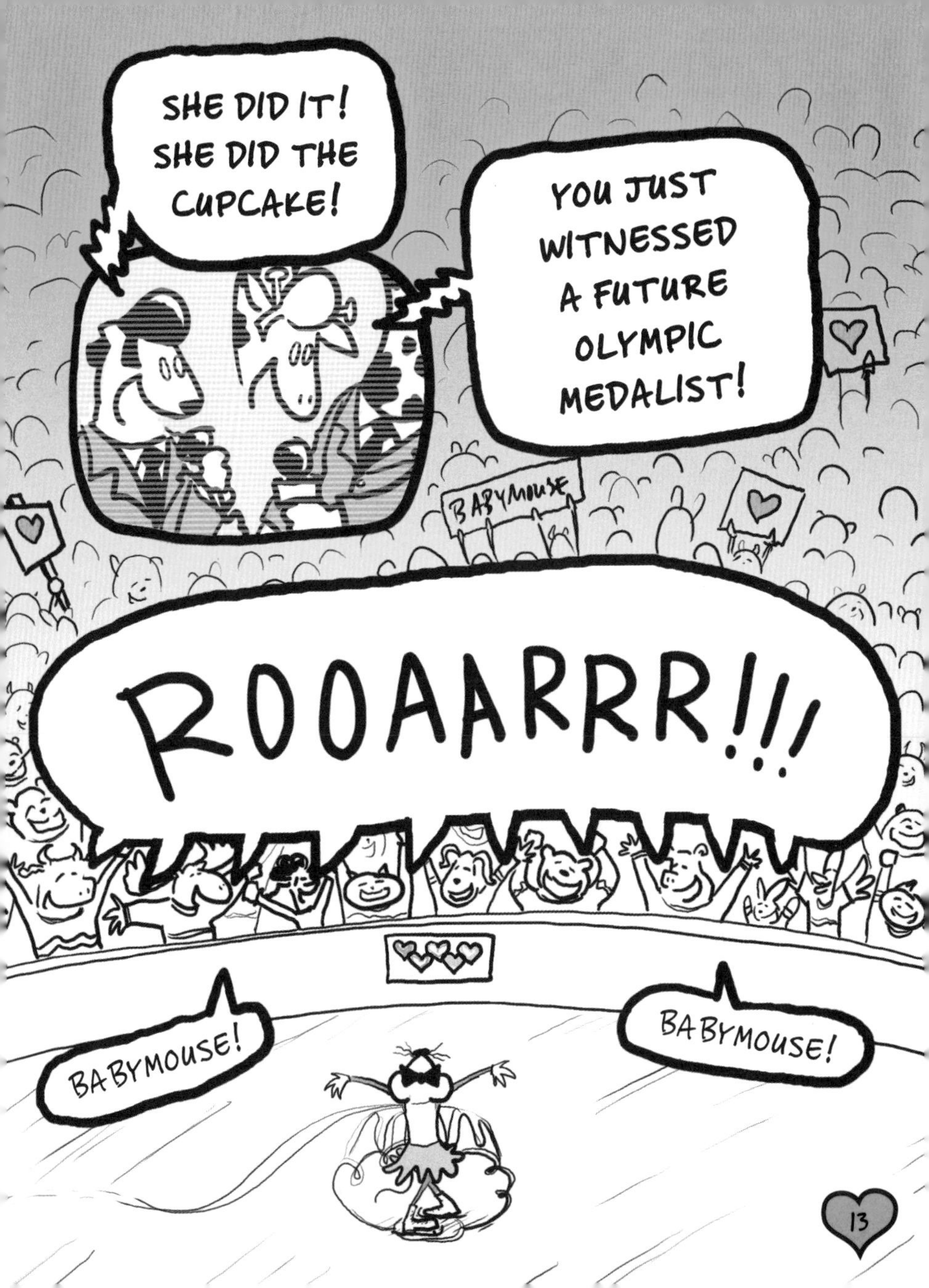
SHE DID IT! SHE DID THE CUPCAKE!
YOU JUST WITNESSED A FUTURE OLYMPIC MEDALIST!
BABYMOUSE
ROOARRRR!!!
BABYMOUSE!
BABYMOUSE!

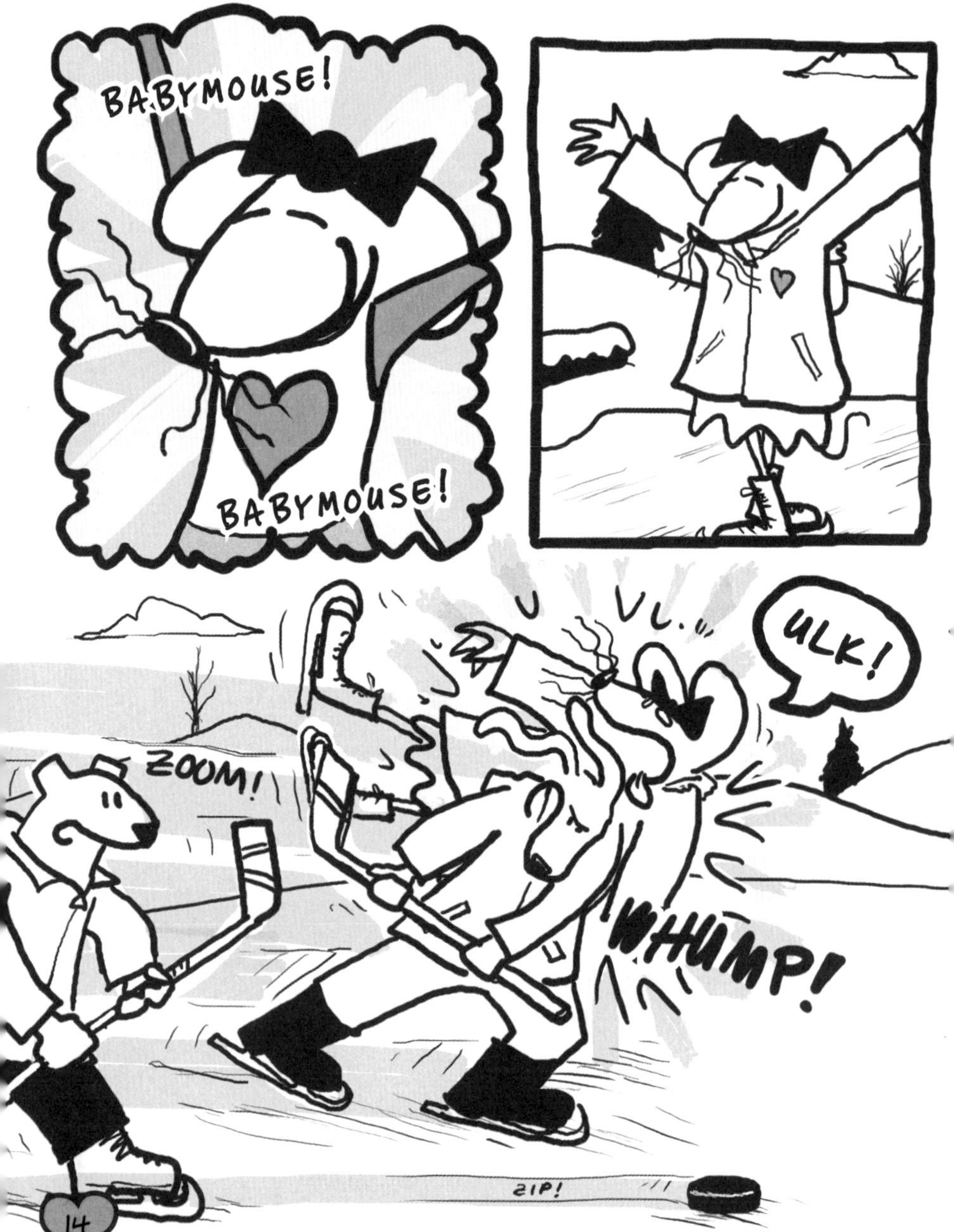
BABYMOUSE!
BABYMOUSE!
ZOOM!
ULK!
WHUMP!
ZIP!

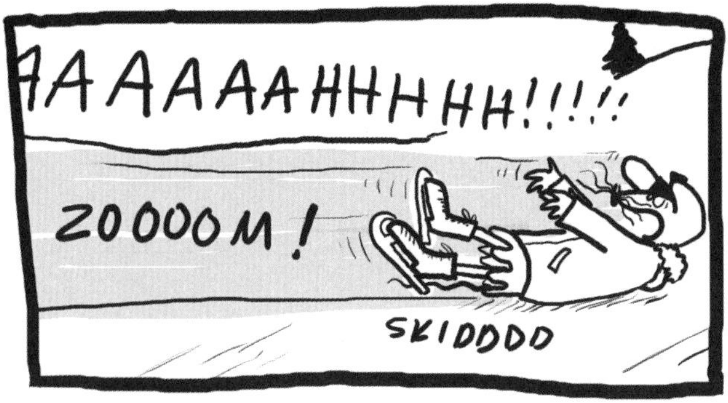
AAAAAAHHHHH!!!!!
ZOOOOM!
SKIDDDD

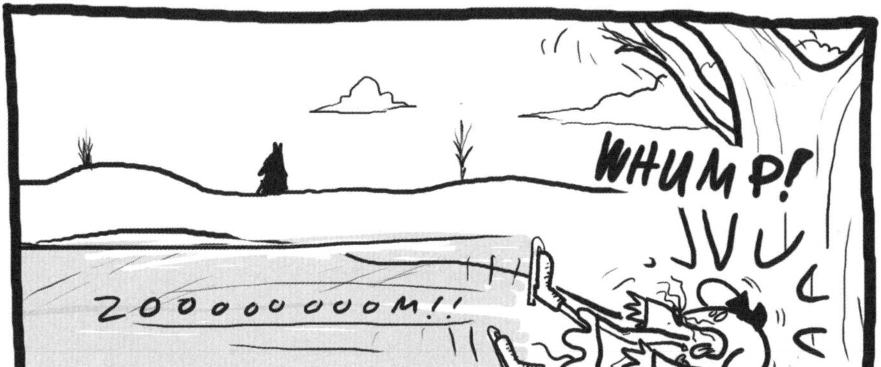
WHUMP!
ZOOOOOOOOOM!!

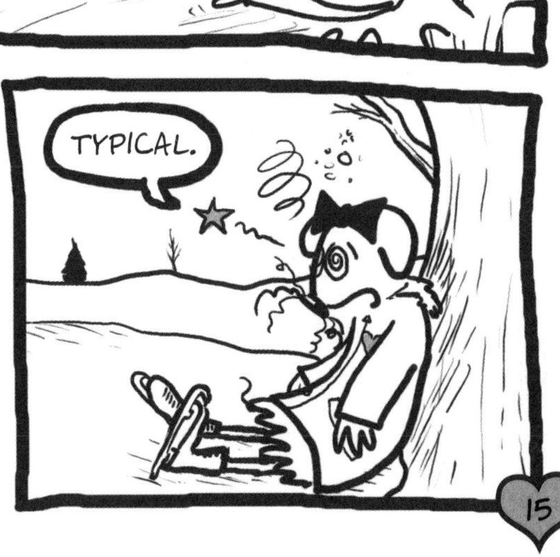
TYPICAL.

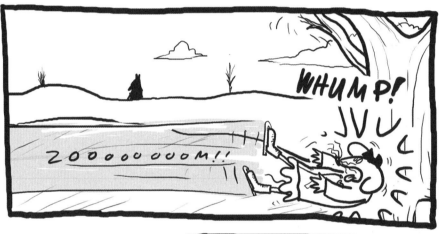

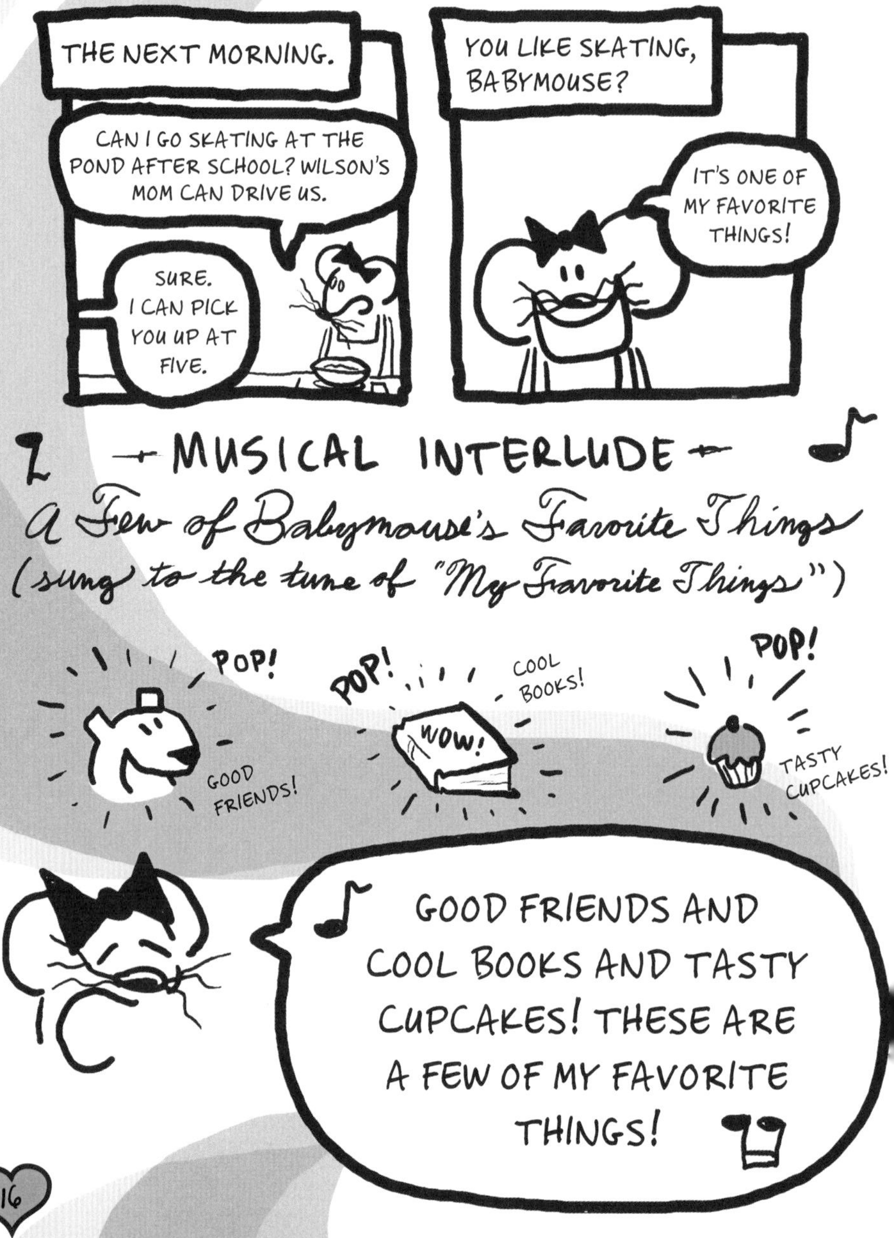
THE NEXT MORNING.
CAN I GO SKATING AT THE POND AFTER SCHOOL? WILSON'S MOM CAN DRIVE US.
SURE. I CAN PICK YOU UP AT FIVE.
YOU LIKE SKATING, BABYMOUSE?
IT'S ONE OF MY FAVORITE THINGS!
MUSICAL INTERLUDE
A Few of Babymouse's Favorite Things
(sung to the tune of "My Favorite Things")
POP!
GOOD FRIENDS!
POP!
WOW!
COOL BOOKS!
POP!
TASTY CUPCAKES!
GOOD FRIENDS AND COOL BOOKS AND TASTY CUPCAKES! THESE ARE A FEW OF MY FAVORITE THINGS!

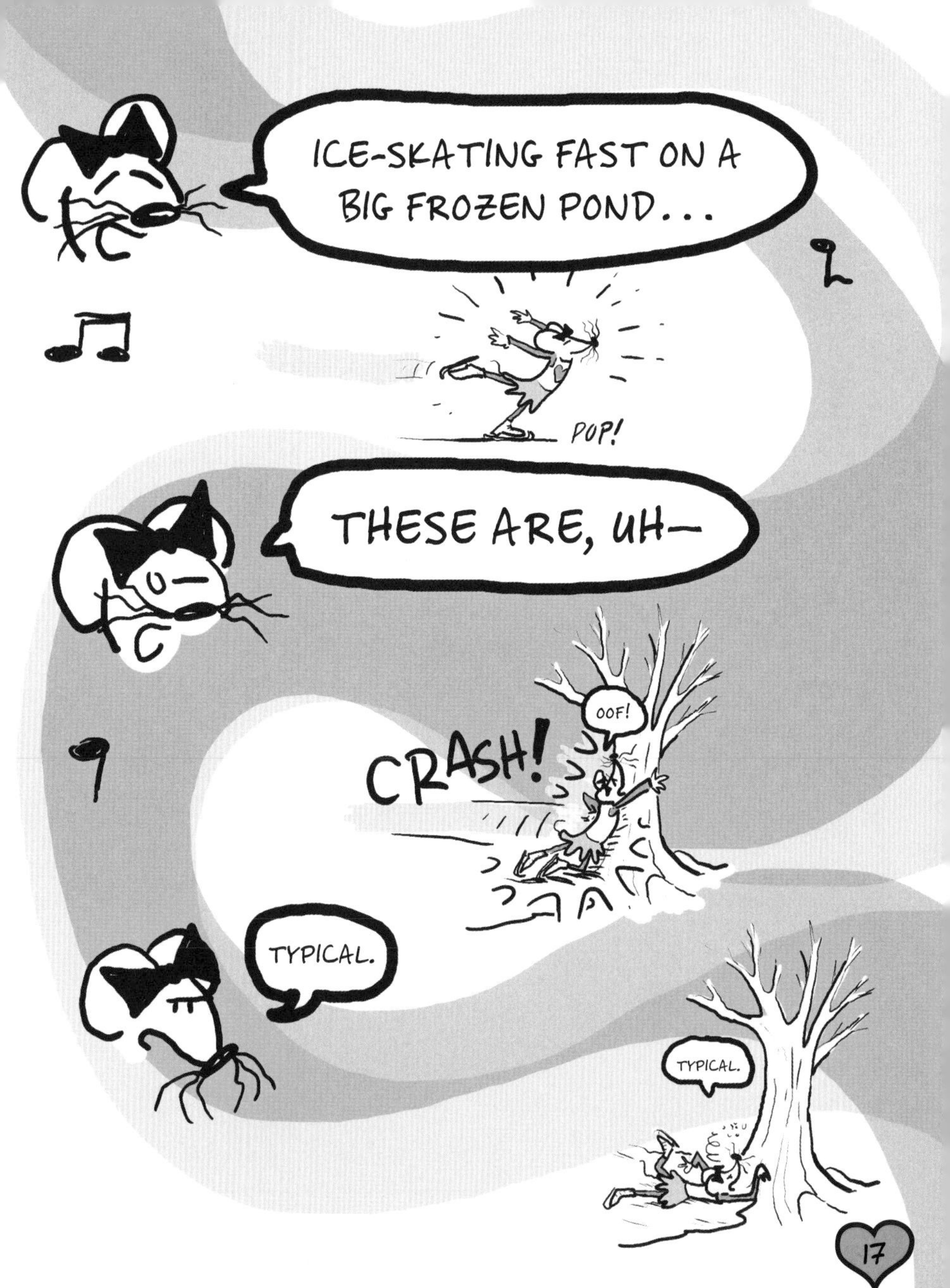
ICE-SKATING FAST ON A BIG FROZEN POND...
POP!
THESE ARE, UH—
OOF!
CRASH!
TYPICAL.
TYPICAL.

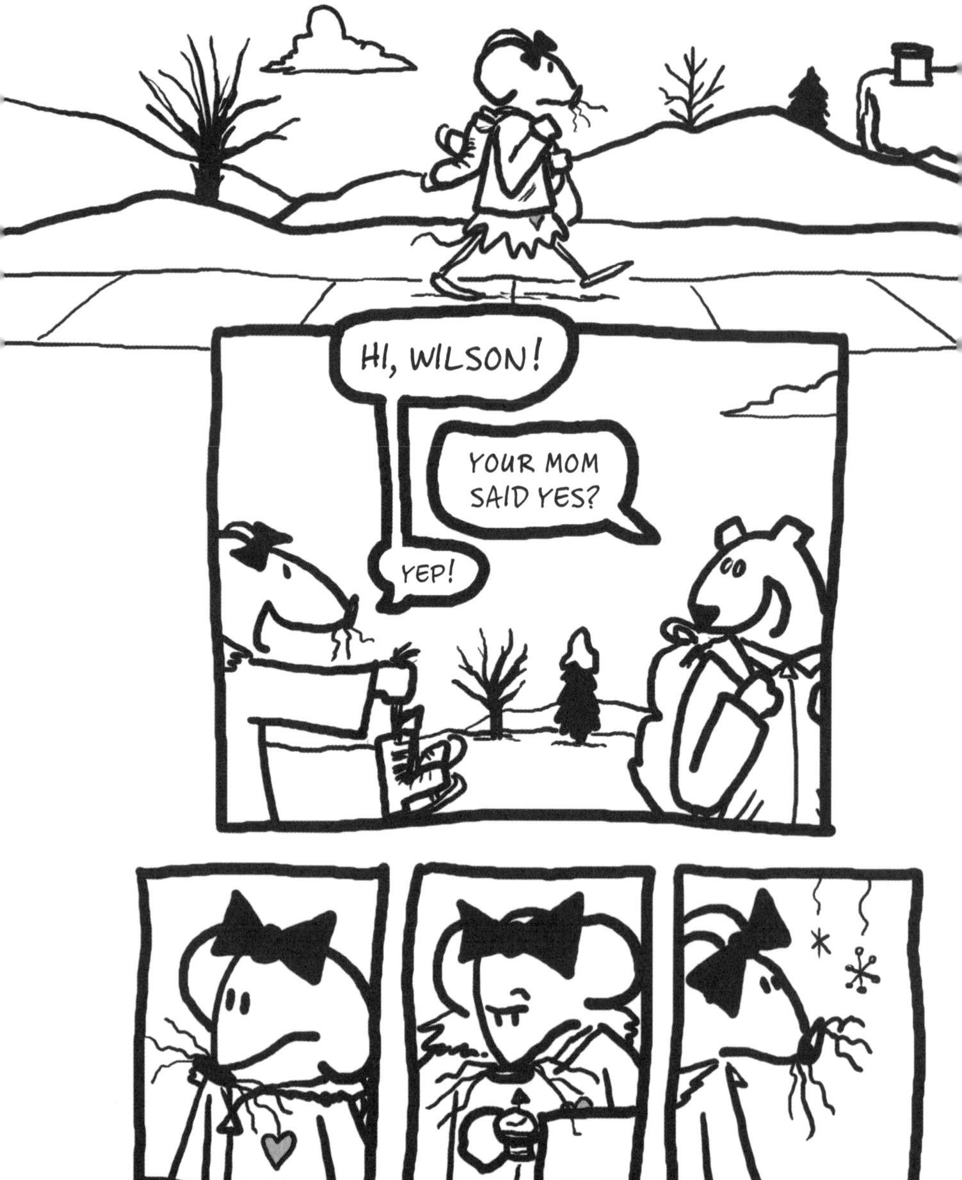
HI, WILSON!
YOUR MOM SAID YES?
YEP!

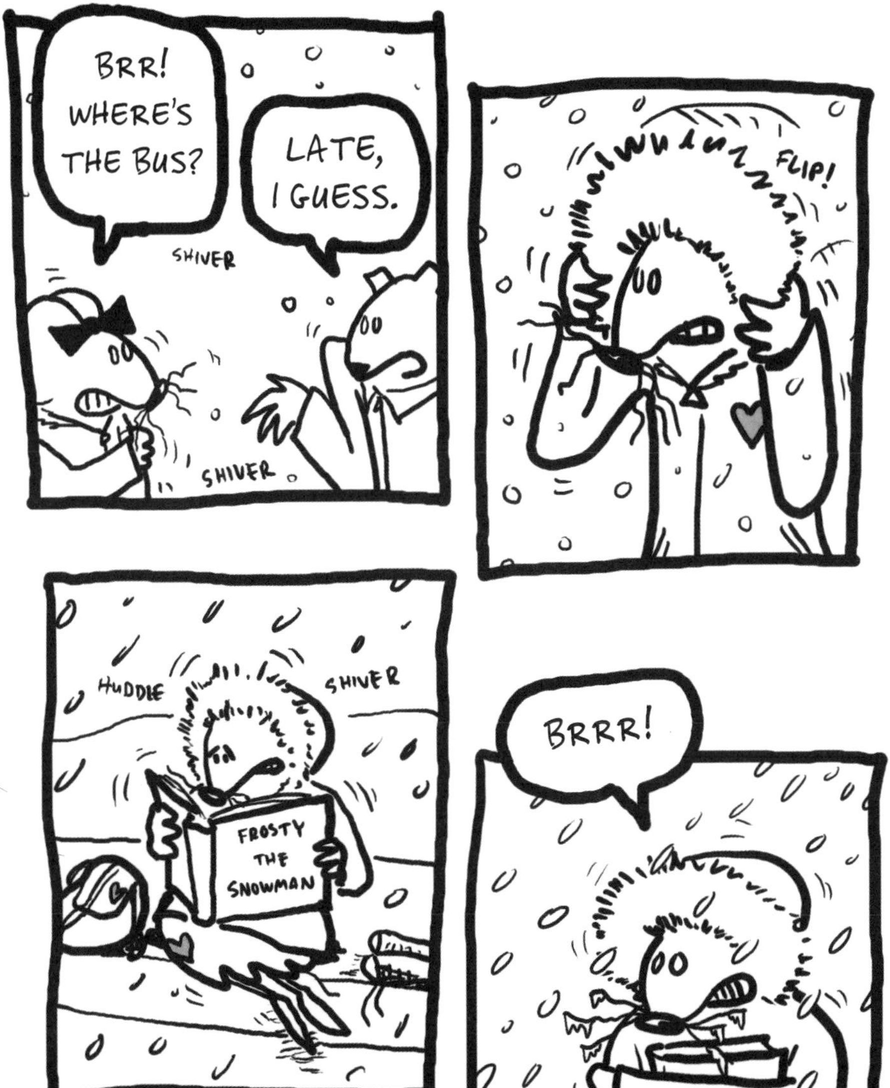
BRR! WHERE'S THE BUS?
LATE, I GUESS.
SHIVER
SHIVER
FLIP!
HUDDLE
SHIVER
FROSTY THE SNOWMAN
BRRR!

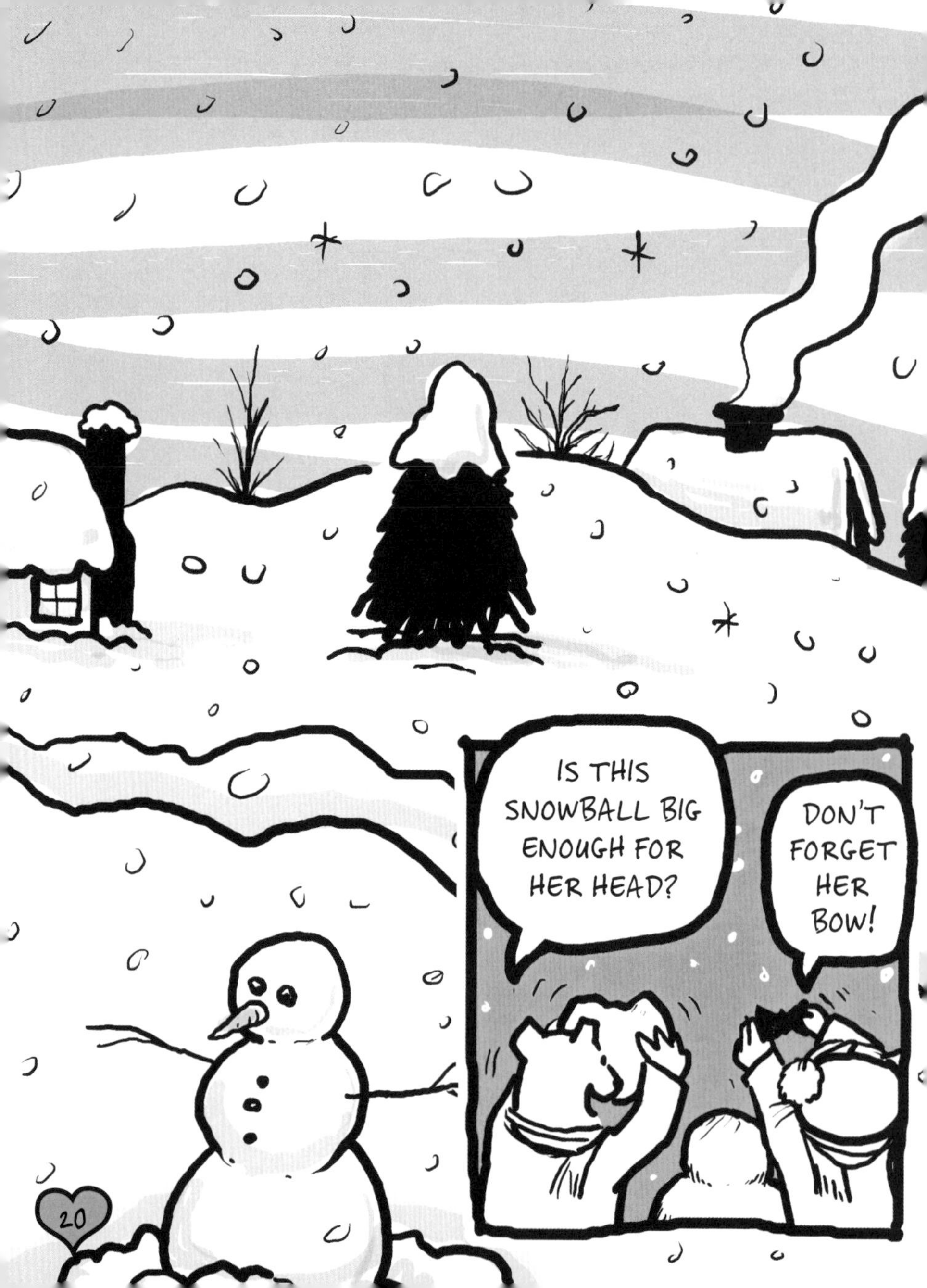
IS THIS SNOWBALL BIG ENOUGH FOR HER HEAD?
DON'T FORGET HER BOW!

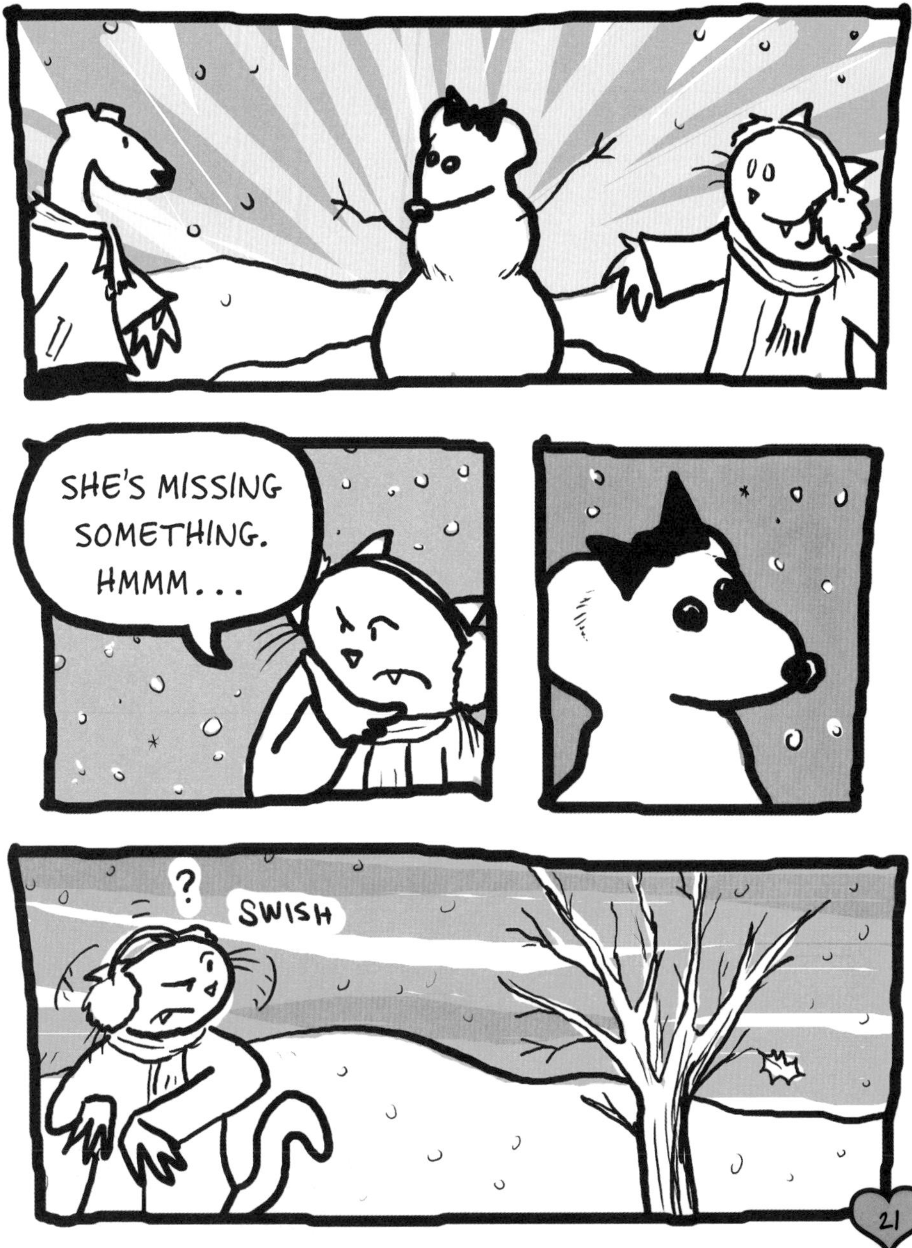
SHE'S MISSING SOMETHING. HMMM...
?
SWISH

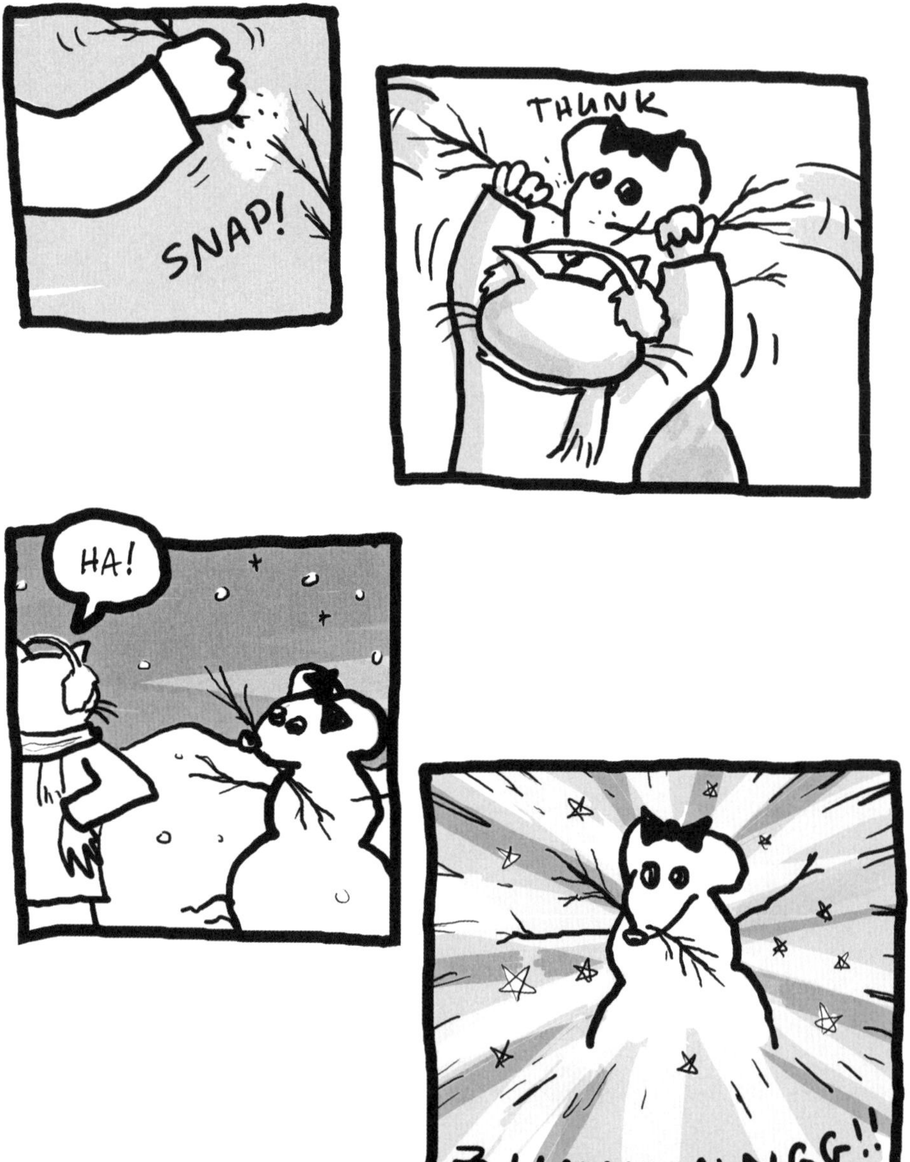
SNAP!
THUNK
HA!
ZIINNNNNGG!!

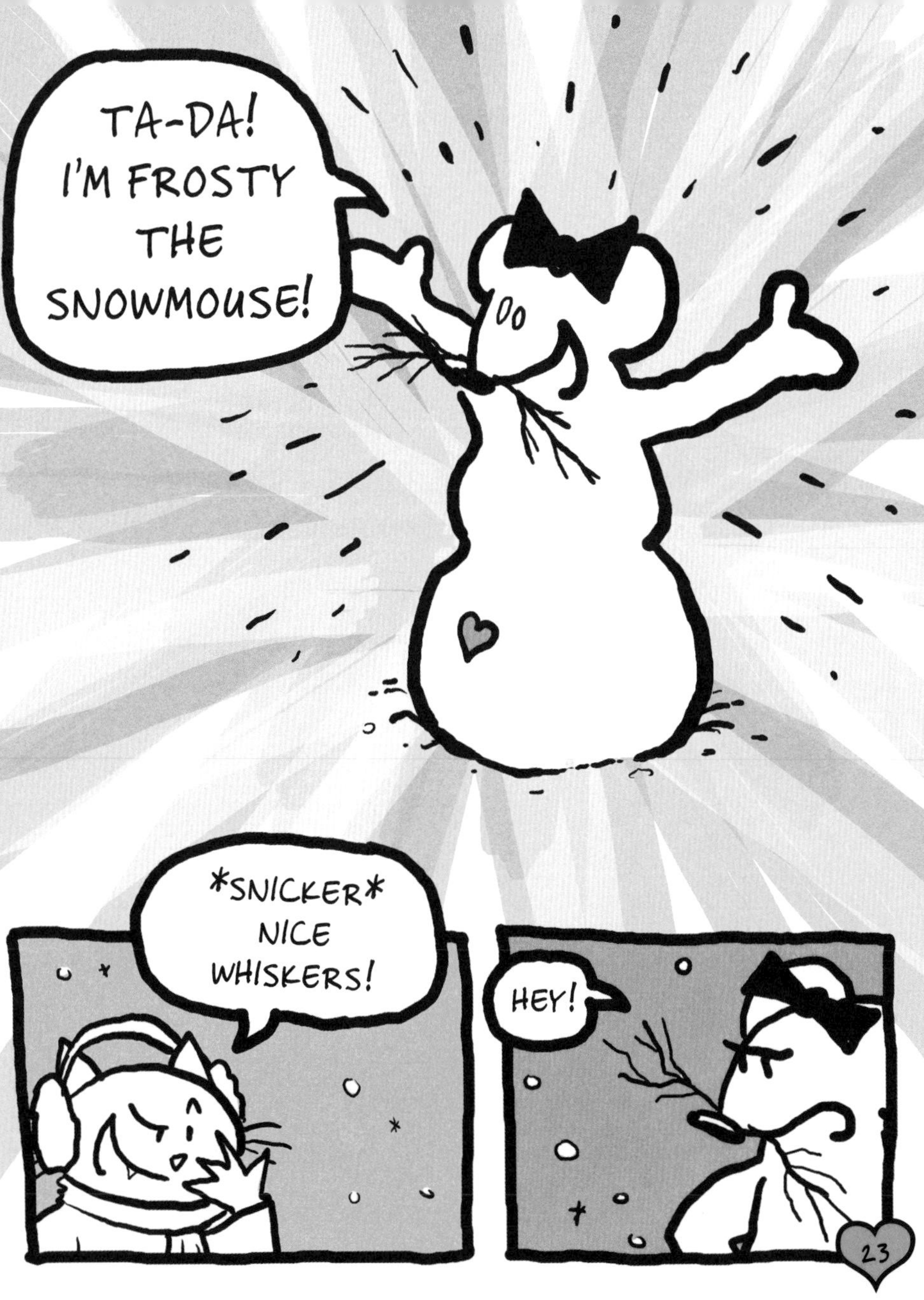
TA-DA! I'M FROSTY THE SNOWMOUSE!
SNICKER NICE WHISKERS!
HEY!

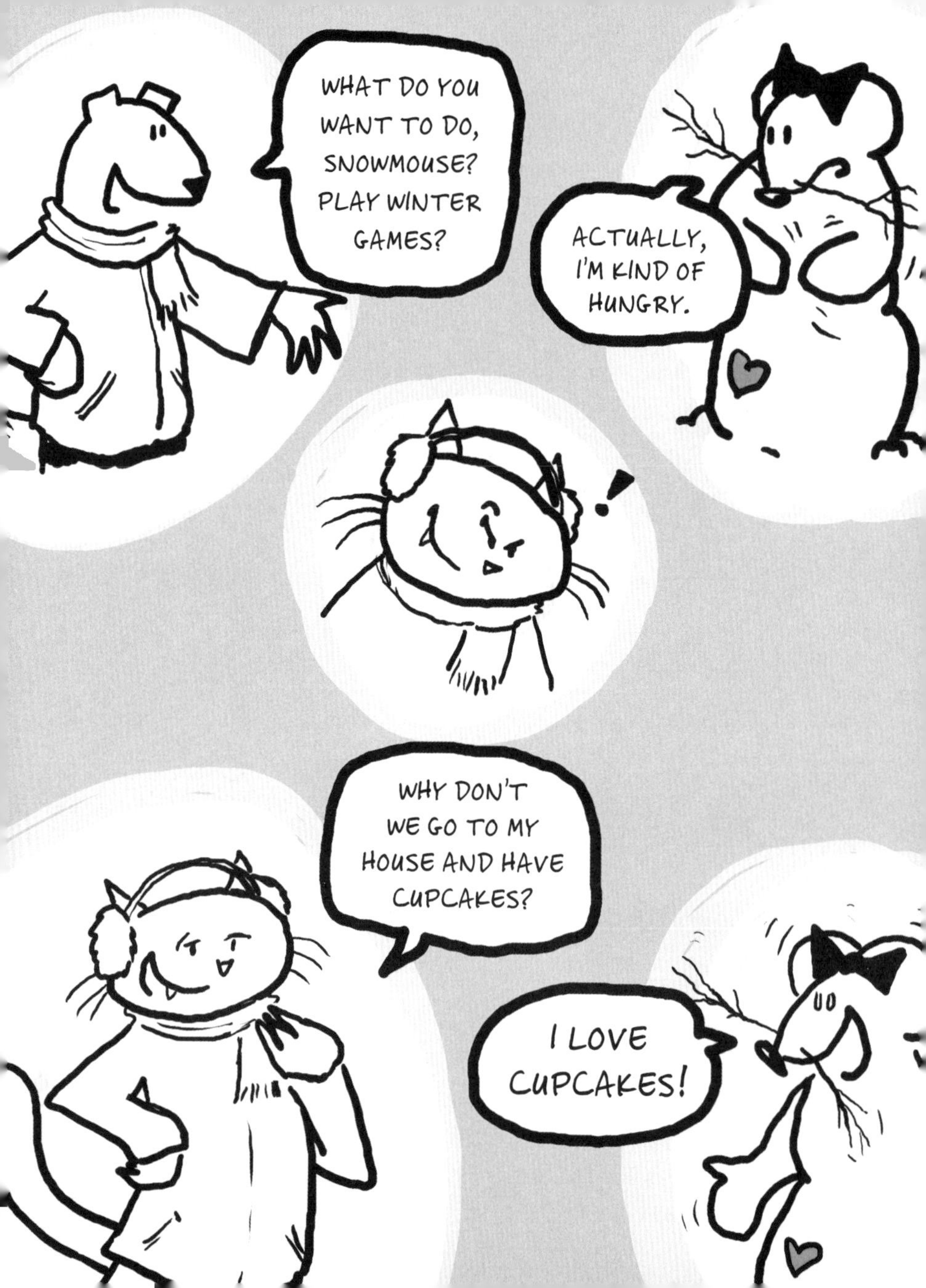
WHAT DO YOU WANT TO DO, SNOWMOUSE? PLAY WINTER GAMES?
ACTUALLY, I'M KIND OF HUNGRY.
!
WHY DON'T WE GO TO MY HOUSE AND HAVE CUPCAKES?
I LOVE CUPCAKES!

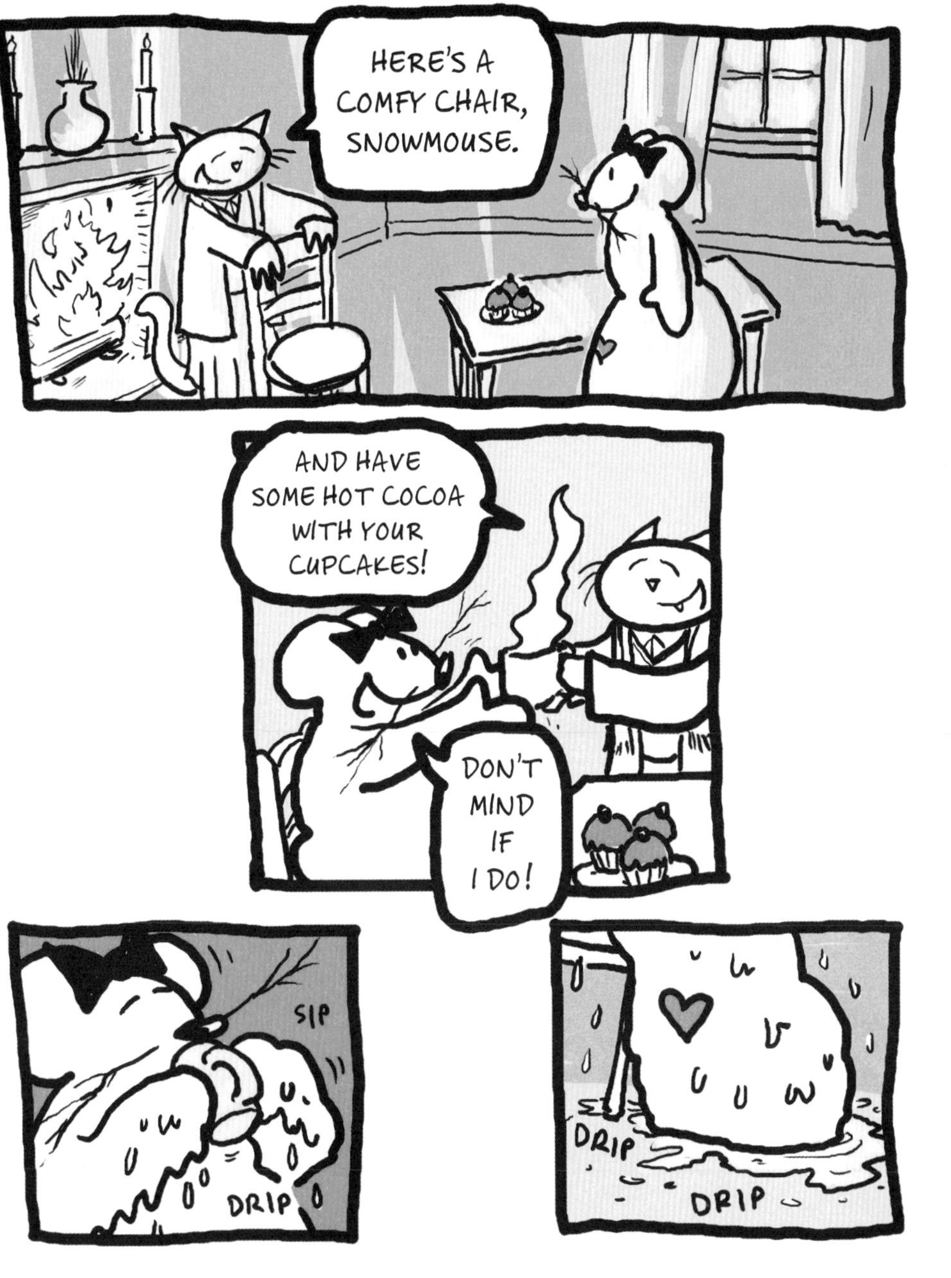
HERE'S A COMFY CHAIR, SNOWMOUSE.
AND HAVE SOME HOT COCOA WITH YOUR CUPCAKES!
DON'T MIND IF I DO!
SIP
DRIP
DRIP
DRIP

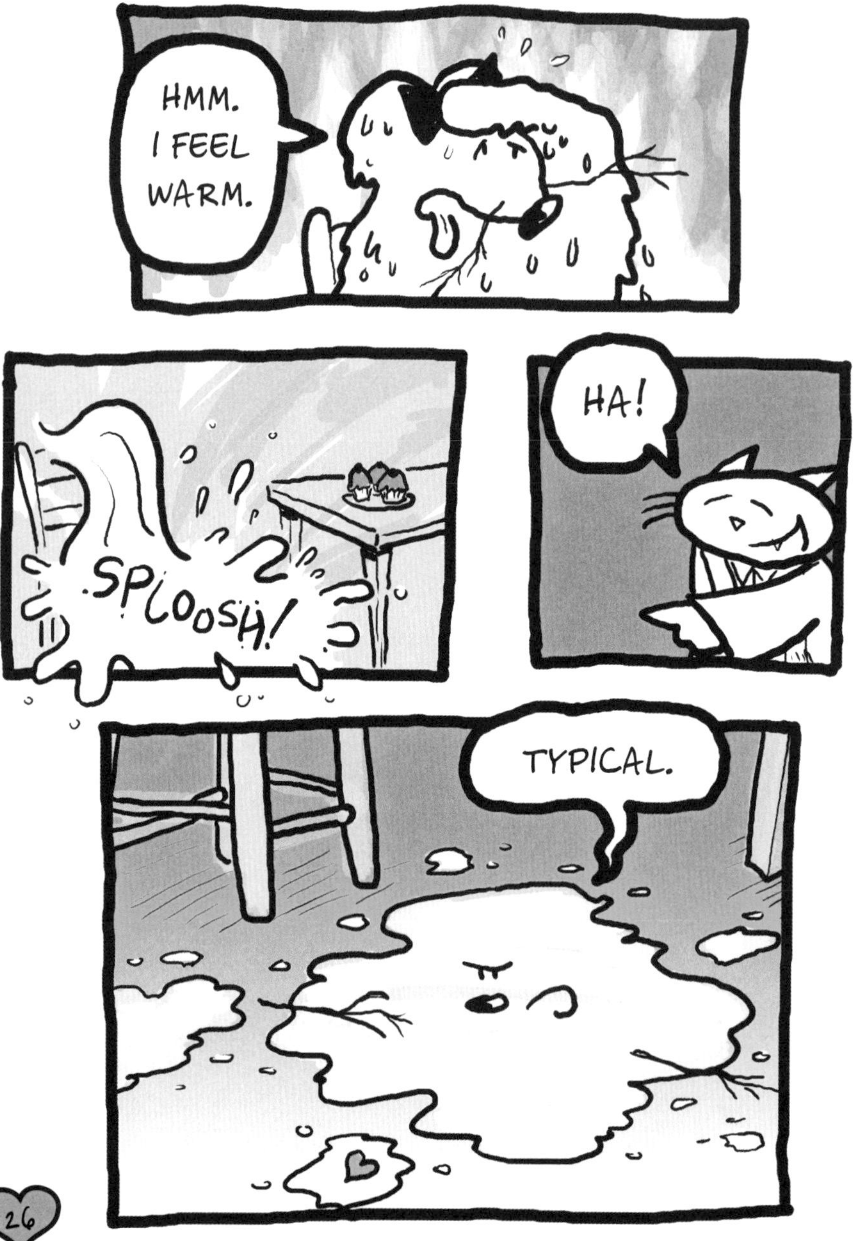
HMM. I FEEL WARM.
SPLOOSH!
HA!
TYPICAL.

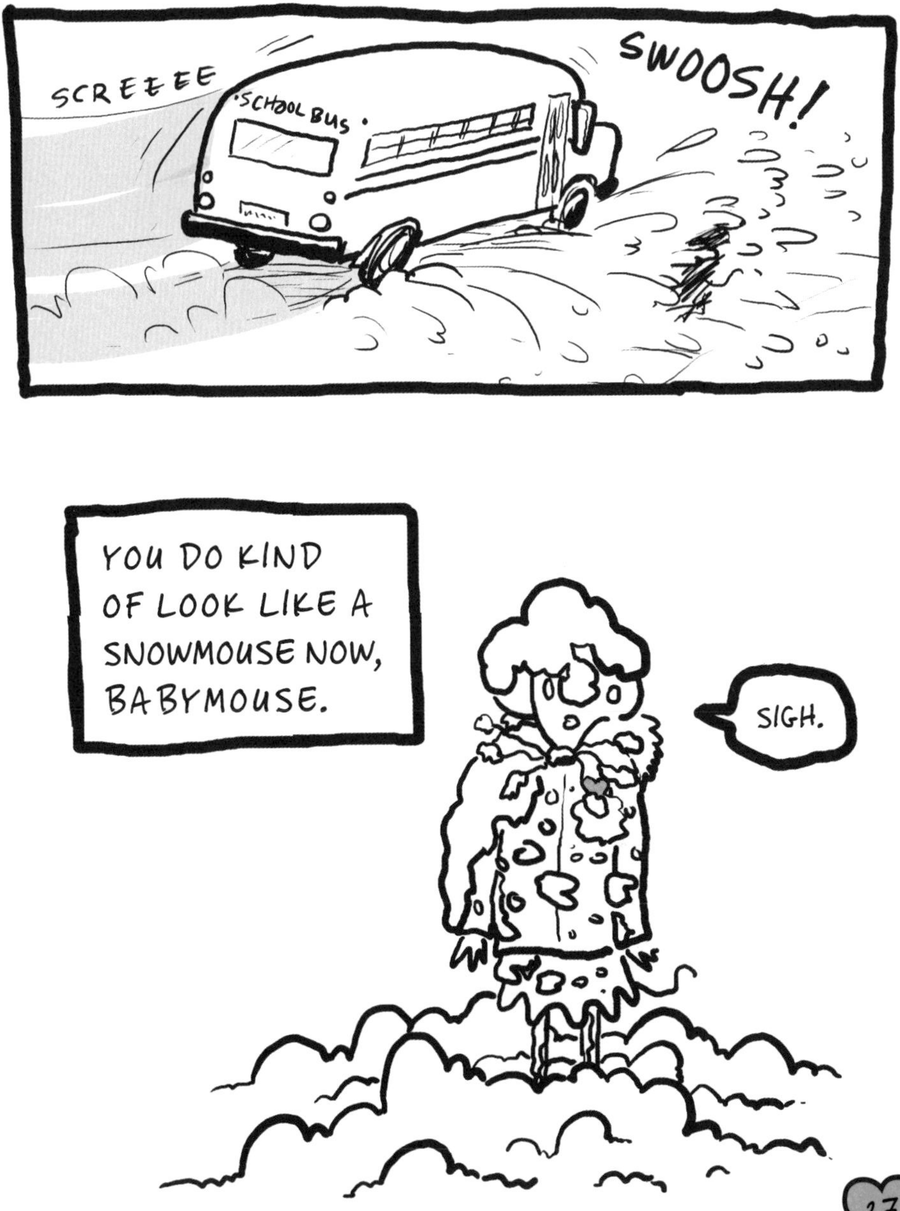
SCREEEE
SCHOOL BUS
SWOOSH!
YOU DO KIND OF LOOK LIKE A SNOWMOUSE NOW, BABYMOUSE.
SIGH.

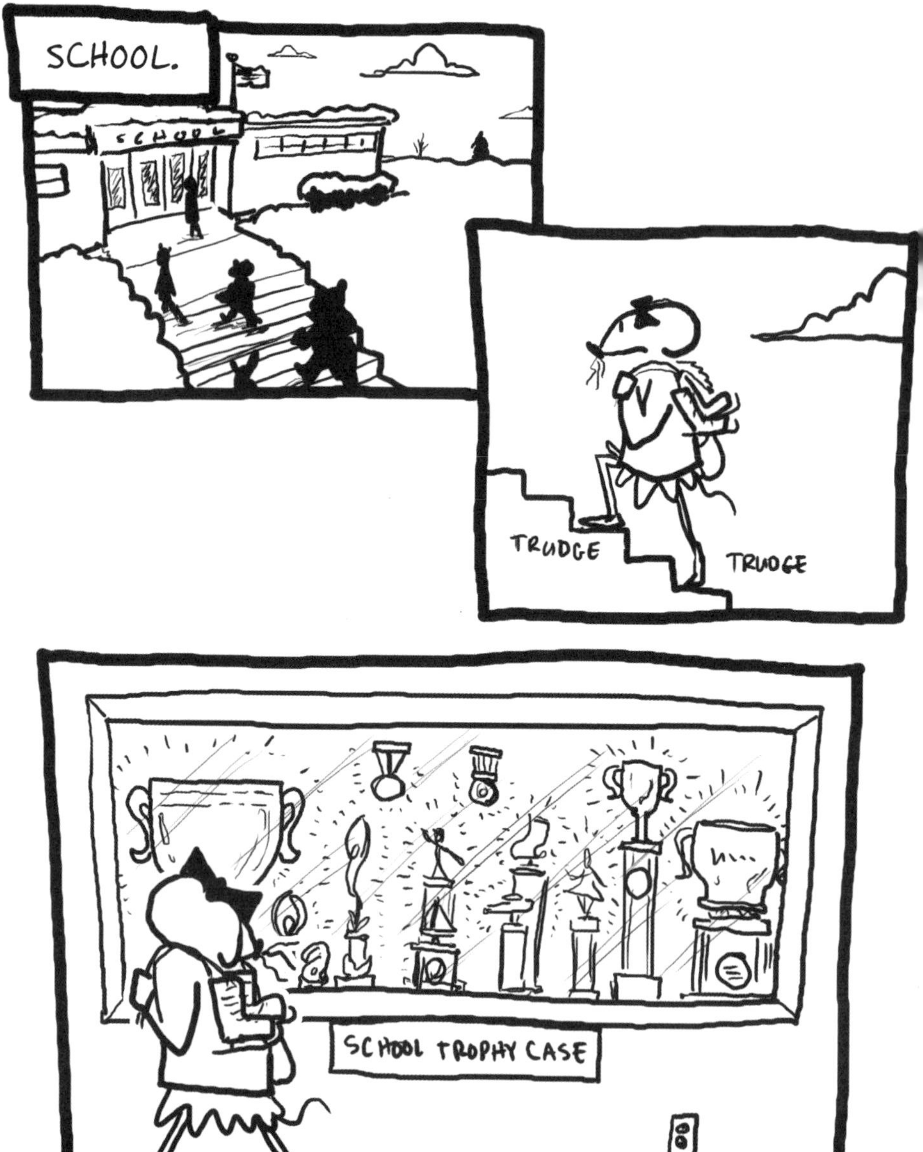
SCHOOL.
SCHOOL
TRUDGE
TRUDGE
SCHOOL TROPHY CASE

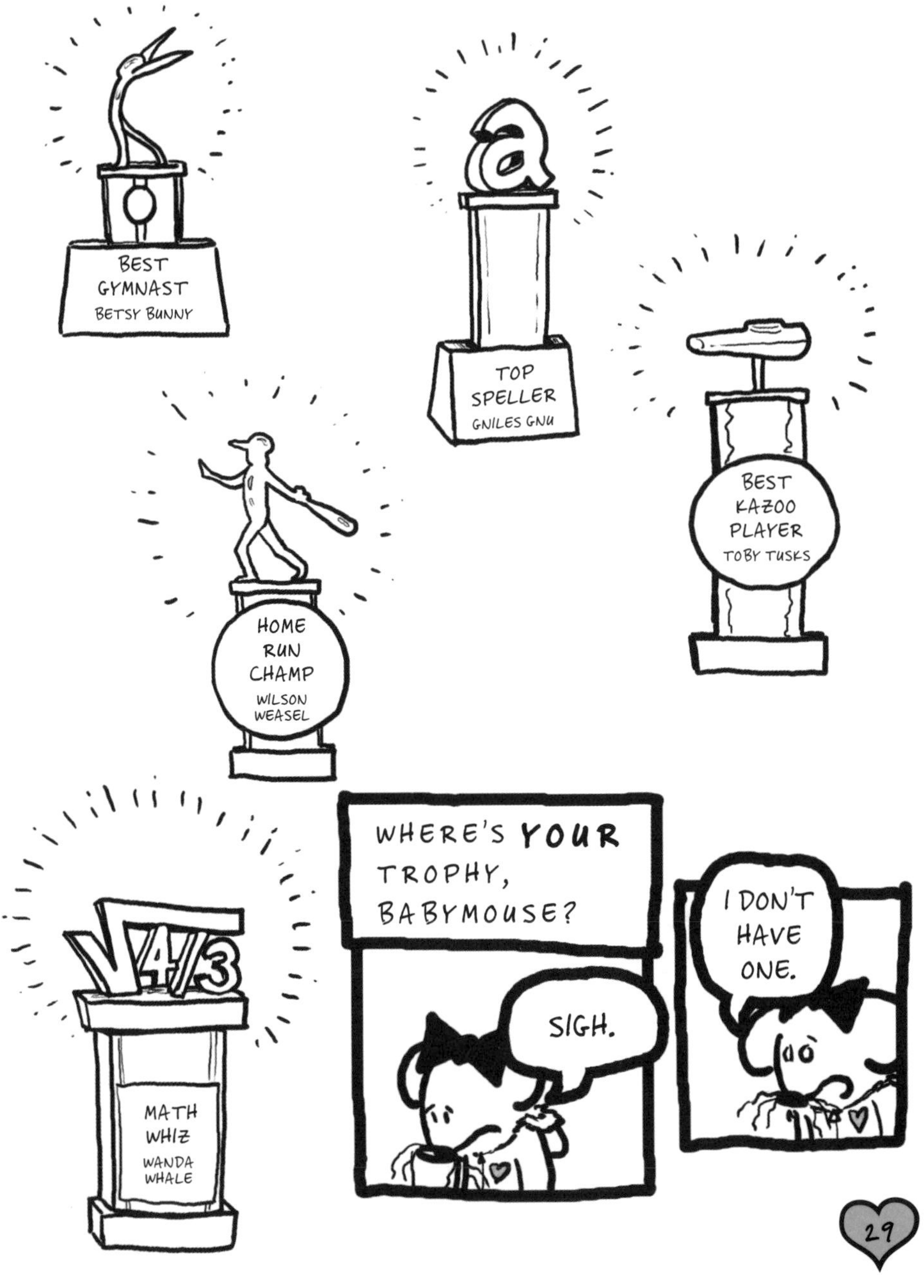
BEST GYMNAST
BETSY BUNNY
TOP SPELLER
GNILES GNU
BEST KAZOO PLAYER
TOBY TUSKS
HOME RUN CHAMP
WILSON WEASEL
MATH WHIZ
WANDA WHALE
WHERE'S **YOUR** TROPHY, BABYMOUSE?
SIGH.
I DON'T HAVE ONE.

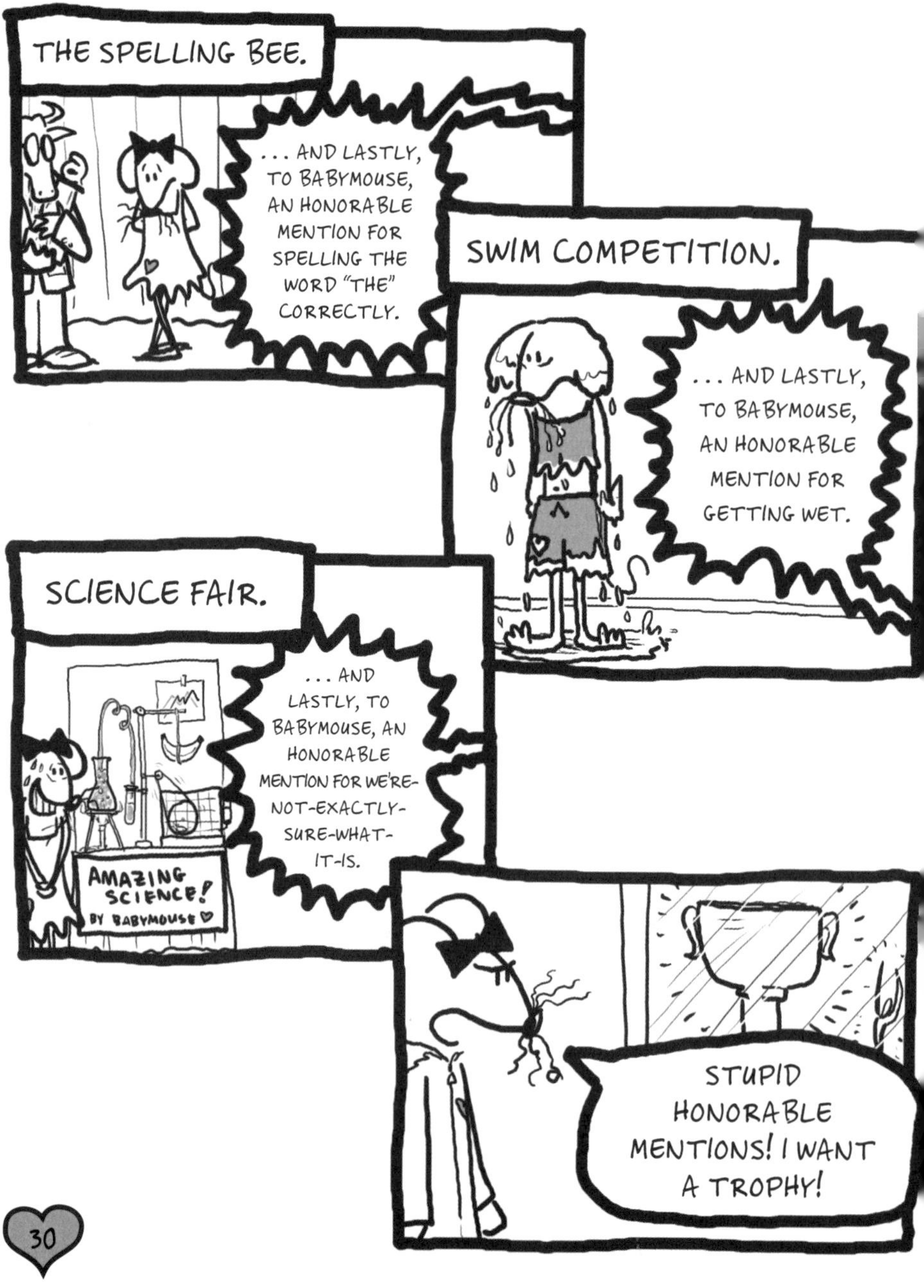
THE SPELLING BEE.
. . . AND LASTLY, TO BABYMOUSE, AN HONORABLE MENTION FOR SPELLING THE WORD "THE" CORRECTLY.
SWIM COMPETITION.
. . . AND LASTLY, TO BABYMOUSE, AN HONORABLE MENTION FOR GETTING WET.
SCIENCE FAIR.
. . . AND LASTLY, TO BABYMOUSE, AN HONORABLE MENTION FOR WE'RE-NOT-EXACTLY-SURE-WHAT-IT-IS.
AMAZING SCIENCE! BY BABYMOUSE
STUPID HONORABLE MENTIONS! I WANT A TROPHY!

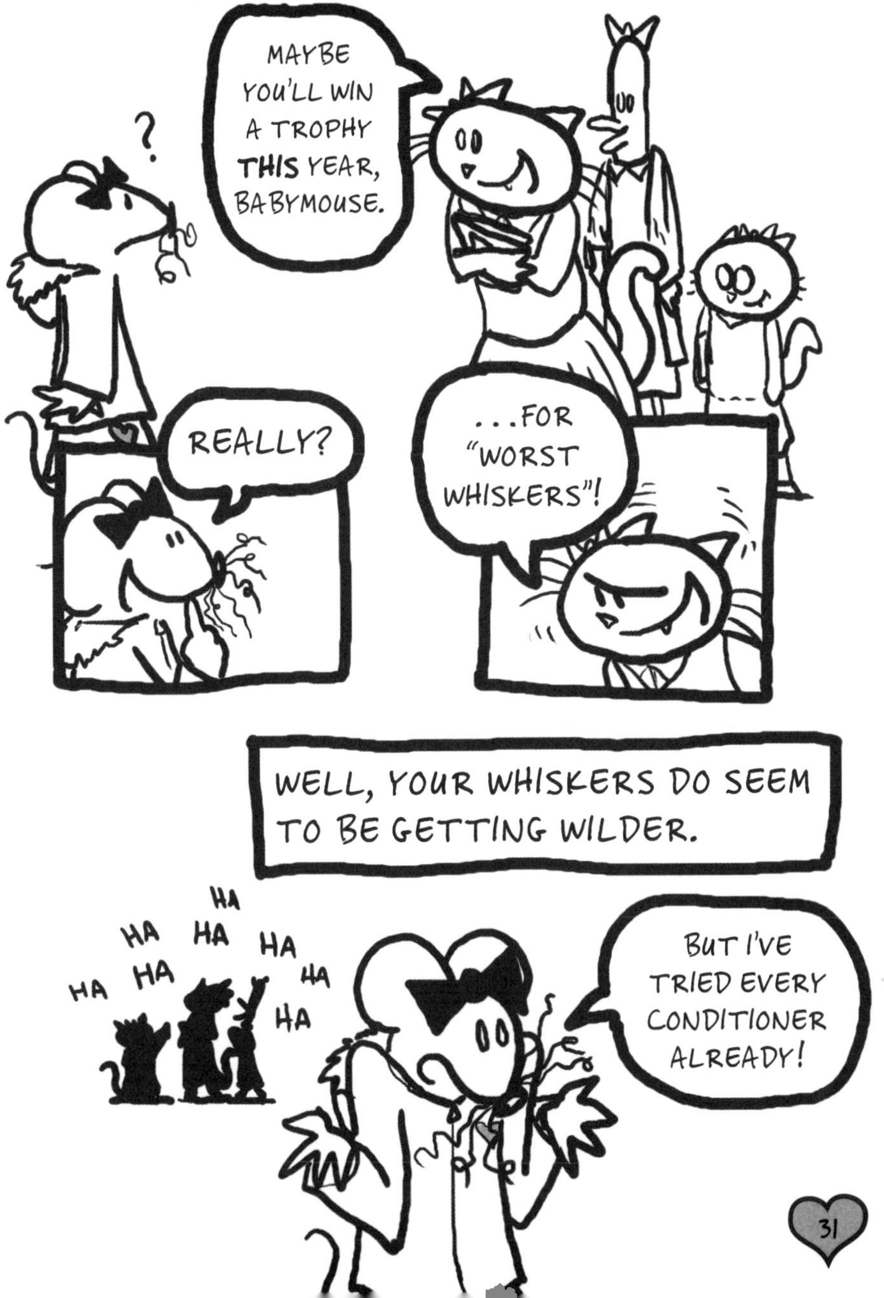

?
MAYBE YOU'LL WIN A TROPHY **THIS** YEAR, BABYMOUSE.
REALLY?
...FOR "WORST WHISKERS"!
WELL, YOUR WHISKERS DO SEEM TO BE GETTING WILDER.
HA HA HA HA HA HA HA HA
BUT I'VE TRIED EVERY CONDITIONER ALREADY!

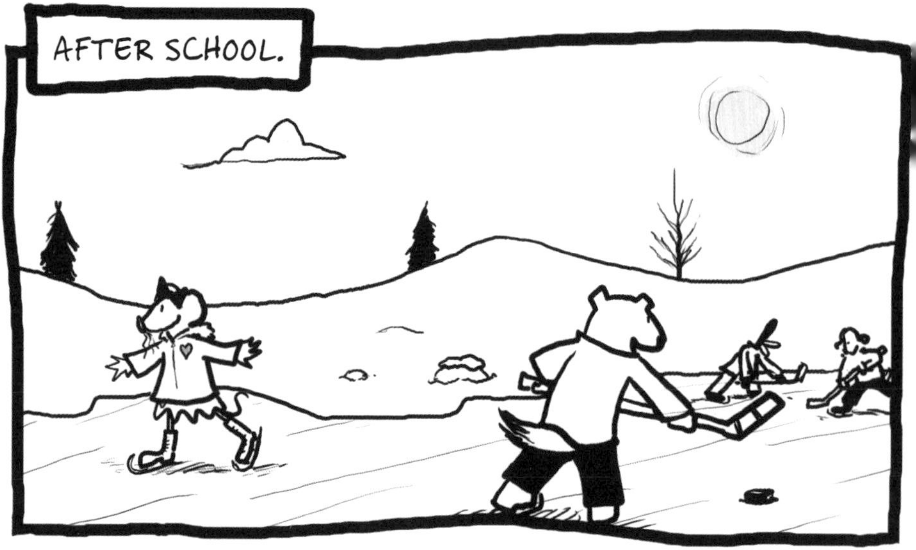
AFTER SCHOOL.

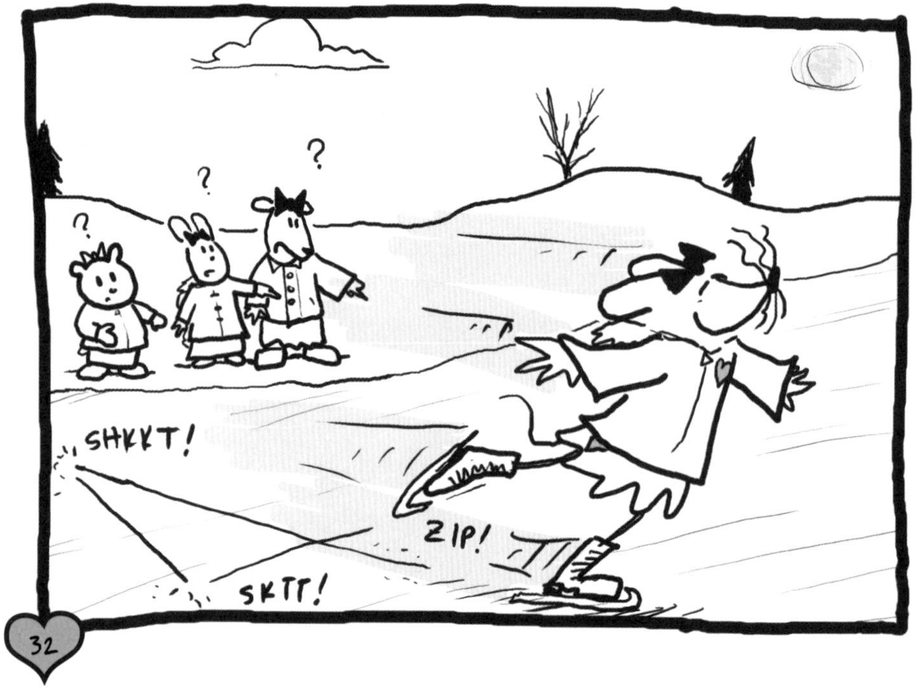
?
?
?
SHKKT!
ZIP!
SKTT!

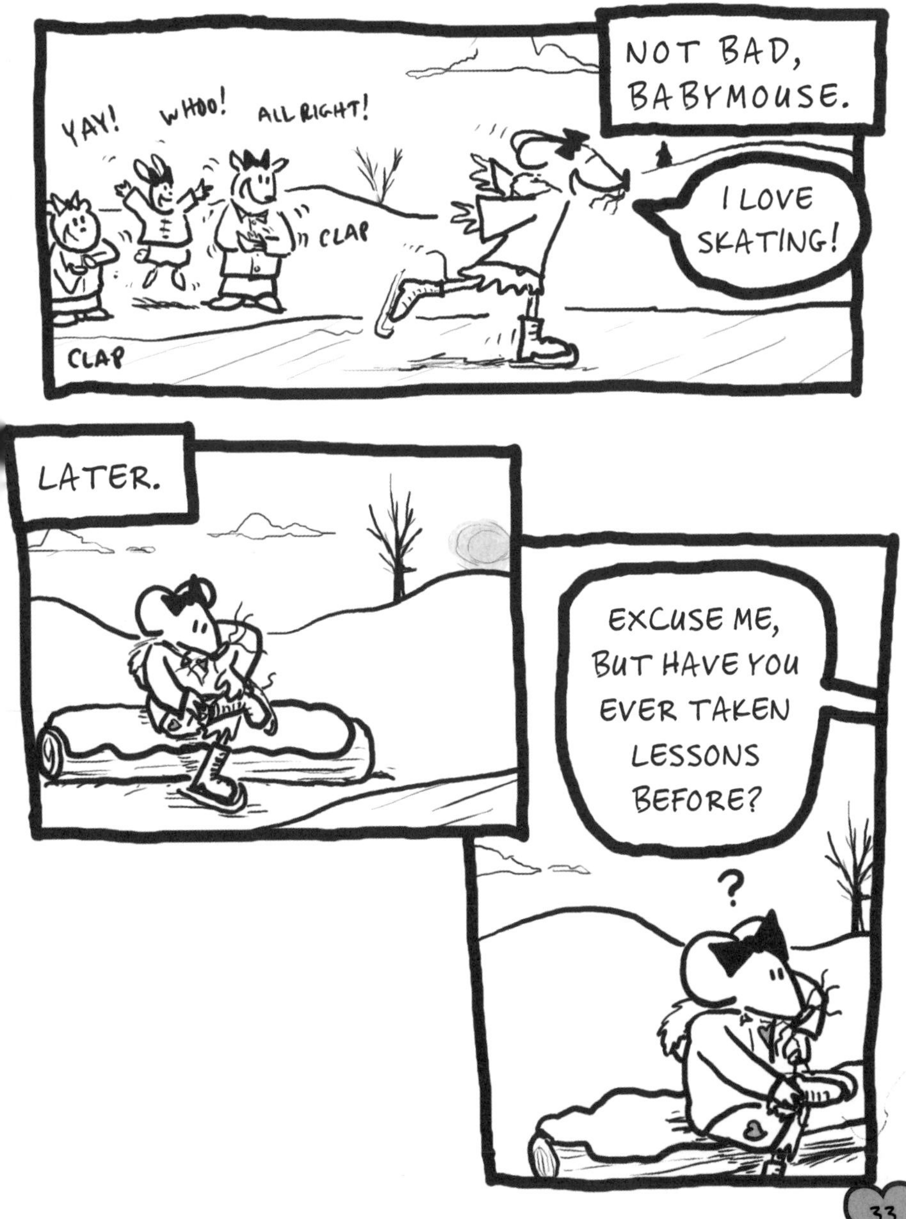
NOT BAD, BABYMOUSE.
YAY!
WHOO!
ALL RIGHT!
CLAP
CLAP
I LOVE SKATING!
LATER.
EXCUSE ME, BUT HAVE YOU EVER TAKEN LESSONS BEFORE?
?

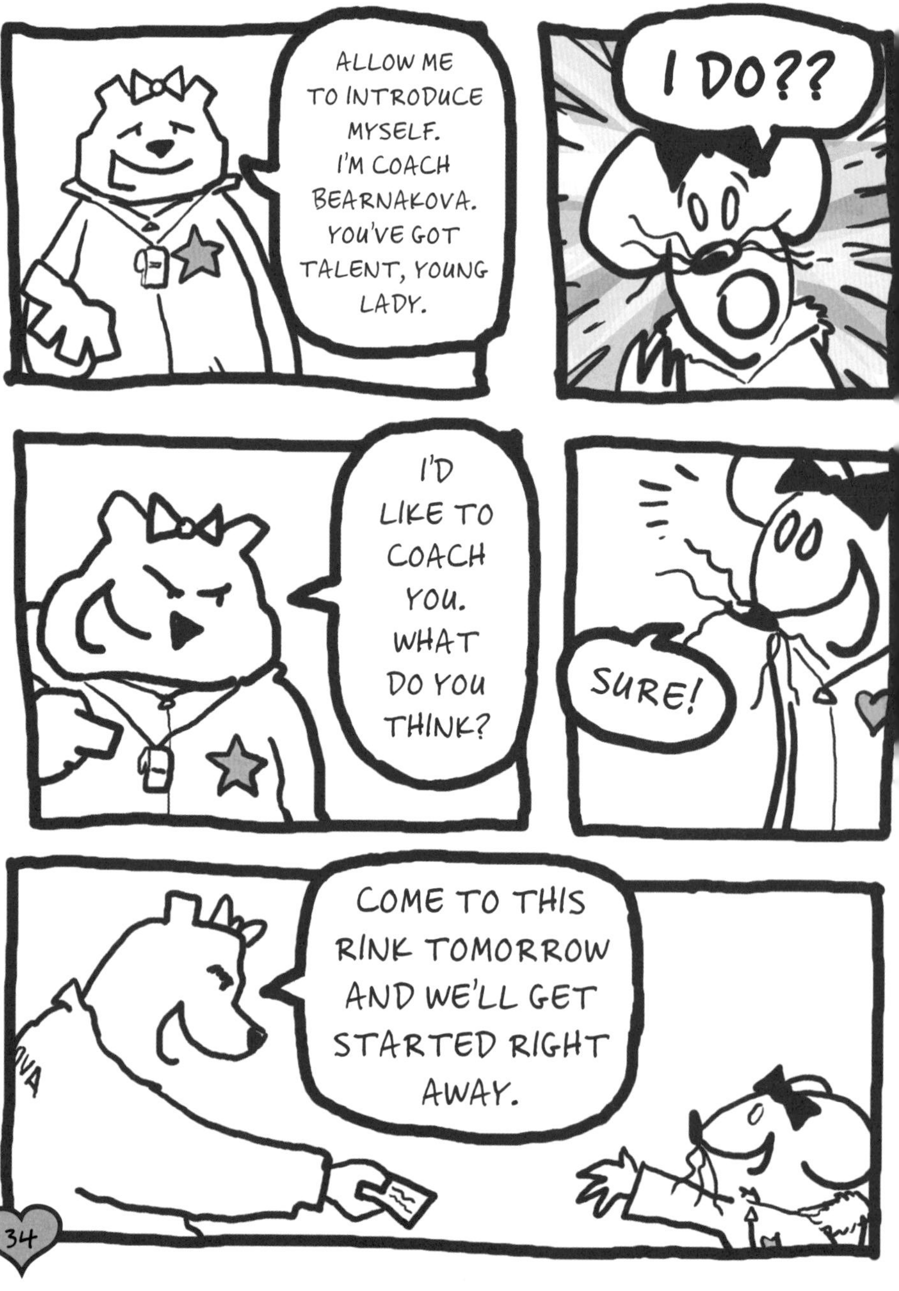
ALLOW ME TO INTRODUCE MYSELF. I'M COACH BEARNAKOVA. YOU'VE GOT TALENT, YOUNG LADY.
I DO??
I'D LIKE TO COACH YOU. WHAT DO YOU THINK?
SURE!
COME TO THIS RINK TOMORROW AND WE'LL GET STARTED RIGHT AWAY.

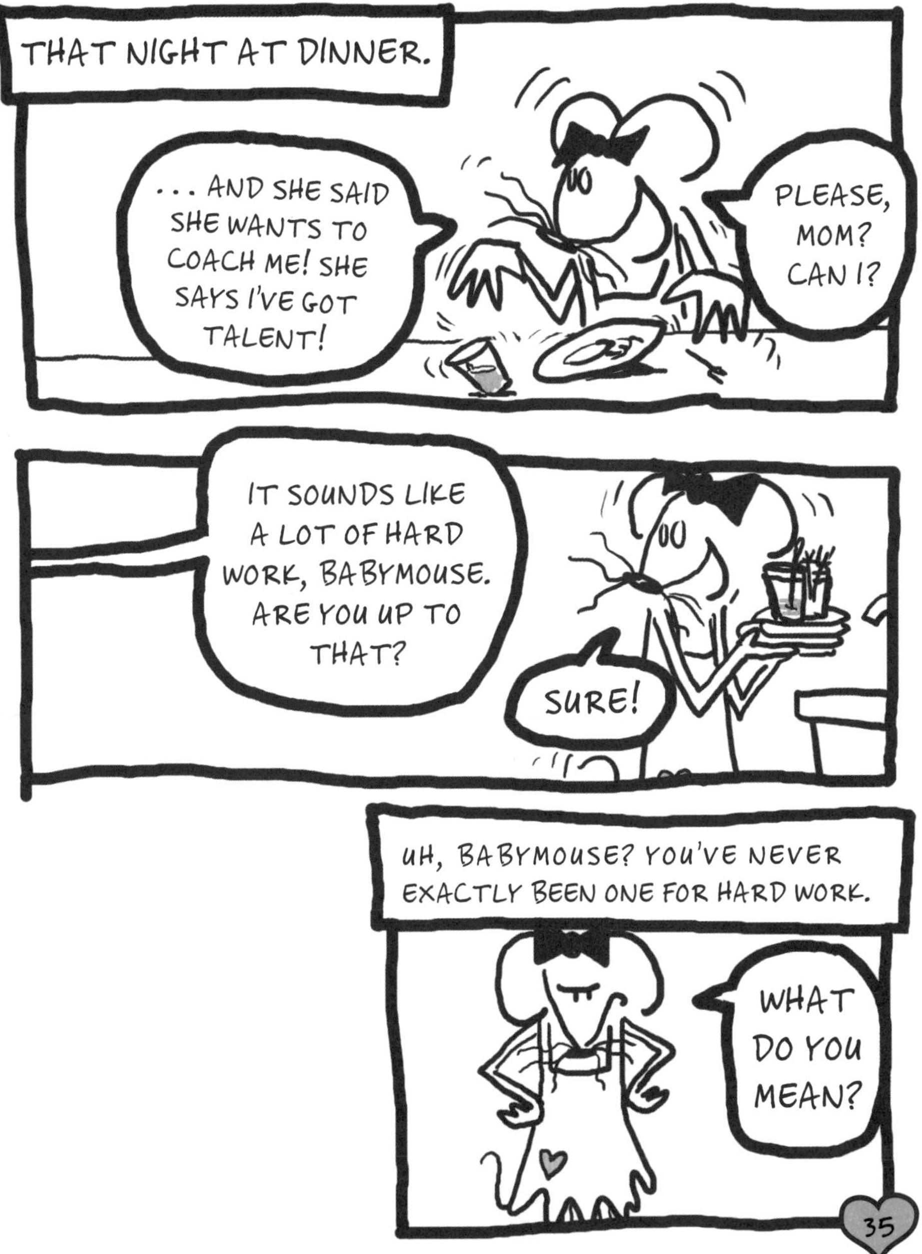
THAT NIGHT AT DINNER.
. . . AND SHE SAID SHE WANTS TO COACH ME! SHE SAYS I'VE GOT TALENT!
PLEASE, MOM? CAN I?
IT SOUNDS LIKE A LOT OF HARD WORK, BABYMOUSE. ARE YOU UP TO THAT?
SURE!
UH, BABYMOUSE? YOU'VE NEVER EXACTLY BEEN ONE FOR HARD WORK.
WHAT DO YOU MEAN?

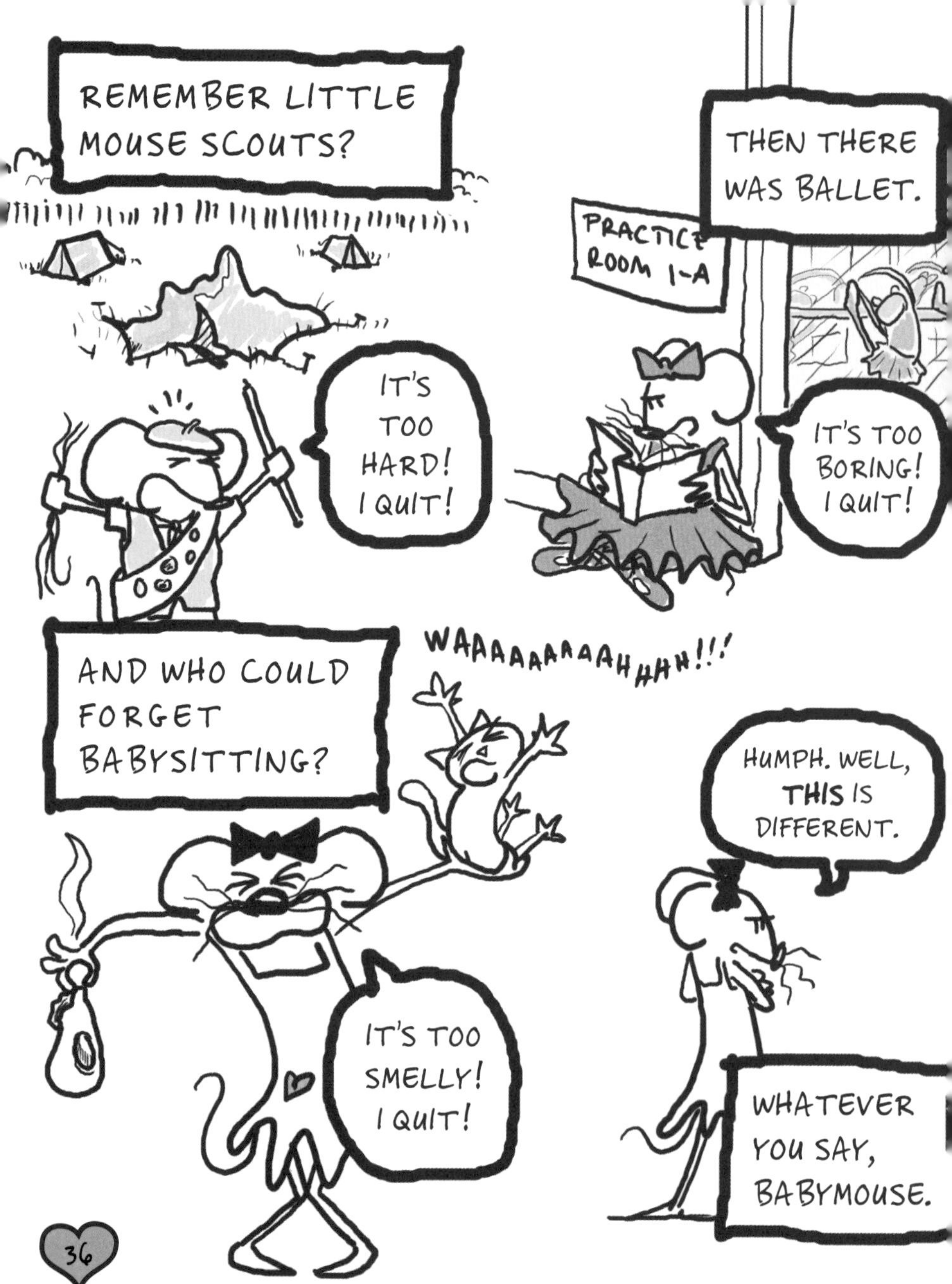
REMEMBER LITTLE MOUSE SCOUTS?
IT'S TOO HARD! I QUIT!
THEN THERE WAS BALLET.
PRACTICE ROOM 1-A
IT'S TOO BORING! I QUIT!
AND WHO COULD FORGET BABYSITTING?
WAAAAAAAAAHHHH!!!
IT'S TOO SMELLY! I QUIT!
HUMPH. WELL, **THIS** IS DIFFERENT.
WHATEVER YOU SAY, BABYMOUSE.

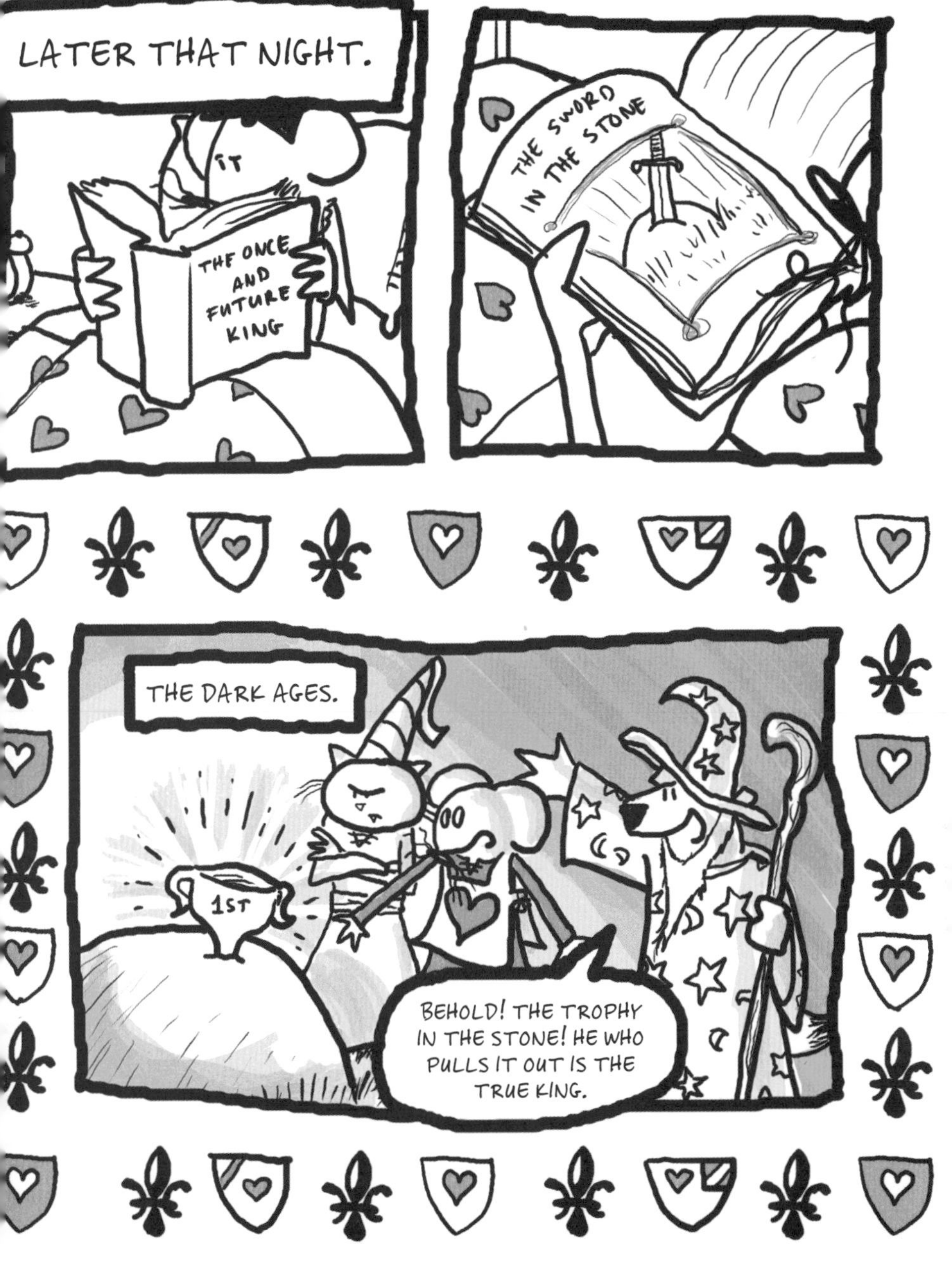
LATER THAT NIGHT.
THE ONCE AND FUTURE KING
THE SWORD IN THE STONE
THE DARK AGES.
1ST
BEHOLD! THE TROPHY IN THE STONE! HE WHO PULLS IT OUT IS THE TRUE KING.

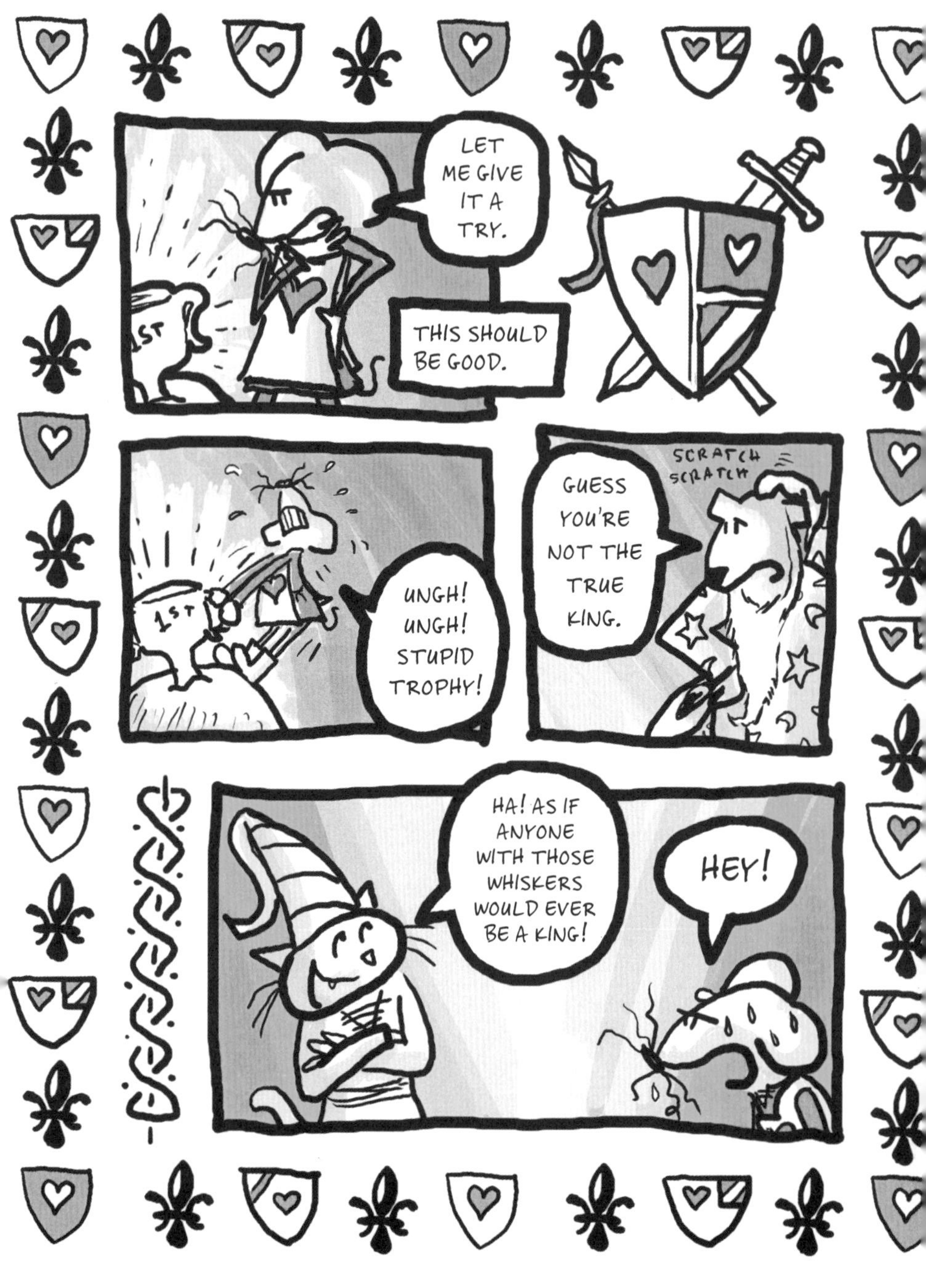
LET ME GIVE IT A TRY.
THIS SHOULD BE GOOD.
1ST
1ST
UNGH! UNGH! STUPID TROPHY!
SCRATCH SCRATCH
GUESS YOU'RE NOT THE TRUE KING.
HA! AS IF ANYONE WITH THOSE WHISKERS WOULD EVER BE A KING!
HEY!

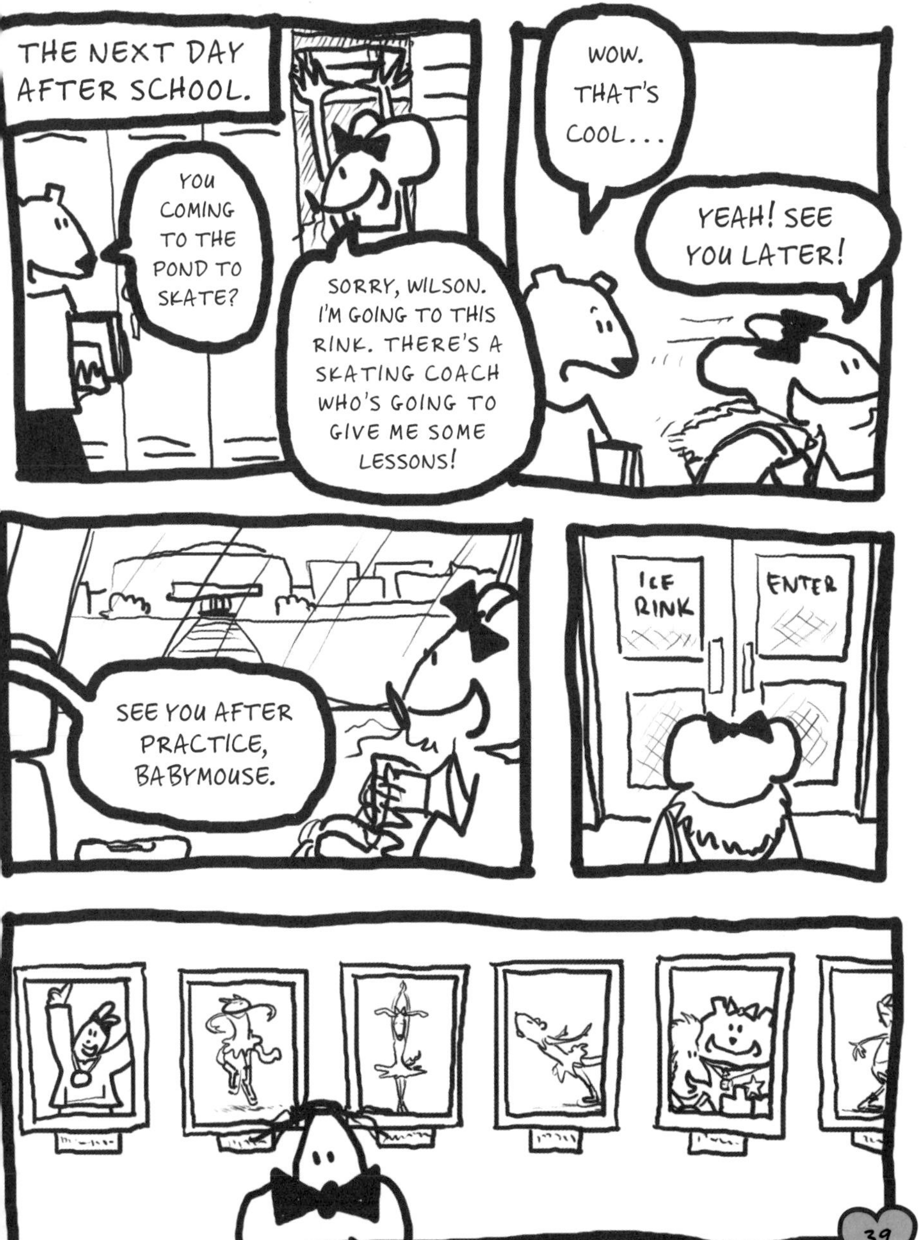
THE NEXT DAY AFTER SCHOOL.
YOU COMING TO THE POND TO SKATE?
SORRY, WILSON. I'M GOING TO THIS RINK. THERE'S A SKATING COACH WHO'S GOING TO GIVE ME SOME LESSONS!
WOW. THAT'S COOL...
YEAH! SEE YOU LATER!
SEE YOU AFTER PRACTICE, BABYMOUSE.
ICE RINK
ENTER

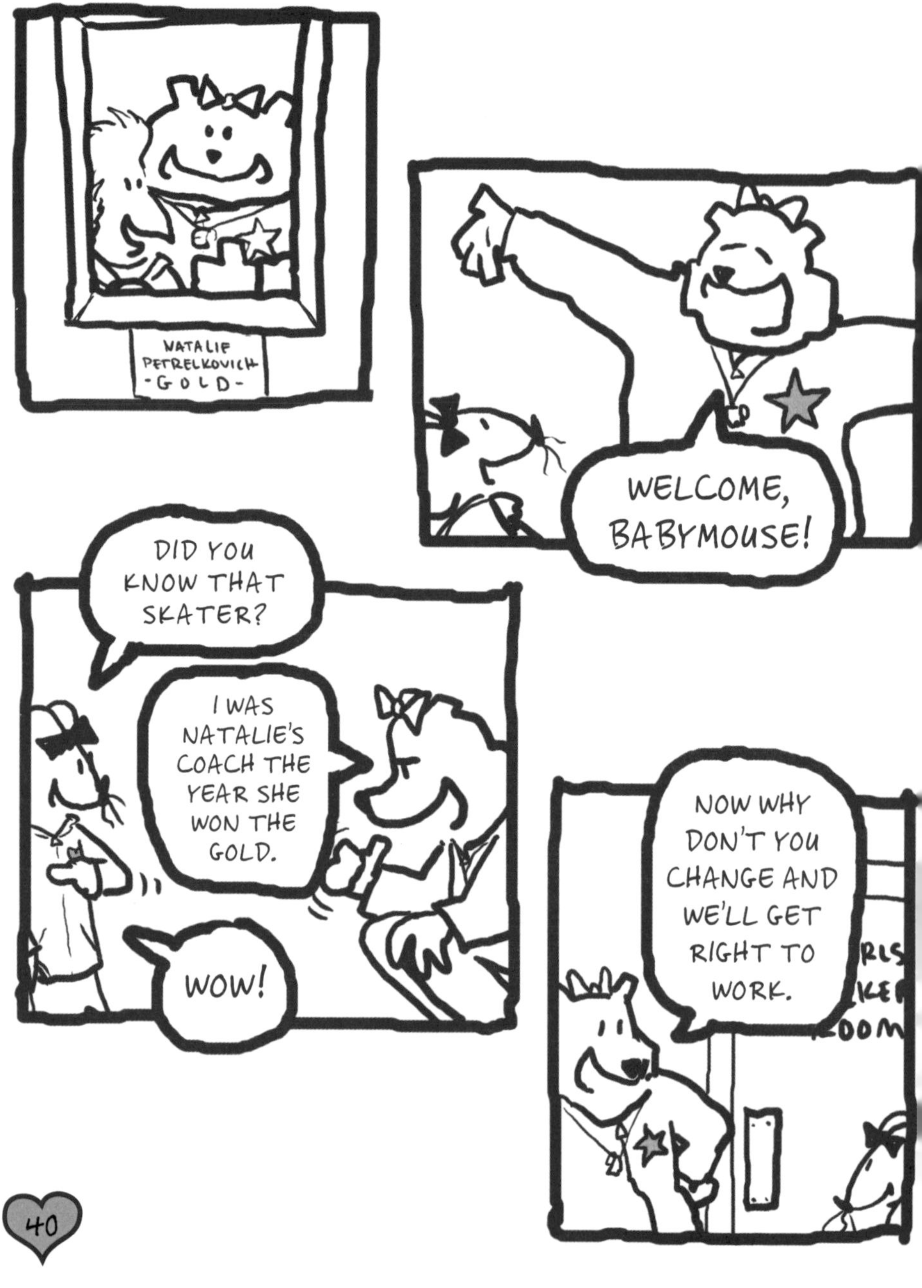
NATALIE PETRELKOVICH -GOLD-
WELCOME, BABYMOUSE!
DID YOU KNOW THAT SKATER?
I WAS NATALIE'S COACH THE YEAR SHE WON THE GOLD.
WOW!
NOW WHY DON'T YOU CHANGE AND WE'LL GET RIGHT TO WORK.

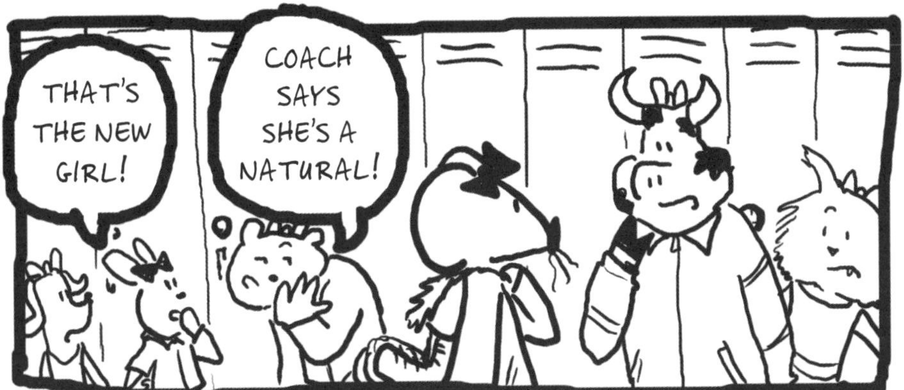
THAT'S THE NEW GIRL!
COACH SAYS SHE'S A NATURAL!

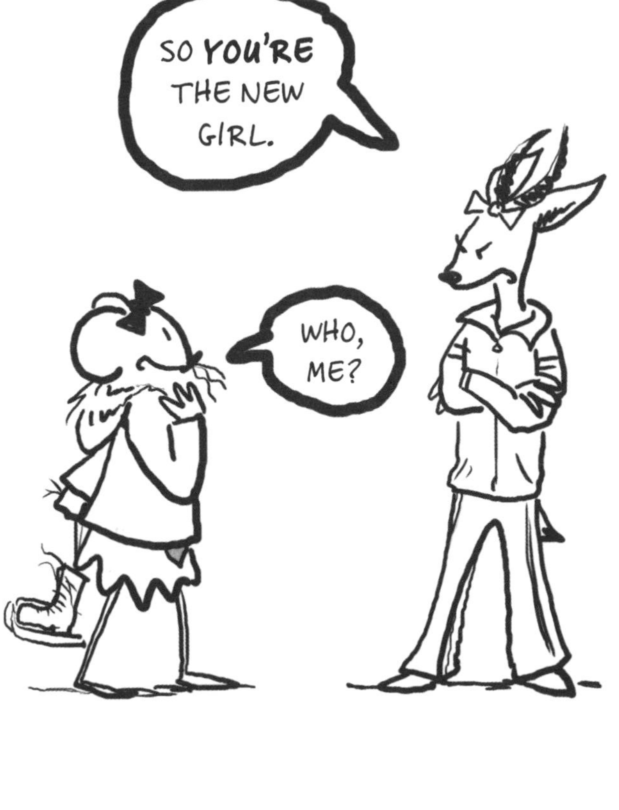
SO **YOU'RE** THE NEW GIRL.
WHO, ME?

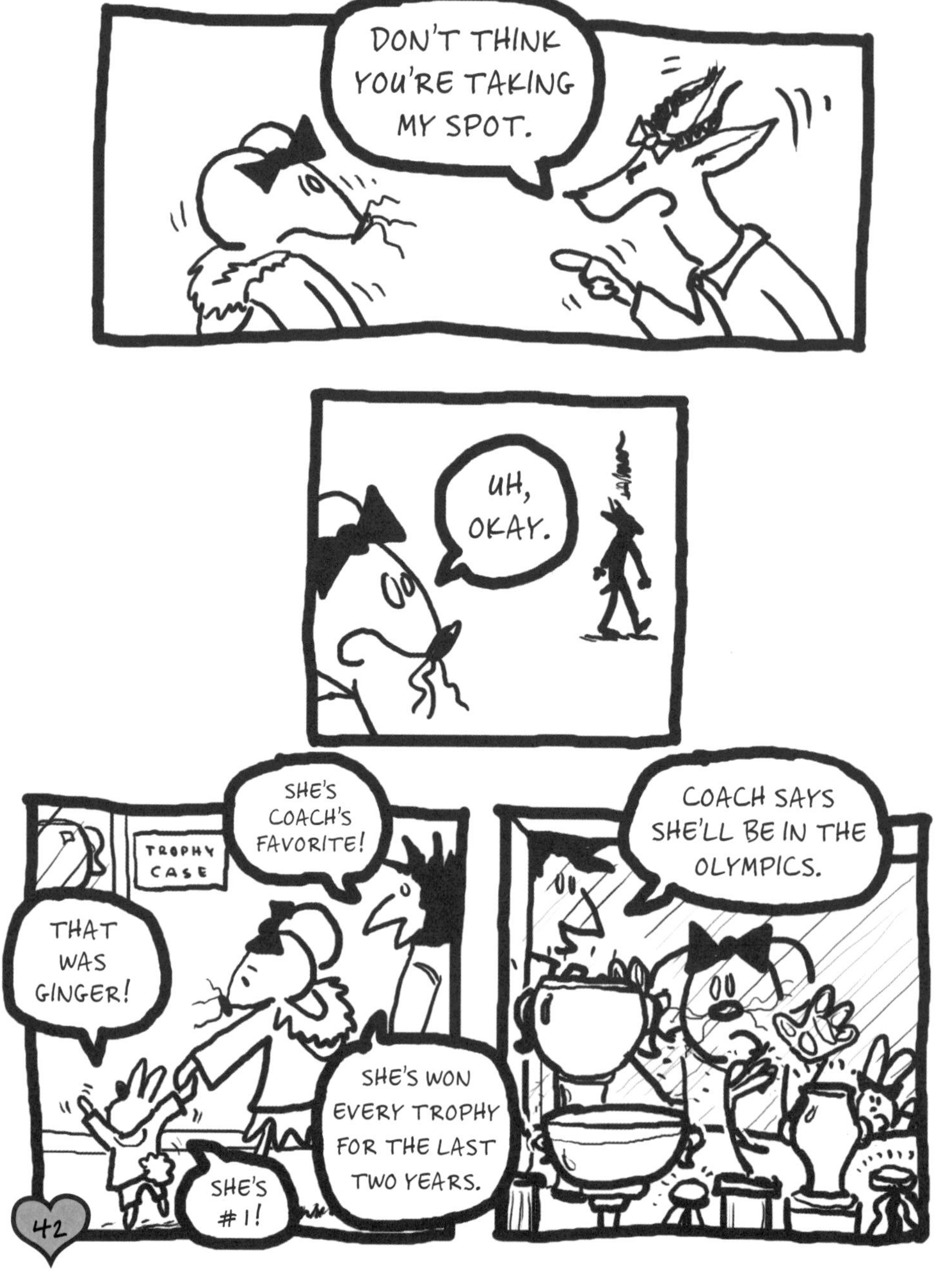
DON'T THINK YOU'RE TAKING MY SPOT.
UH, OKAY.
TROPHY CASE
SHE'S COACH'S FAVORITE!
THAT WAS GINGER!
SHE'S WON EVERY TROPHY FOR THE LAST TWO YEARS.
SHE'S #1!
COACH SAYS SHE'LL BE IN THE OLYMPICS.

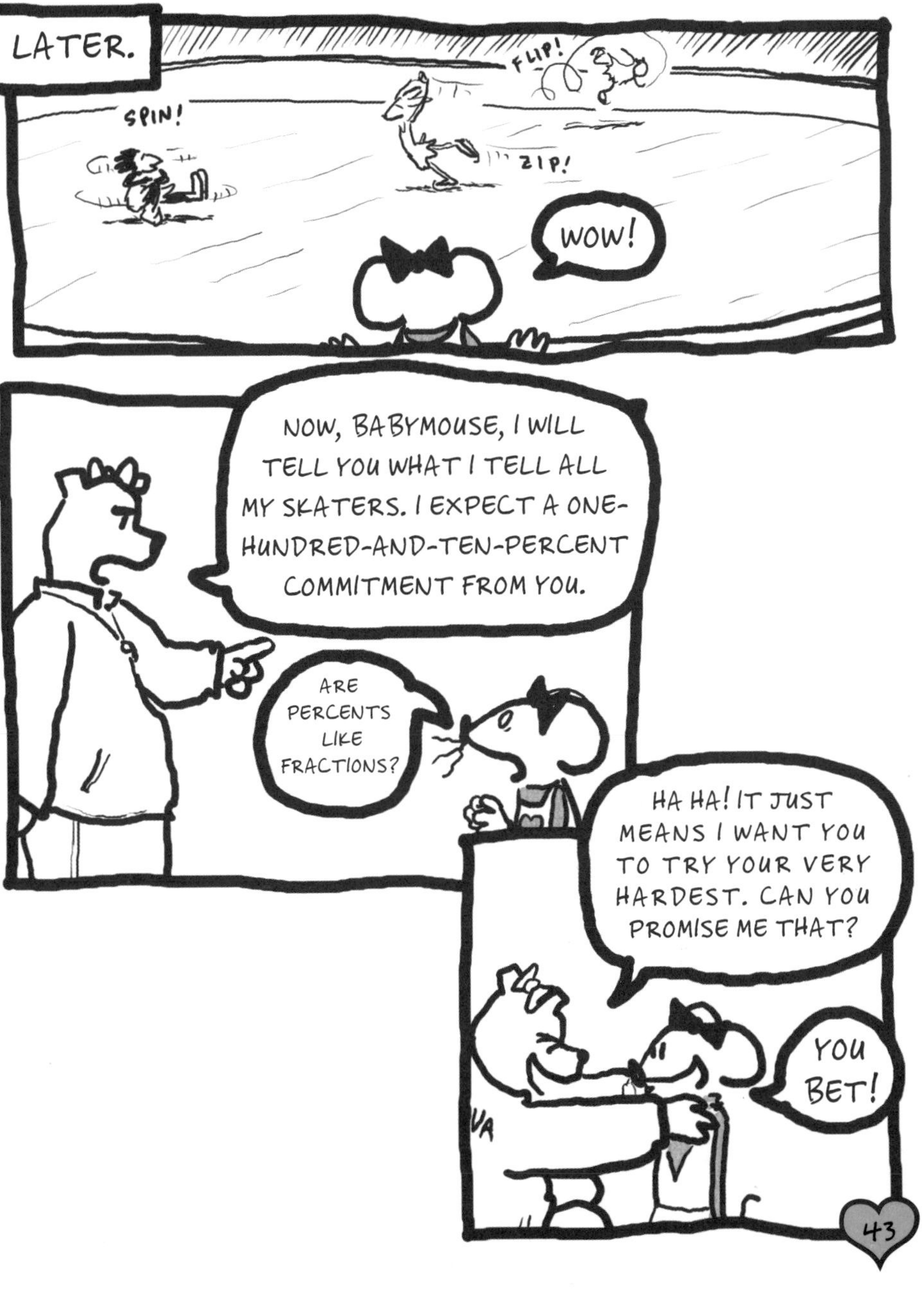
LATER.
SPIN!
FLIP!
ZIP!
WOW!
NOW, BABYMOUSE, I WILL TELL YOU WHAT I TELL ALL MY SKATERS. I EXPECT A ONE-HUNDRED-AND-TEN-PERCENT COMMITMENT FROM YOU.
ARE PERCENTS LIKE FRACTIONS?
HA HA! IT JUST MEANS I WANT YOU TO TRY YOUR VERY HARDEST. CAN YOU PROMISE ME THAT?
YOU BET!

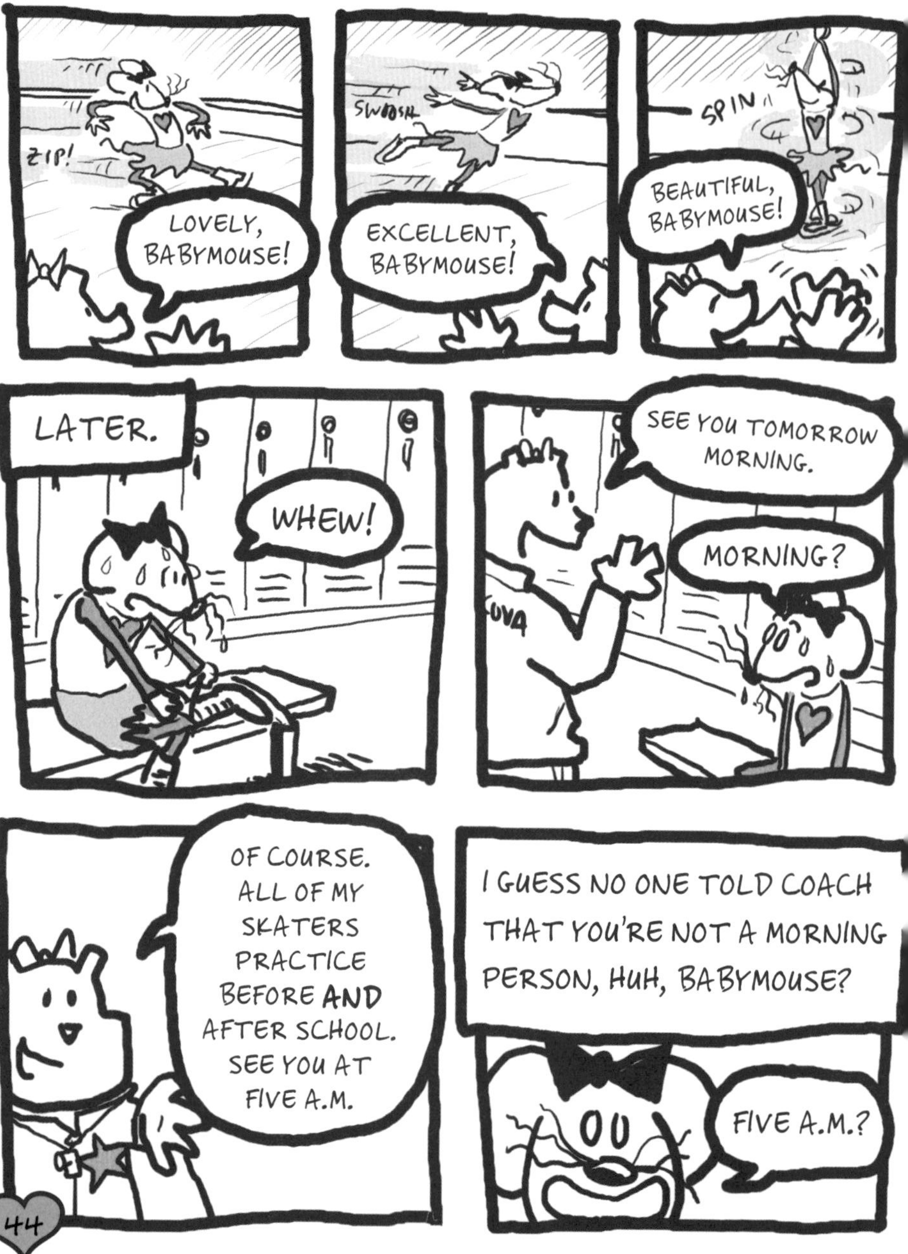
ZIP!
LOVELY, BABYMOUSE!
SWOOSH
EXCELLENT, BABYMOUSE!
SPIN
BEAUTIFUL, BABYMOUSE!
LATER.
WHEW!
SEE YOU TOMORROW MORNING.
MORNING?
OF COURSE. ALL OF MY SKATERS PRACTICE BEFORE AND AFTER SCHOOL. SEE YOU AT FIVE A.M.
I GUESS NO ONE TOLD COACH THAT YOU'RE NOT A MORNING PERSON, HUH, BABYMOUSE?
FIVE A.M.?

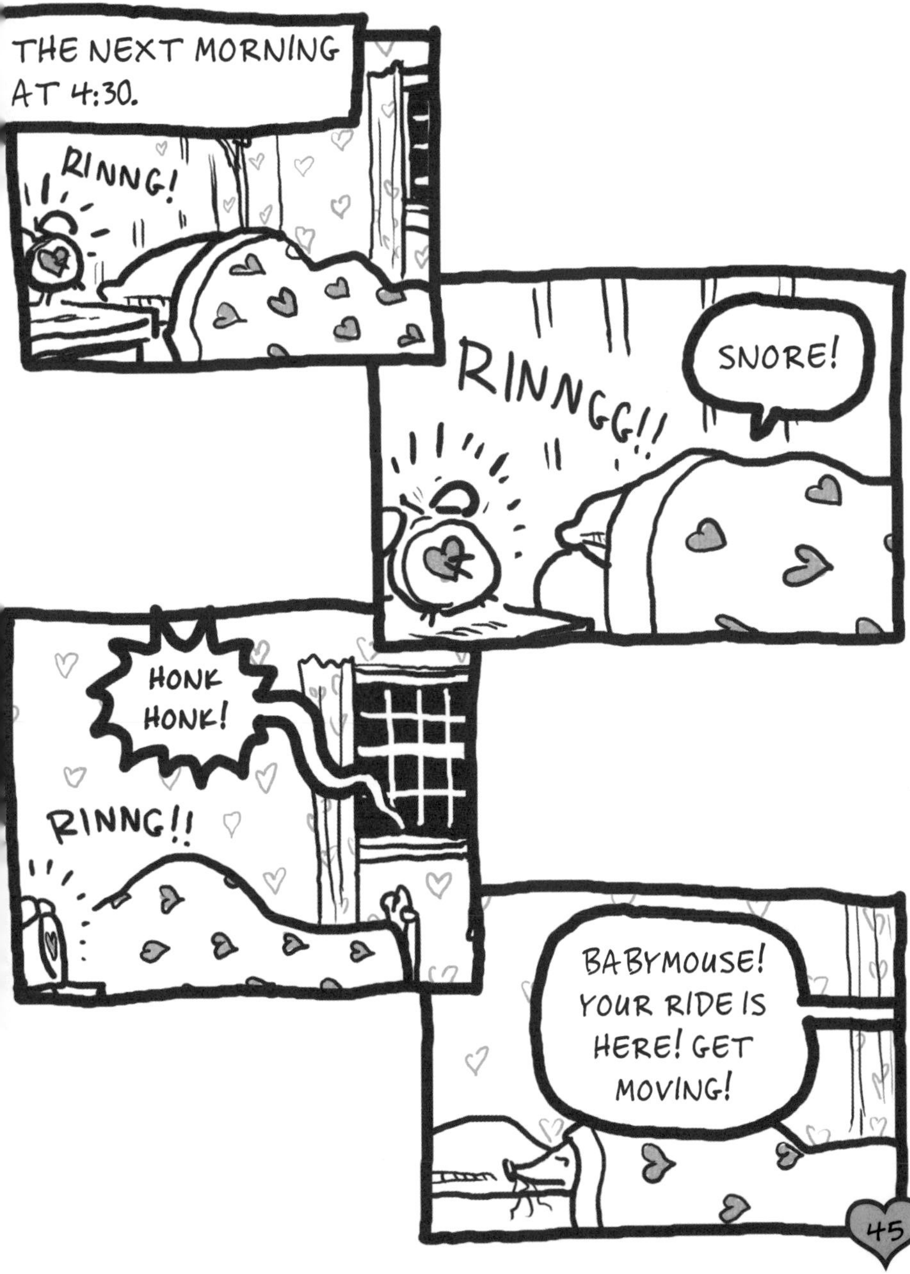
THE NEXT MORNING AT 4:30.
RINNG!
RINNGG!!
SNORE!
HONK HONK!
RINNG!!
BABYMOUSE! YOUR RIDE IS HERE! GET MOVING!

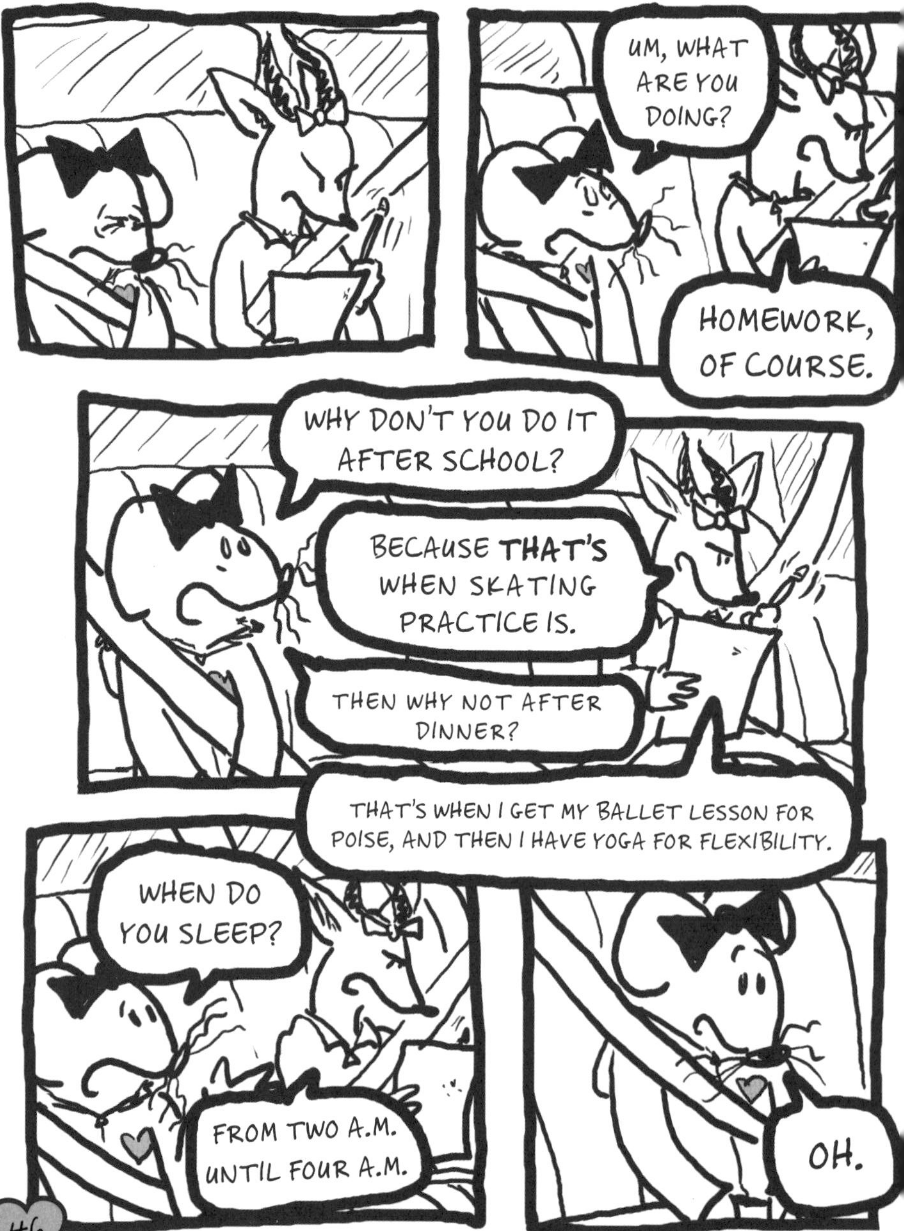
UM, WHAT ARE YOU DOING?
HOMEWORK, OF COURSE.
WHY DON'T YOU DO IT AFTER SCHOOL?
BECAUSE THAT'S WHEN SKATING PRACTICE IS.
THEN WHY NOT AFTER DINNER?
THAT'S WHEN I GET MY BALLET LESSON FOR POISE, AND THEN I HAVE YOGA FOR FLEXIBILITY.
WHEN DO YOU SLEEP?
FROM TWO A.M. UNTIL FOUR A.M.
OH.

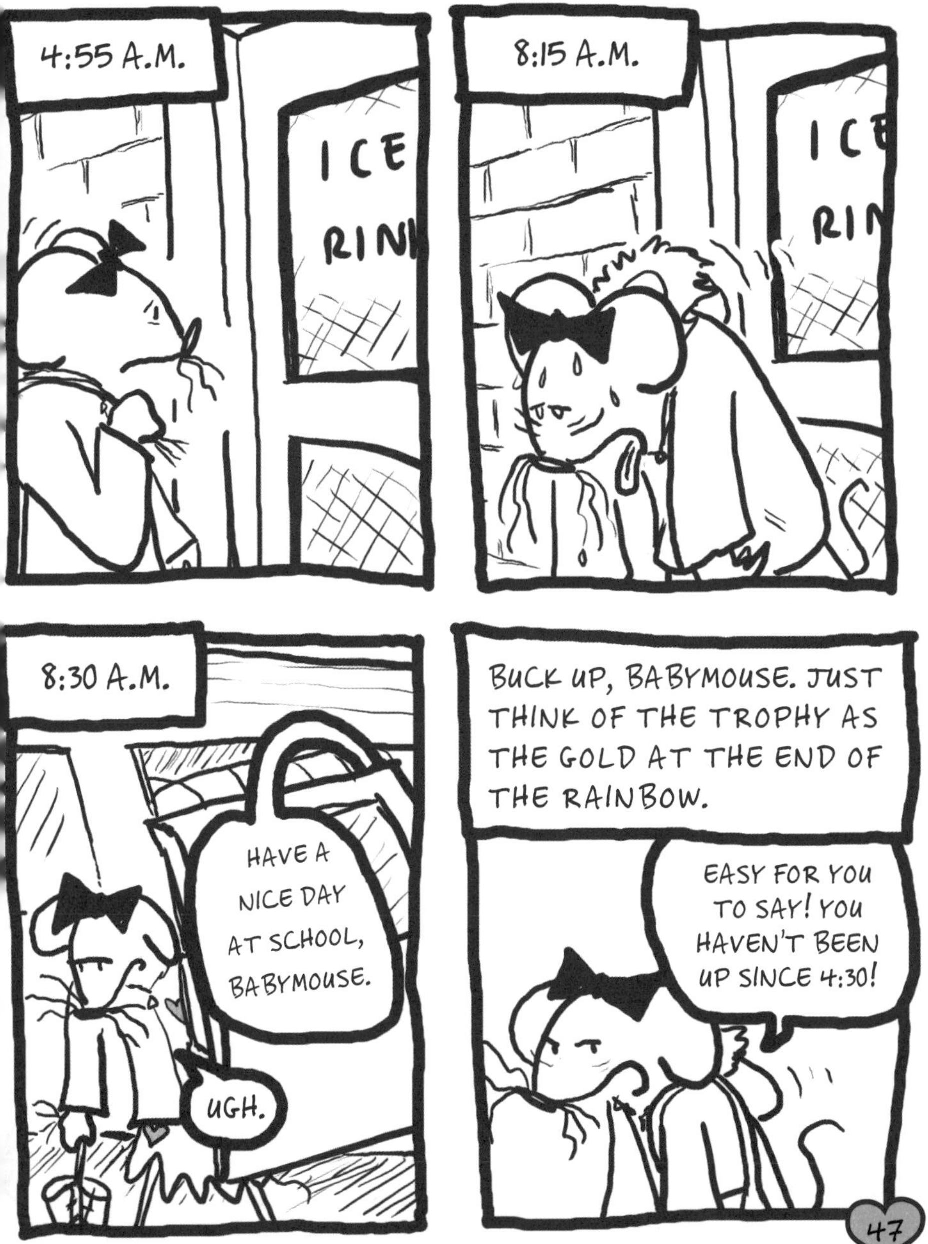
4:55 A.M.
ICE RINK
8:15 A.M.
ICE RINK
8:30 A.M.
HAVE A NICE DAY AT SCHOOL, BABYMOUSE.
UGH.
BUCK UP, BABYMOUSE. JUST THINK OF THE TROPHY AS THE GOLD AT THE END OF THE RAINBOW.
EASY FOR YOU TO SAY! YOU HAVEN'T BEEN UP SINCE 4:30!

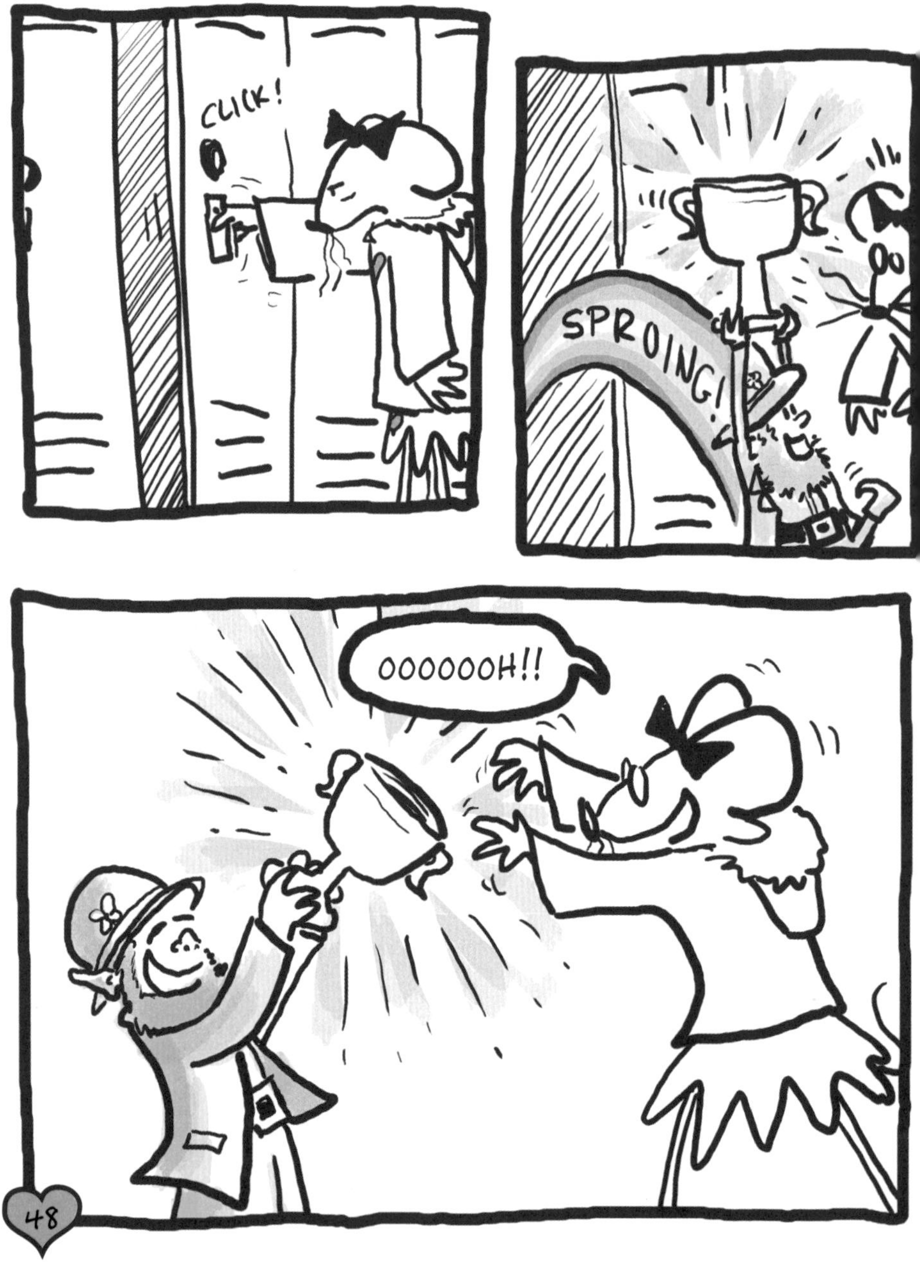
CLICK!
SPROING!
OOOOOOH!!

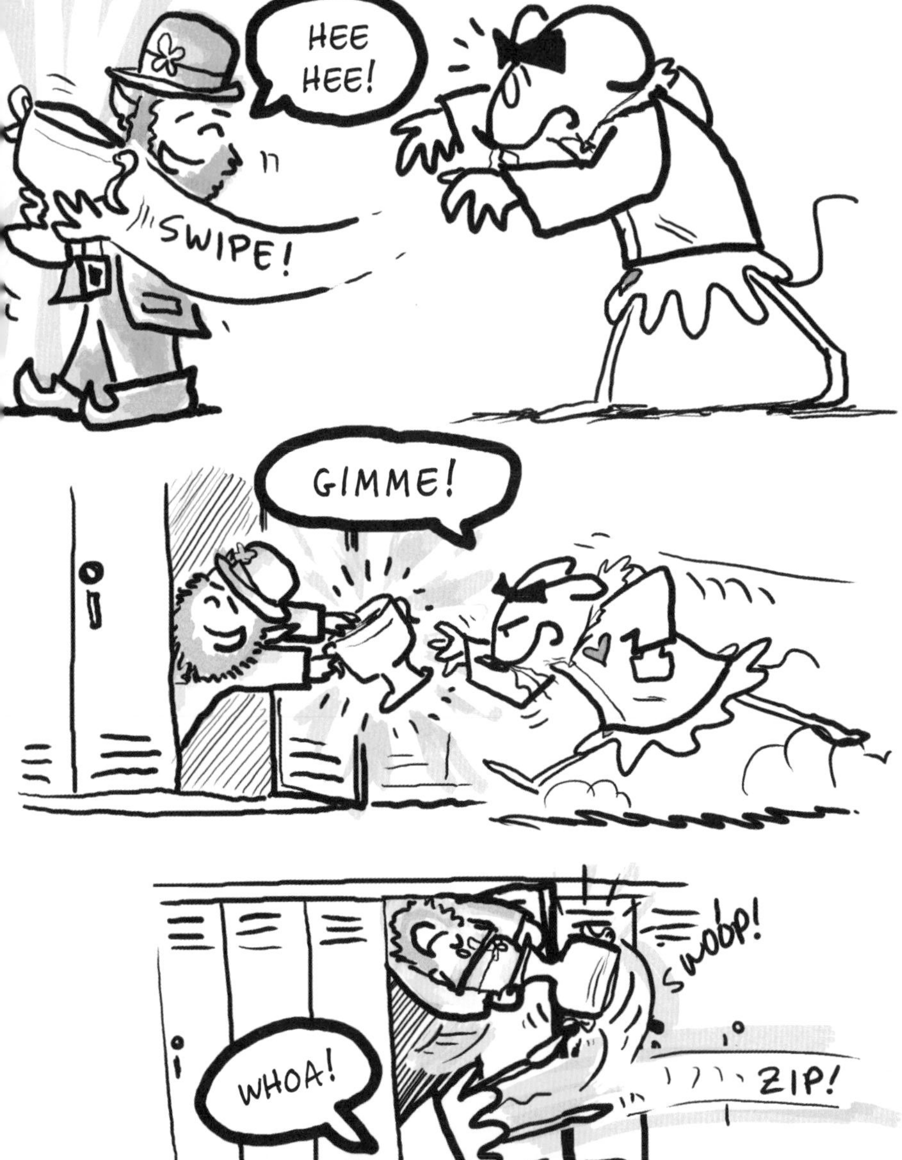
HEE HEE!
SWIPE!
GIMME!
SWOOP!
WHOA!
ZIP!

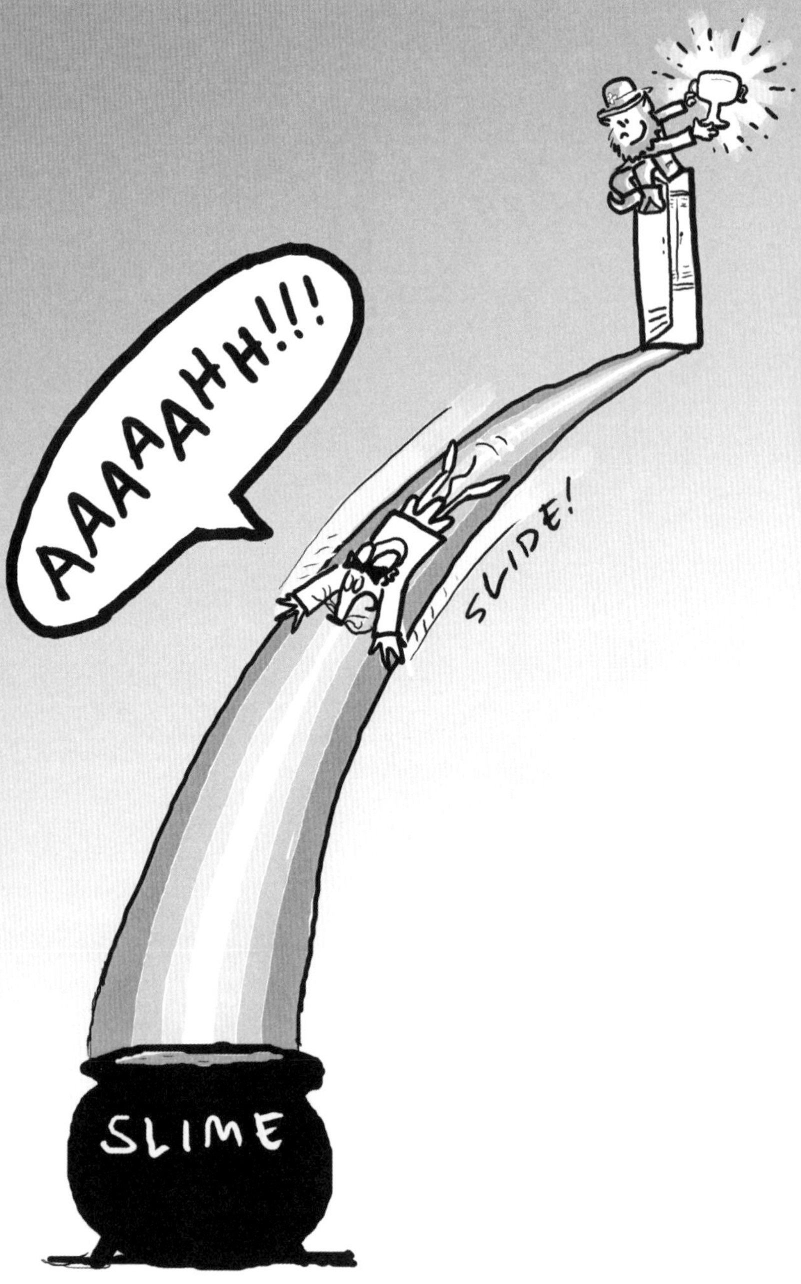
AAAAAH!!!
SLIDE!
SLIME

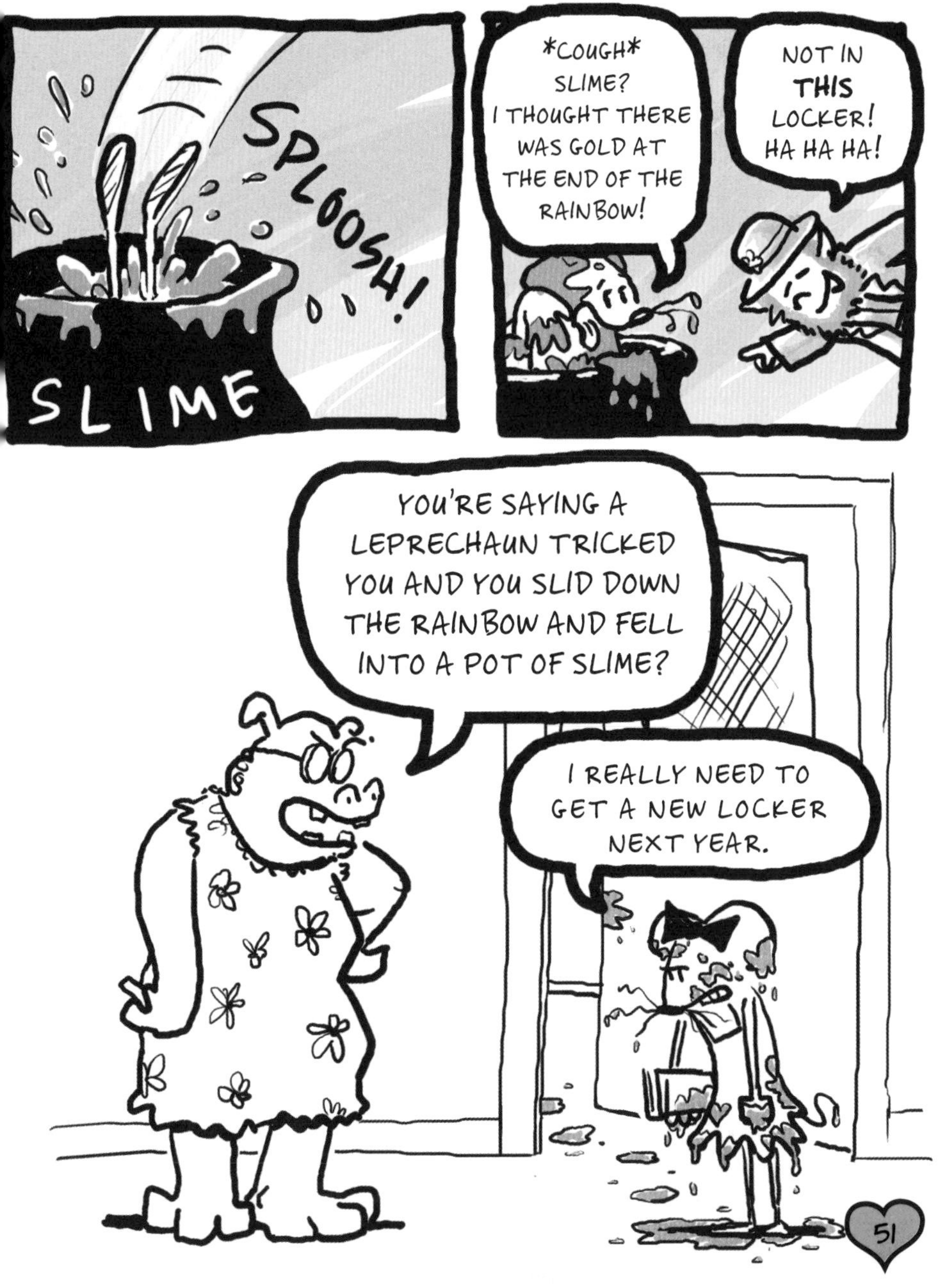
SPLOOSH!
SLIME
COUGH SLIME? I THOUGHT THERE WAS GOLD AT THE END OF THE RAINBOW!
NOT IN THIS LOCKER! HA HA HA!
YOU'RE SAYING A LEPRECHAUN TRICKED YOU AND YOU SLID DOWN THE RAINBOW AND FELL INTO A POT OF SLIME?
I REALLY NEED TO GET A NEW LOCKER NEXT YEAR.

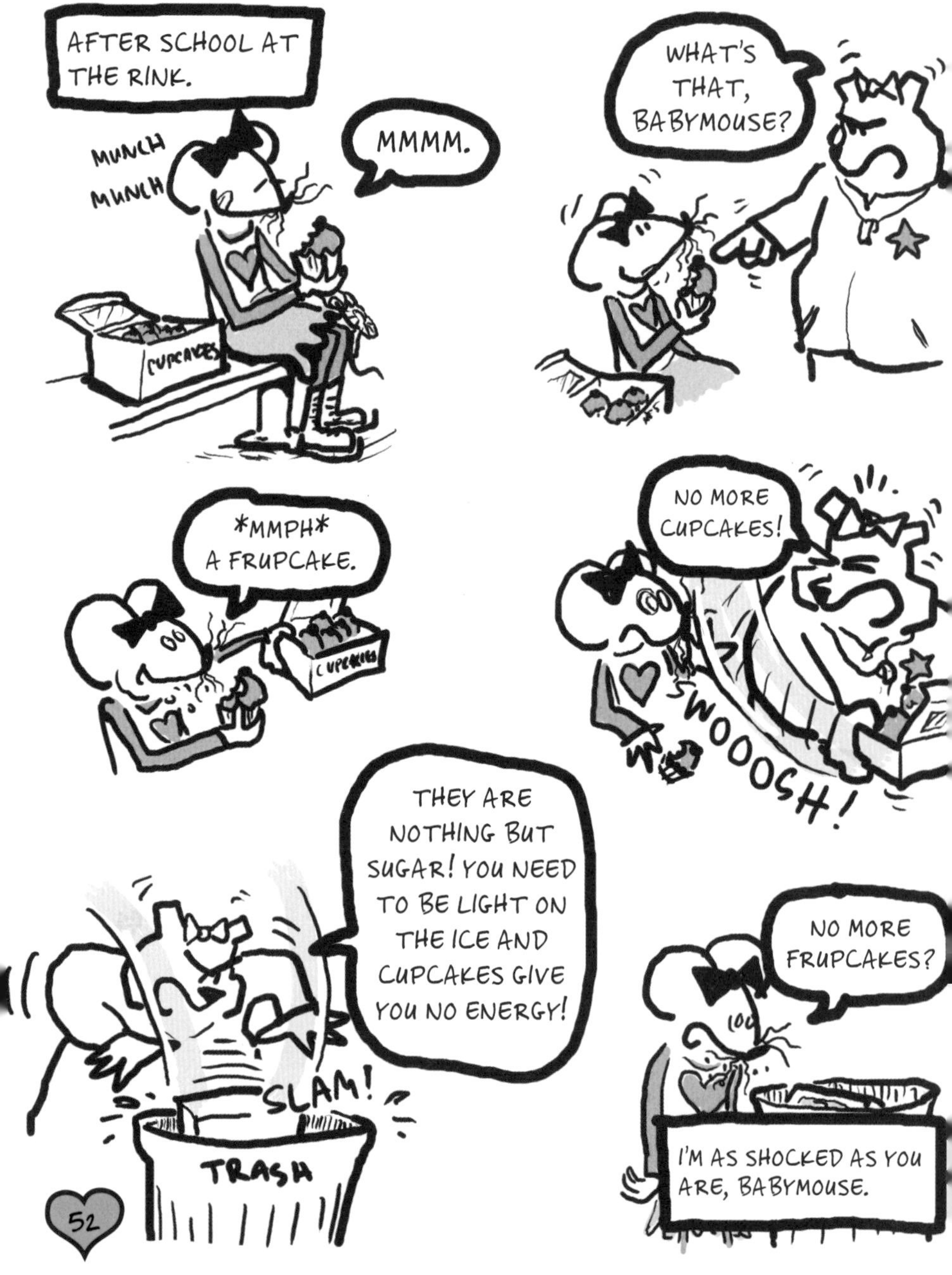
AFTER SCHOOL AT THE RINK.
MUNCH MUNCH
MMMM.
CUPCAKES
WHAT'S THAT, BABYMOUSE?
MMPH A FRUPCAKE.
CUPCAKES
NO MORE CUPCAKES!
SWOOOOSH!
THEY ARE NOTHING BUT SUGAR! YOU NEED TO BE LIGHT ON THE ICE AND CUPCAKES GIVE YOU NO ENERGY!
SLAM!
TRASH
NO MORE FRUPCAKES?
I'M AS SHOCKED AS YOU ARE, BABYMOUSE.

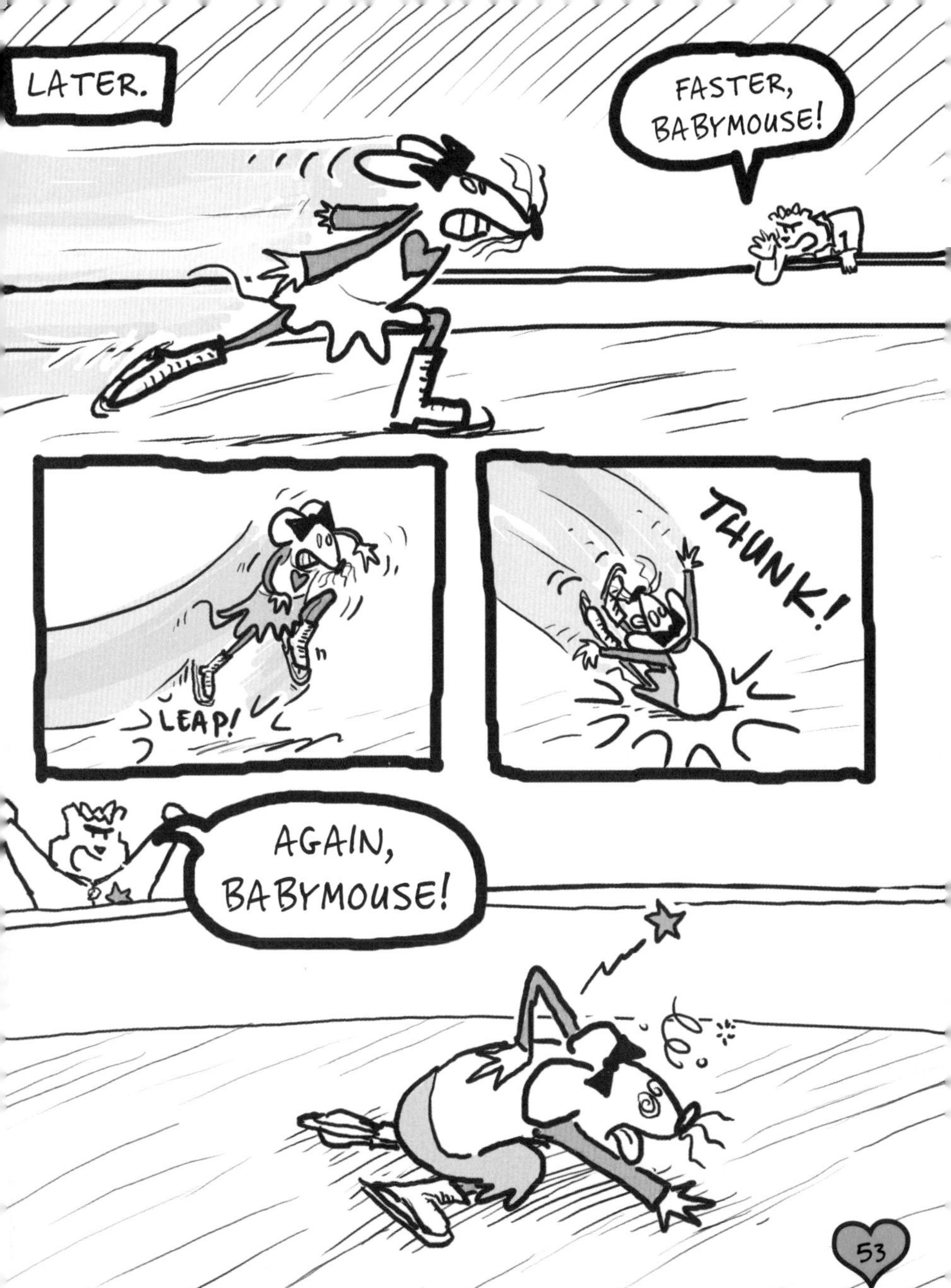
LATER.
FASTER, BABYMOUSE!
LEAP!
THUNK!
AGAIN, BABYMOUSE!

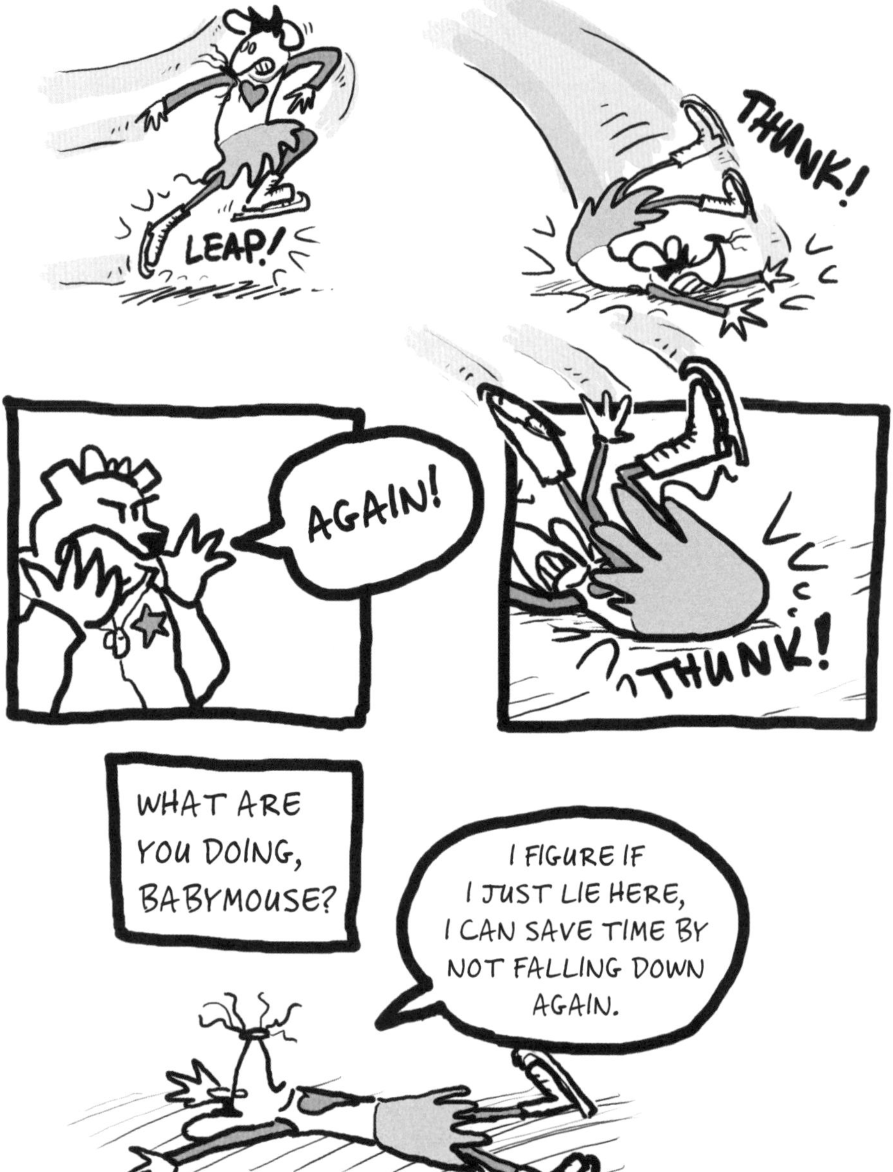
LEAP!
THUNK!
AGAIN!
THUNK!
WHAT ARE YOU DOING, BABYMOUSE?
I FIGURE IF I JUST LIE HERE, I CAN SAVE TIME BY NOT FALLING DOWN AGAIN.

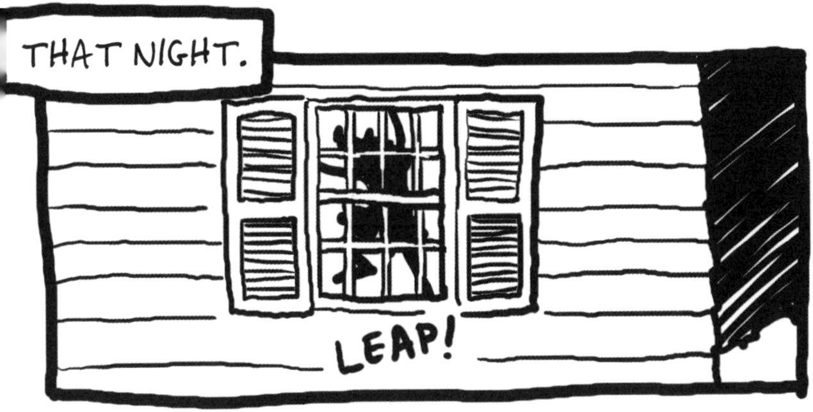
THAT NIGHT.
LEAP!

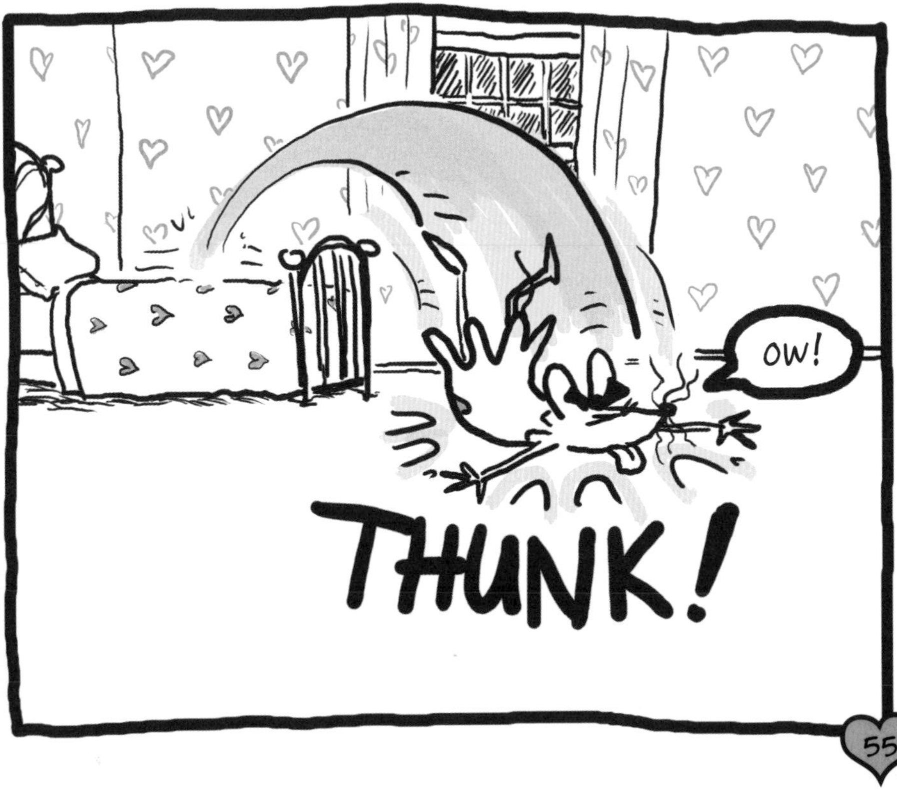
OW!
THUNK!

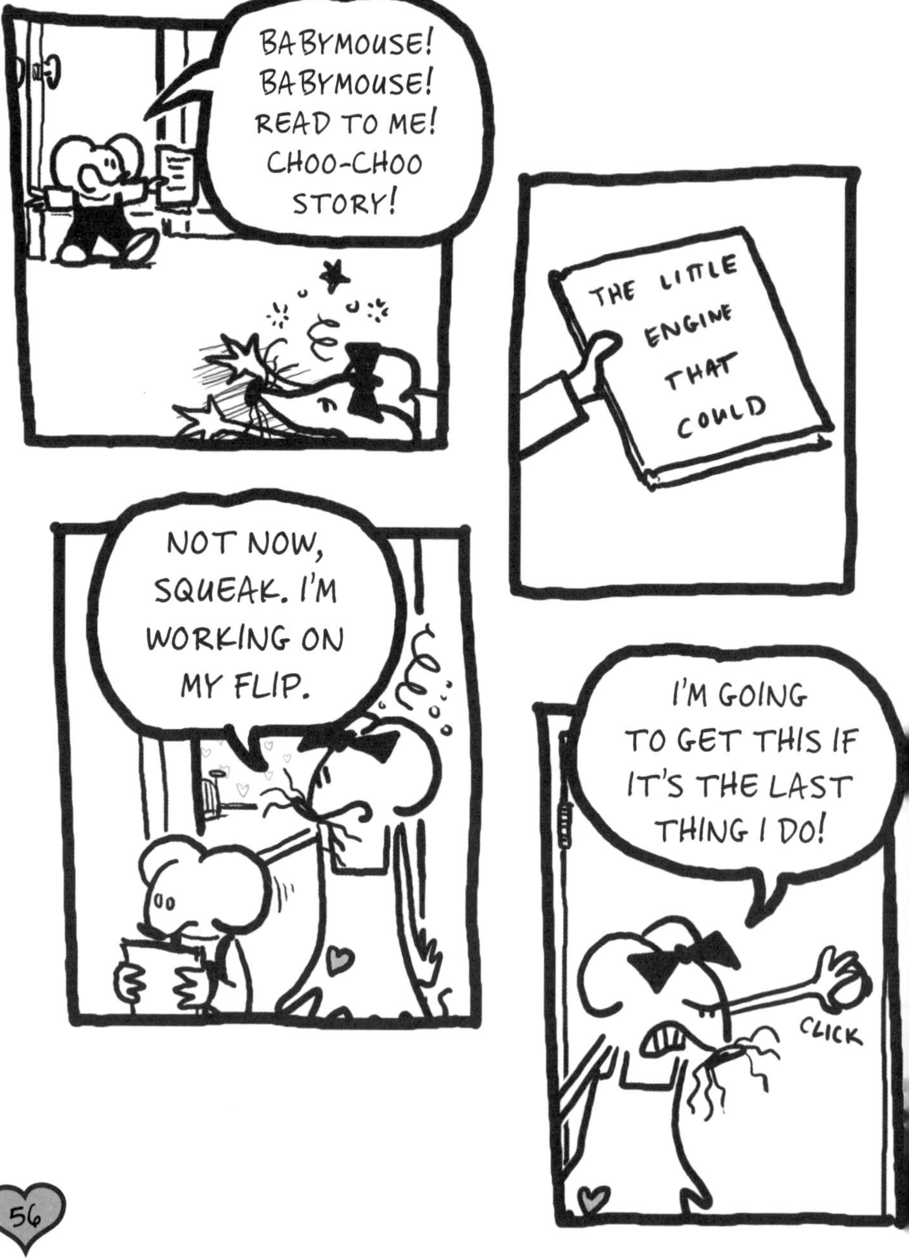
BABYMOUSE! BABYMOUSE! READ TO ME! CHOO-CHOO STORY!
THE LITTLE ENGINE THAT COULD
NOT NOW, SQUEAK. I'M WORKING ON MY FLIP.
I'M GOING TO GET THIS IF IT'S THE LAST THING I DO!
CLICK

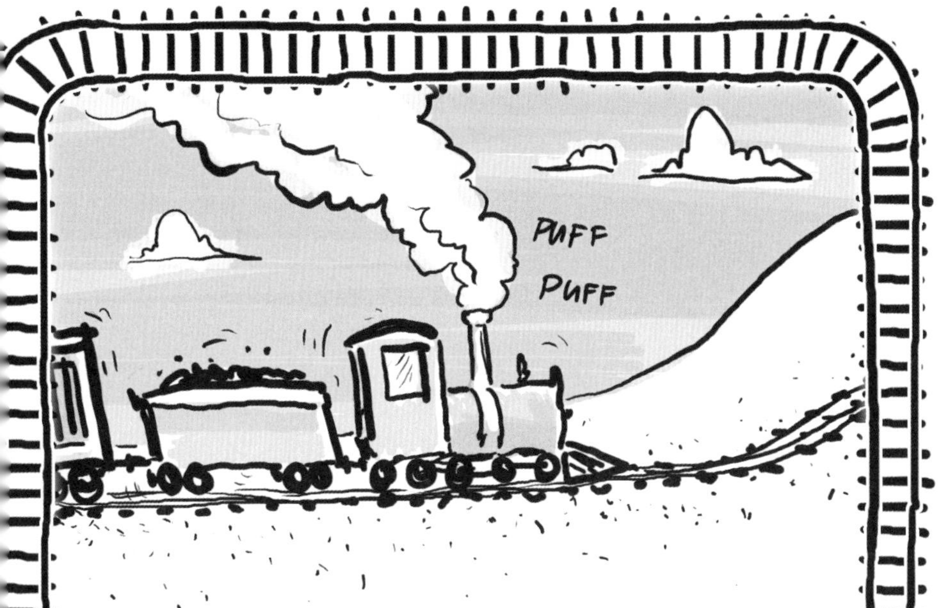
PUFF
PUFF

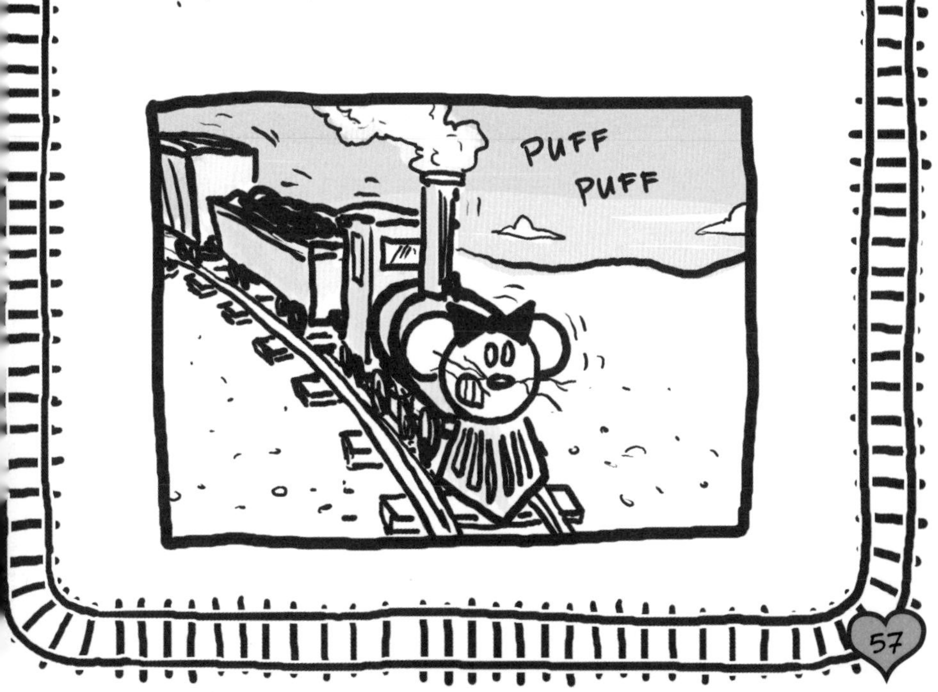
PUFF
PUFF

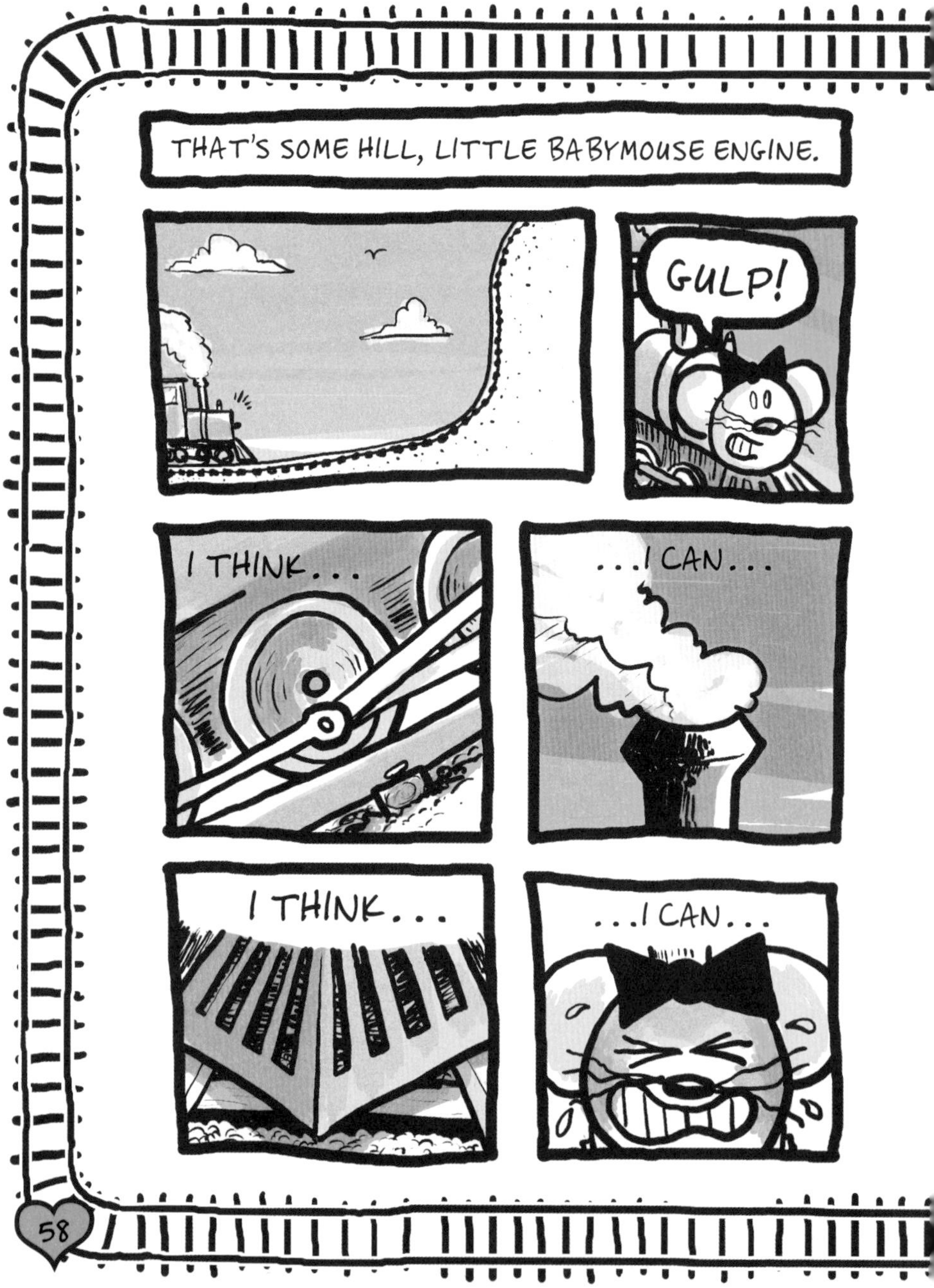
THAT'S SOME HILL, LITTLE BABYMOUSE ENGINE.
GULP!
I THINK...
...I CAN...
I THINK...
...I CAN...

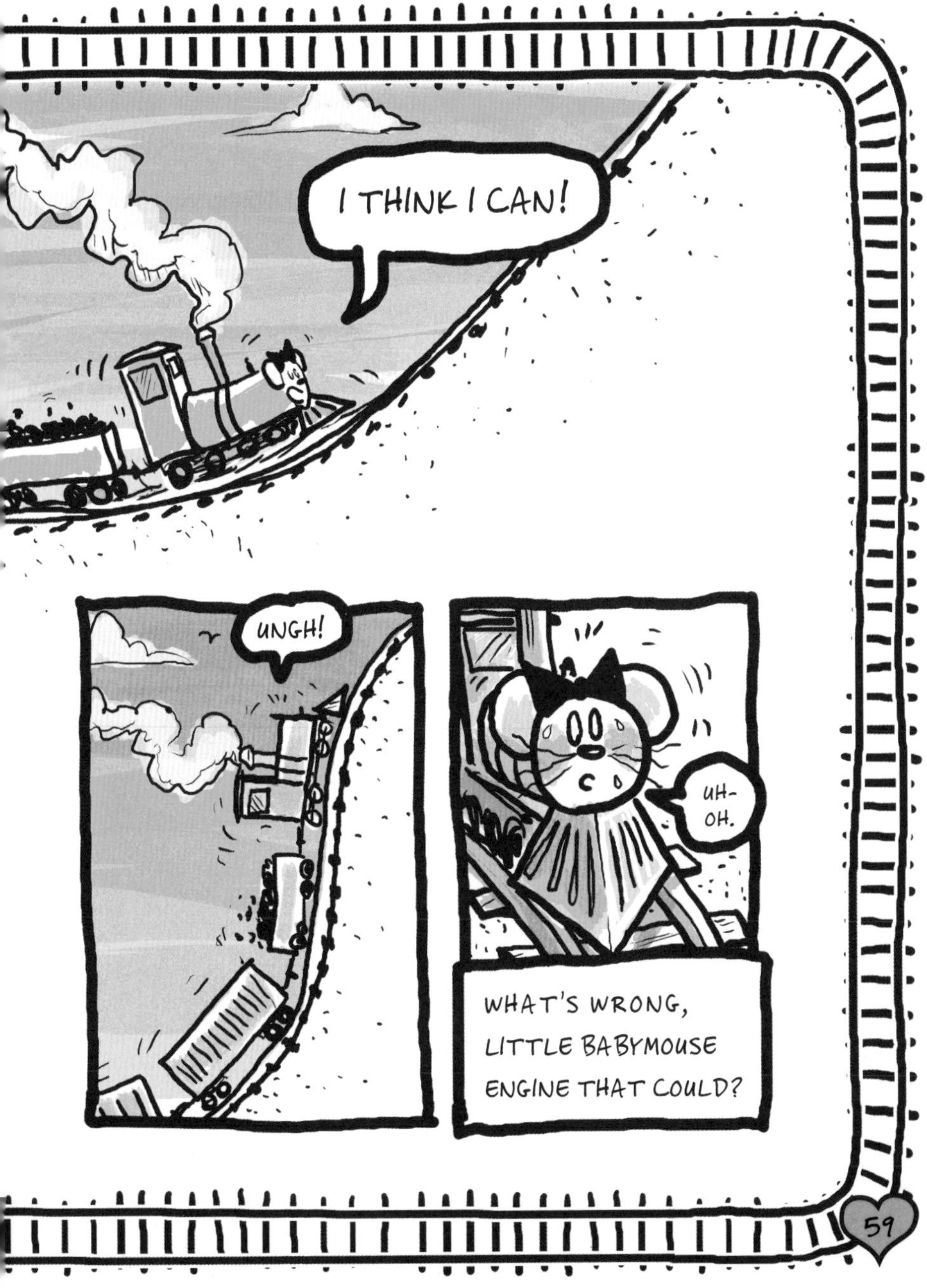
I THINK I CAN!
UNGH!
UH-OH.
WHAT'S WRONG, LITTLE BABYMOUSE ENGINE THAT COULD?

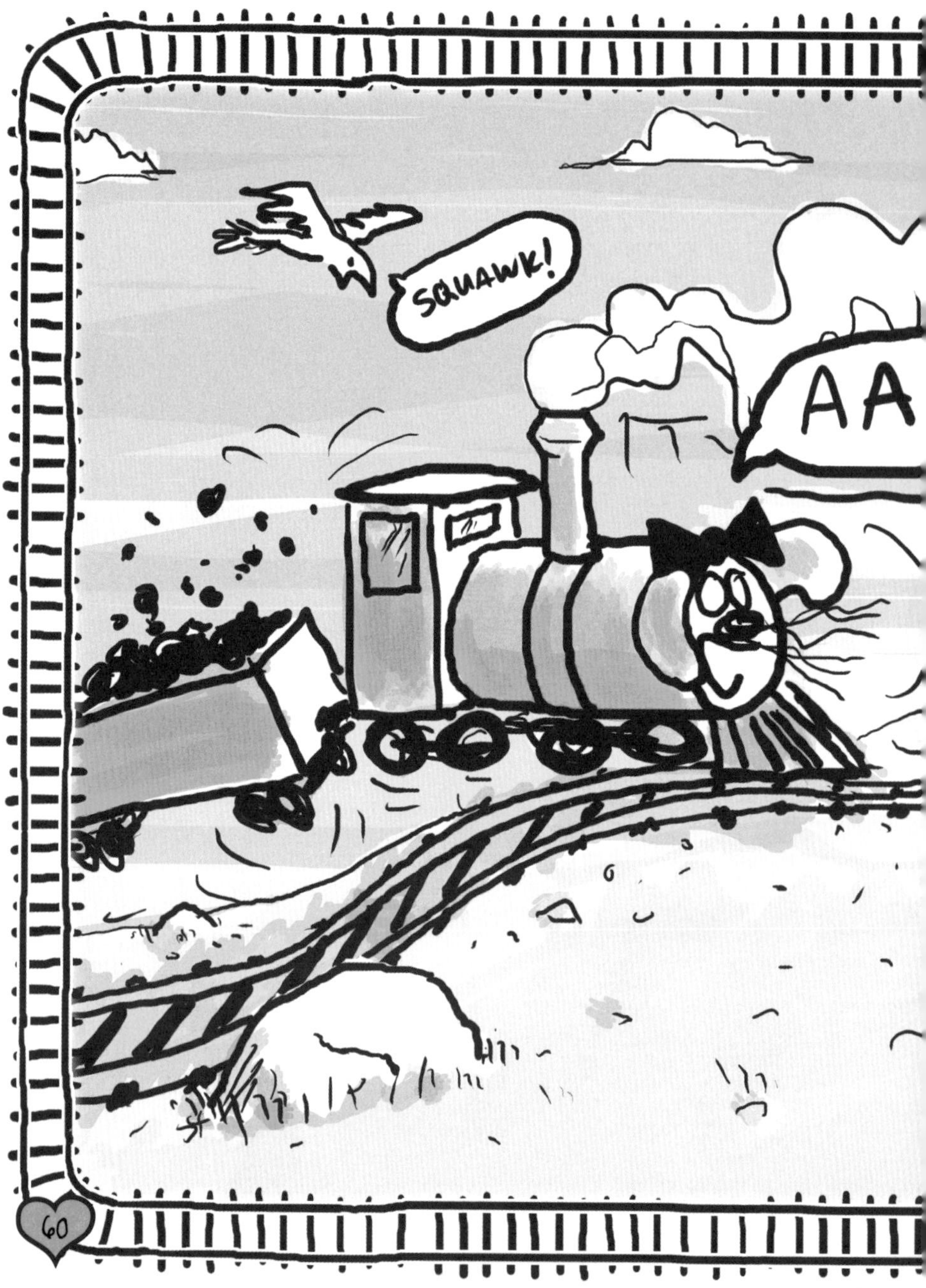
SQUAWK!
AA

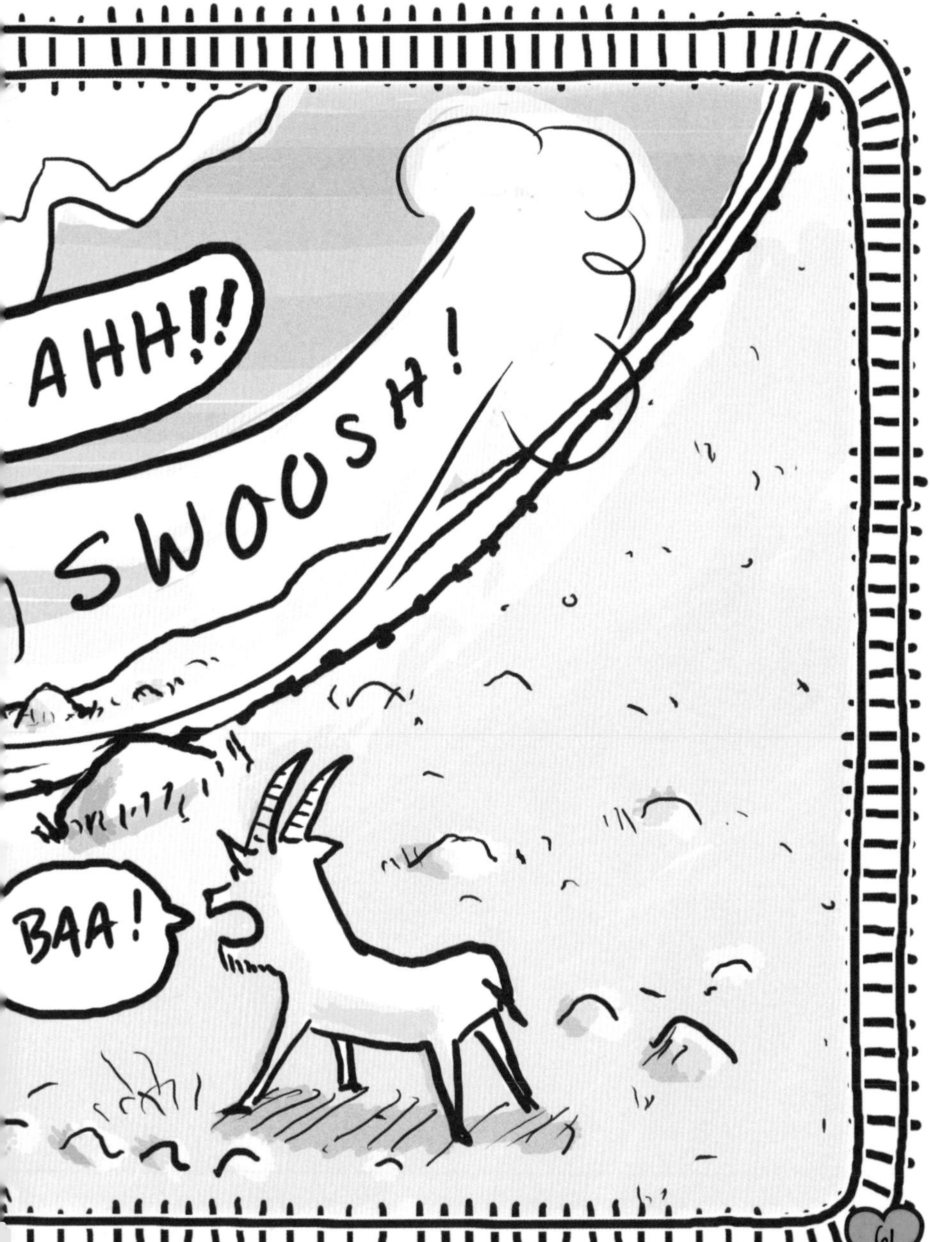
AHH!!!
SWOOSH!
BAA!

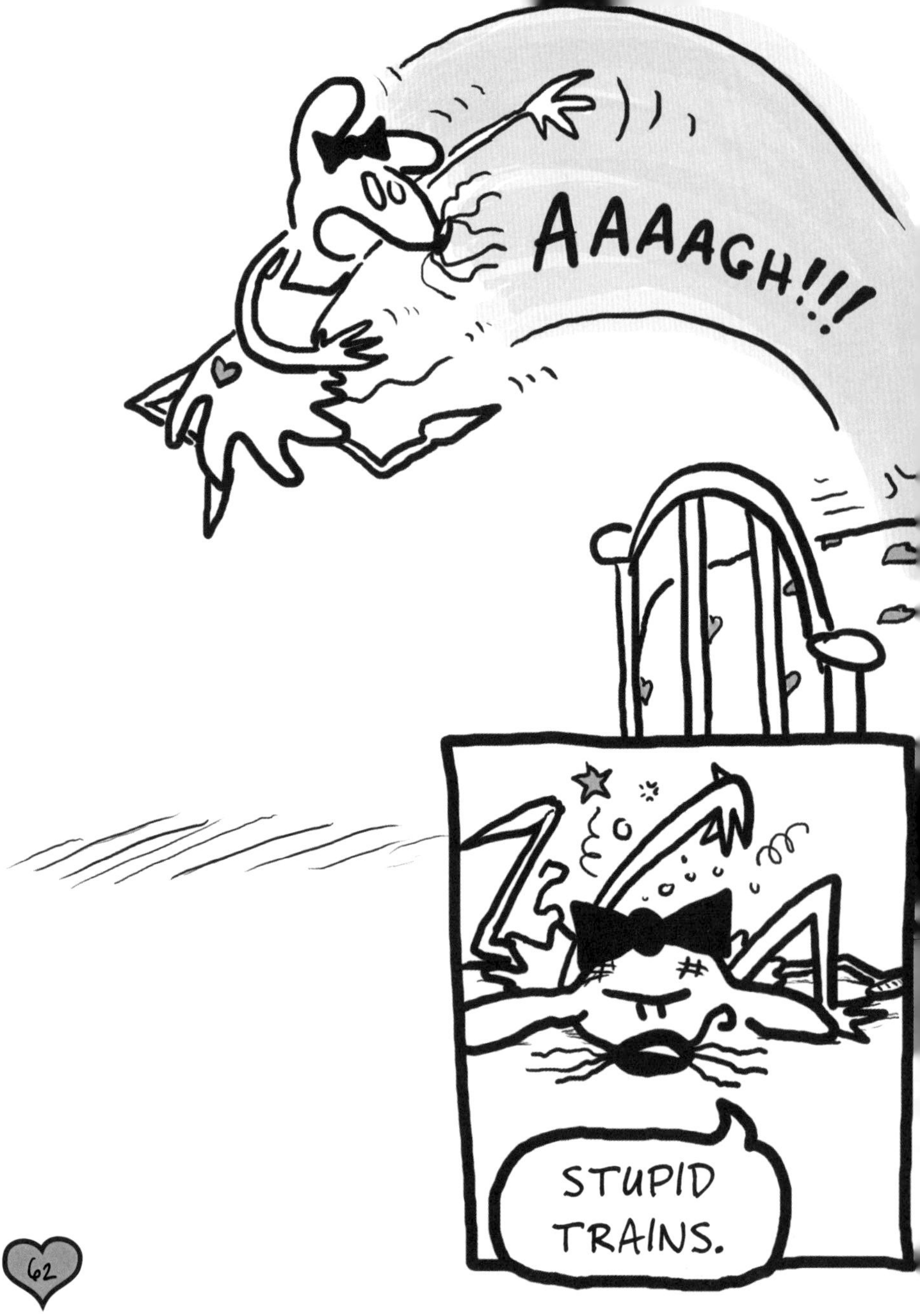
AAAAGH!!!
STUPID TRAINS.

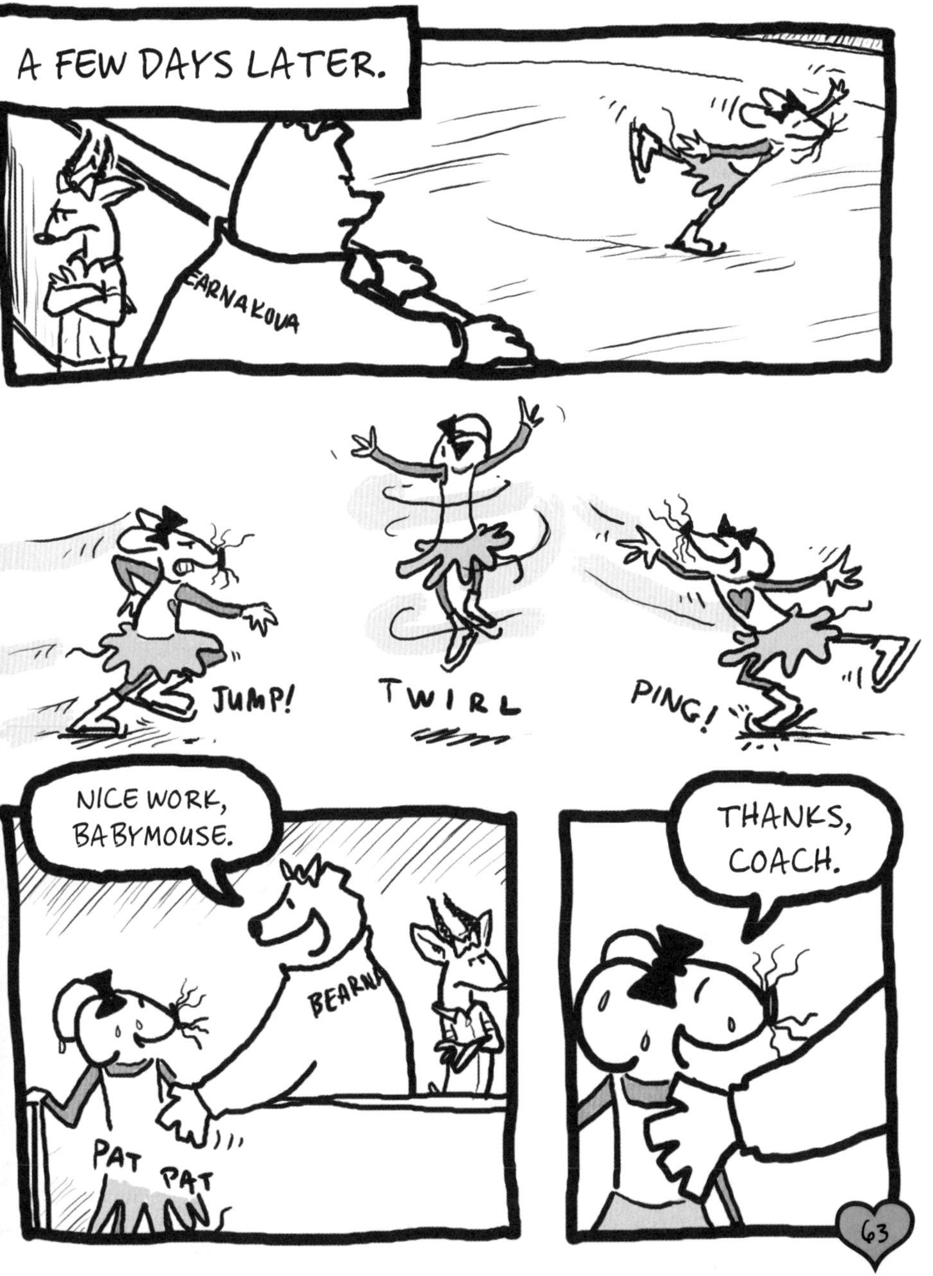
A FEW DAYS LATER.
EARNAKOVA
JUMP!
TWIRL
PING!
NICE WORK, BABYMOUSE.
BEARNA
PAT PAT
THANKS, COACH.

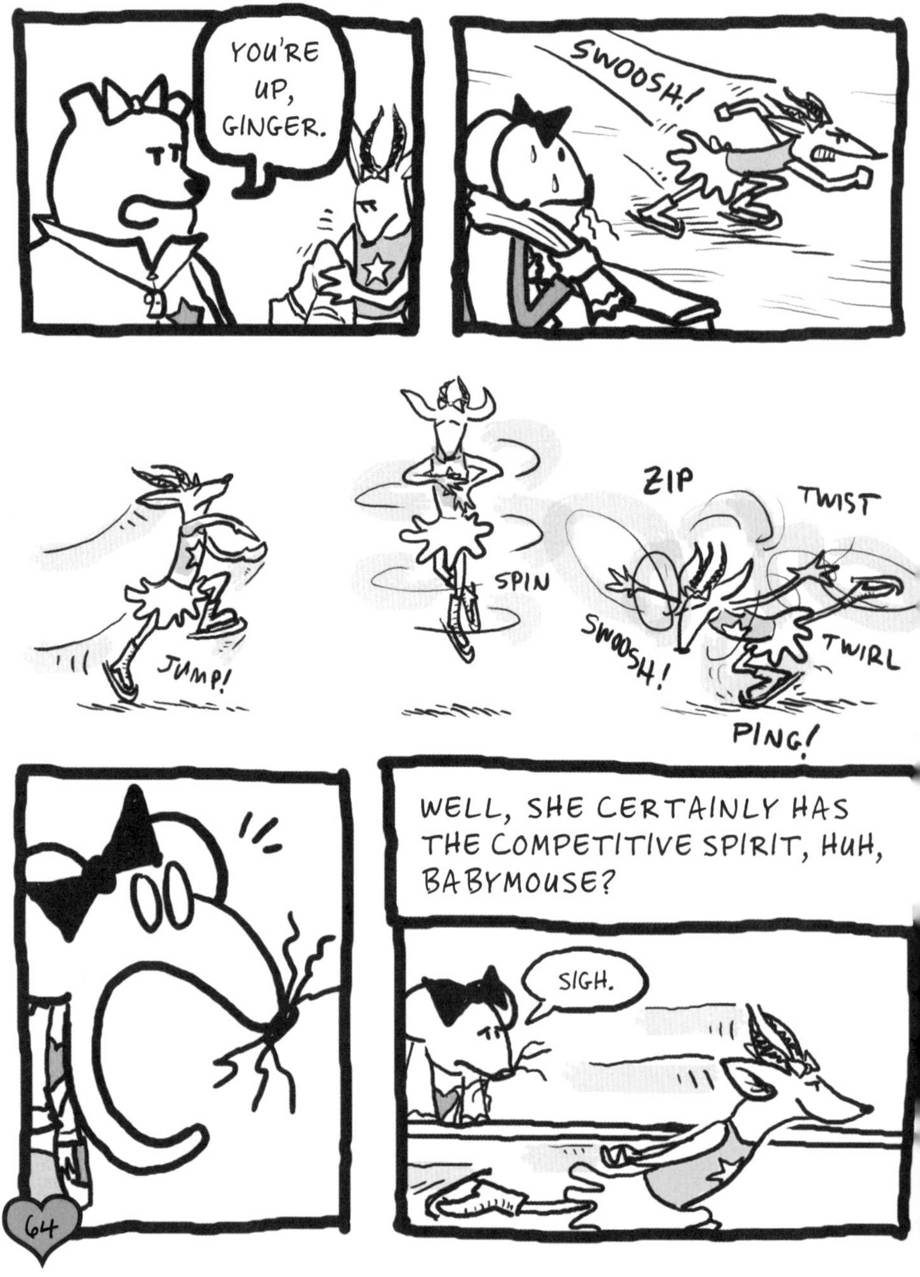
YOU'RE UP, GINGER.
SWOOSH!
JUMP!
SPIN
ZIP
TWIST
SWOOSH!
TWIRL
PING!
WELL, SHE CERTAINLY HAS THE COMPETITIVE SPIRIT, HUH, BABYMOUSE?
SIGH.

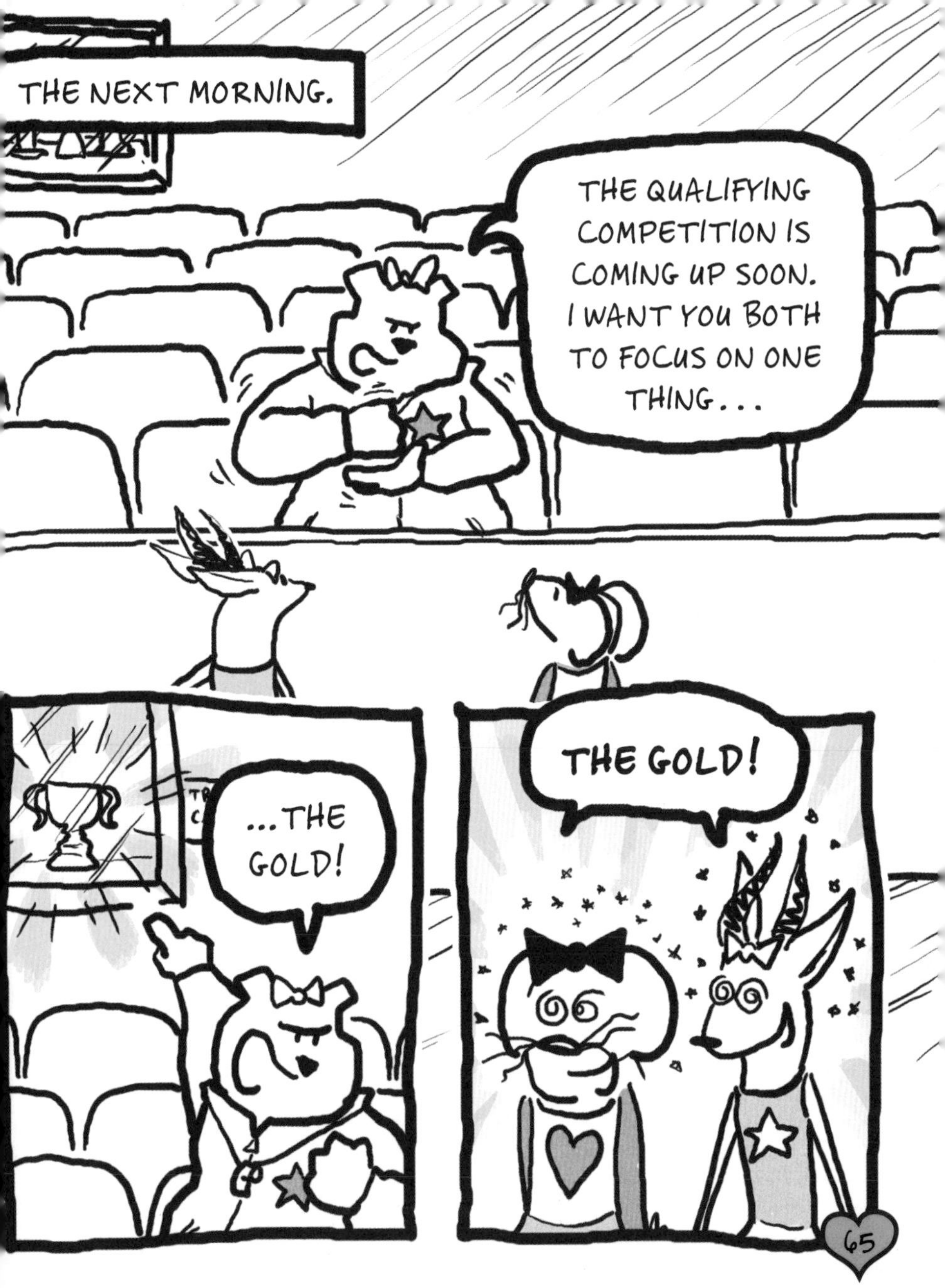
THE NEXT MORNING.
THE QUALIFYING COMPETITION IS COMING UP SOON. I WANT YOU BOTH TO FOCUS ON ONE THING...
...THE GOLD!
THE GOLD!

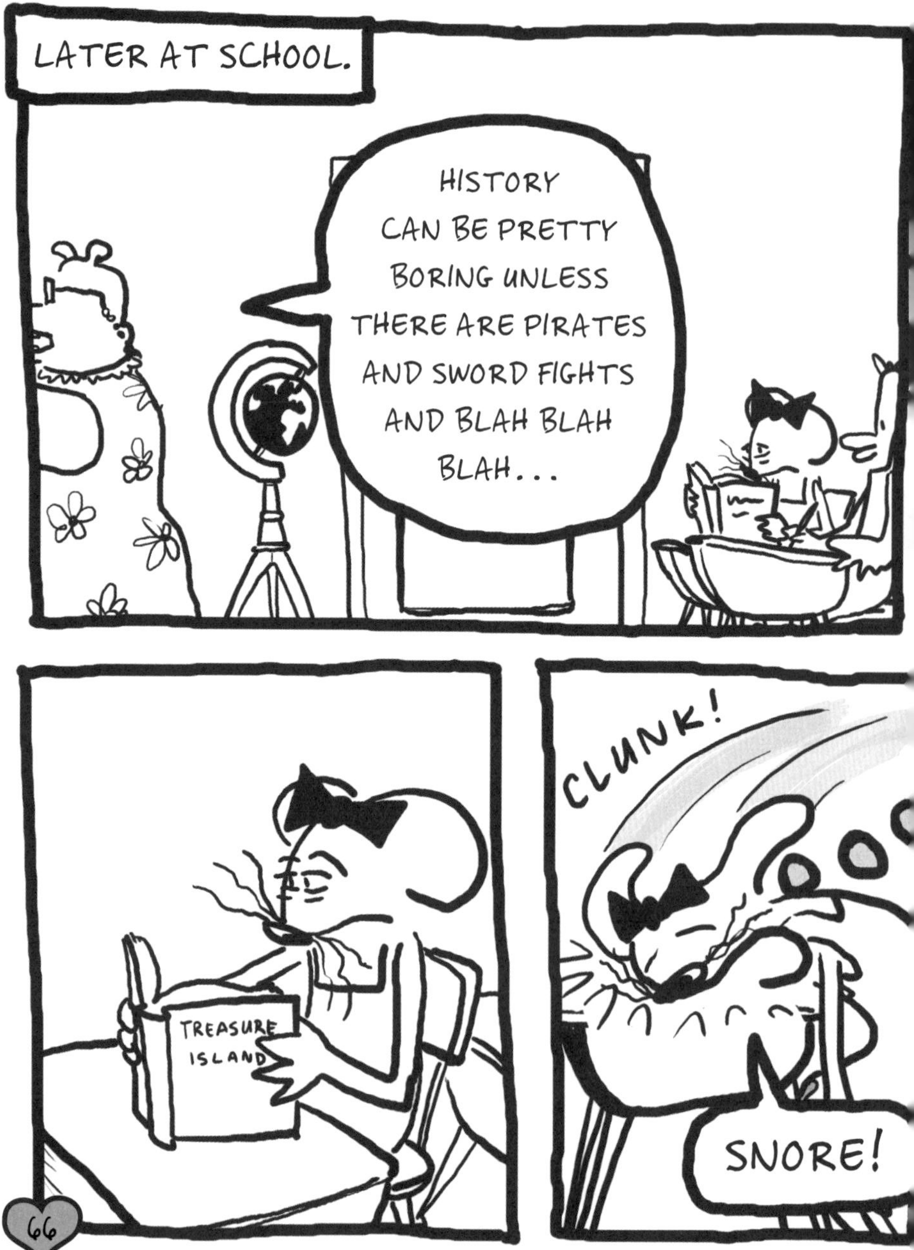
LATER AT SCHOOL.
HISTORY CAN BE PRETTY BORING UNLESS THERE ARE PIRATES AND SWORD FIGHTS AND BLAH BLAH BLAH...
TREASURE ISLAND
CLUNK!
SNORE!

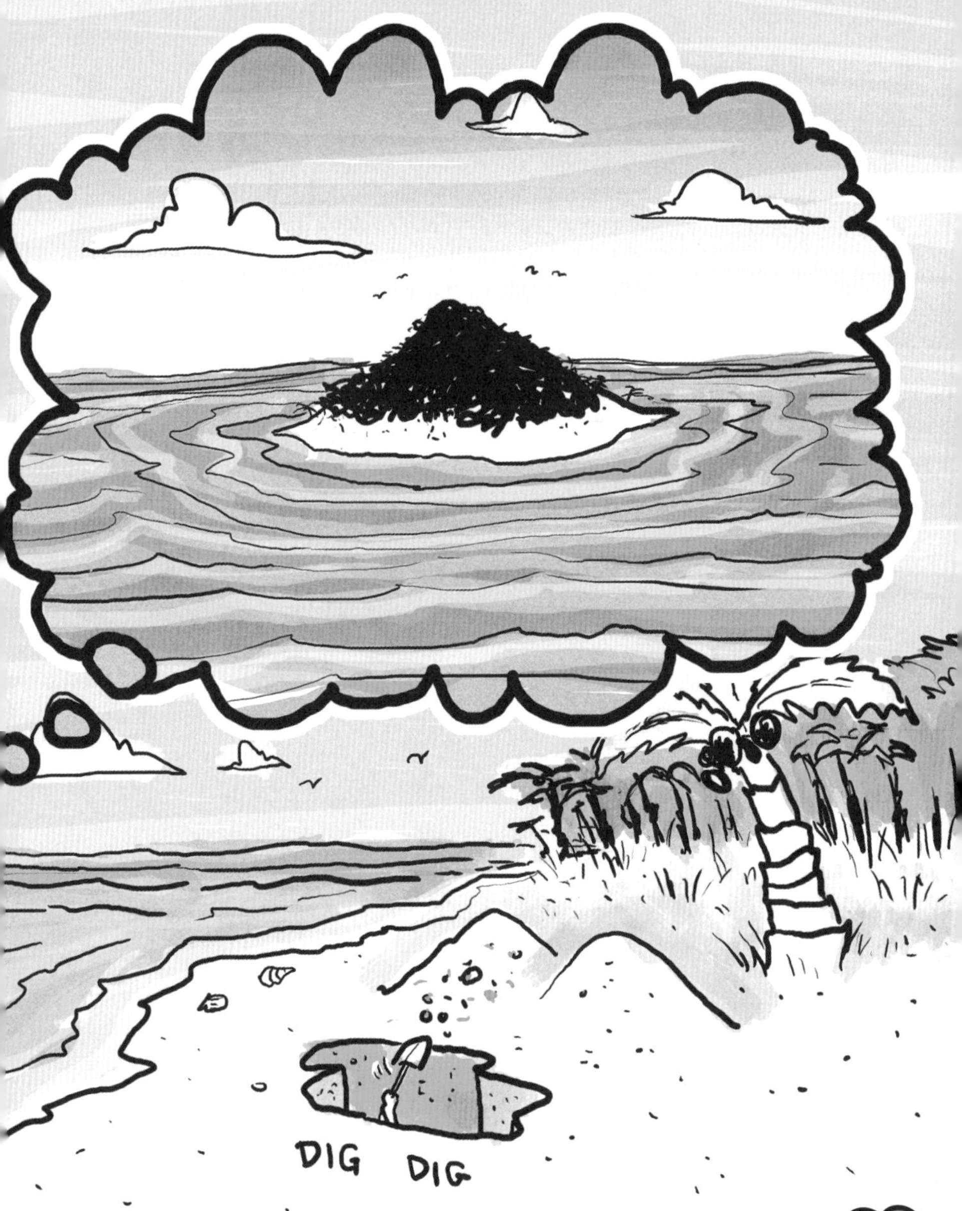
DIG DIG

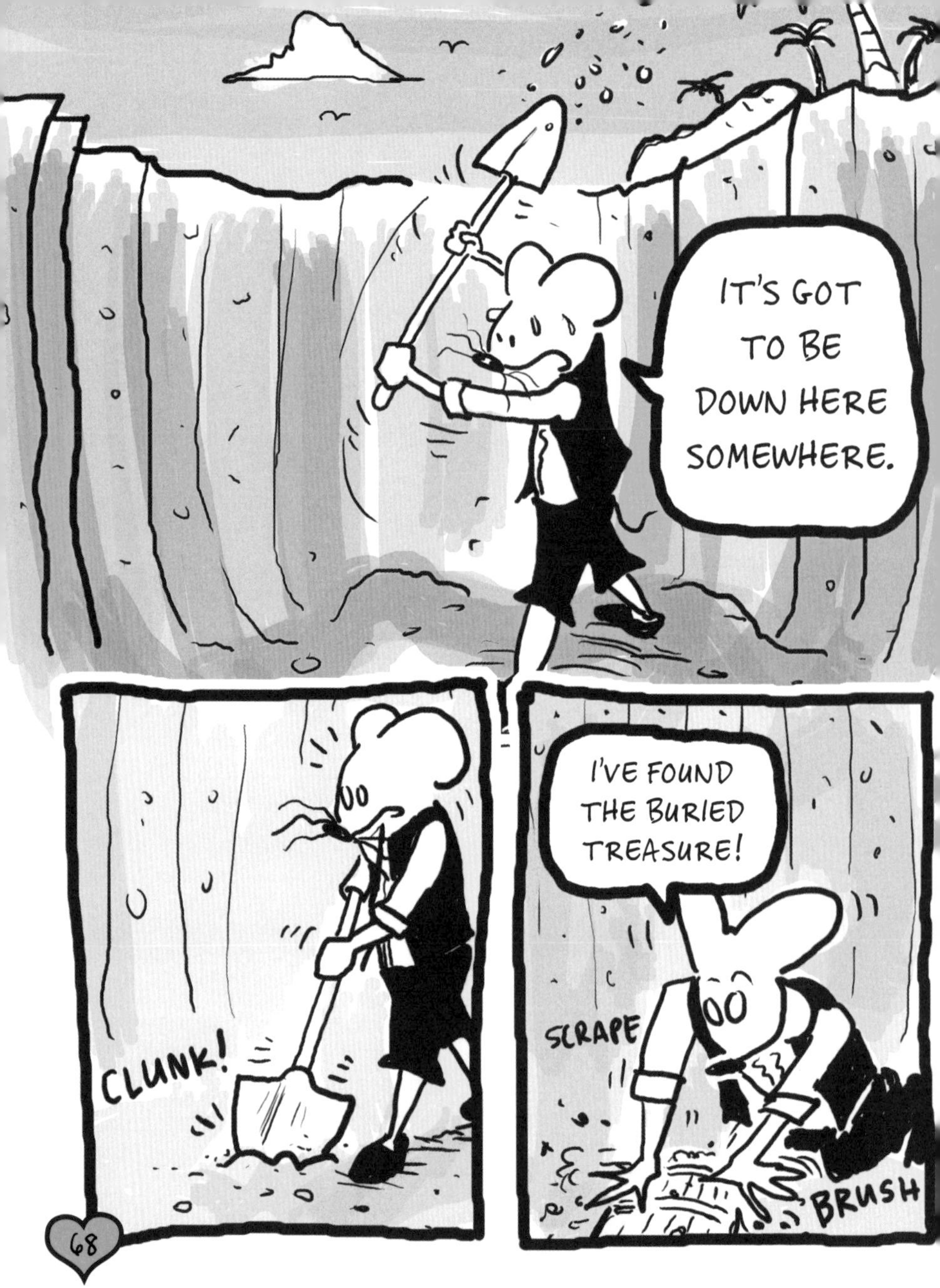
IT'S GOT TO BE DOWN HERE SOMEWHERE.
CLUNK!
I'VE FOUND THE BURIED TREASURE!
SCRAPE
BRUSH

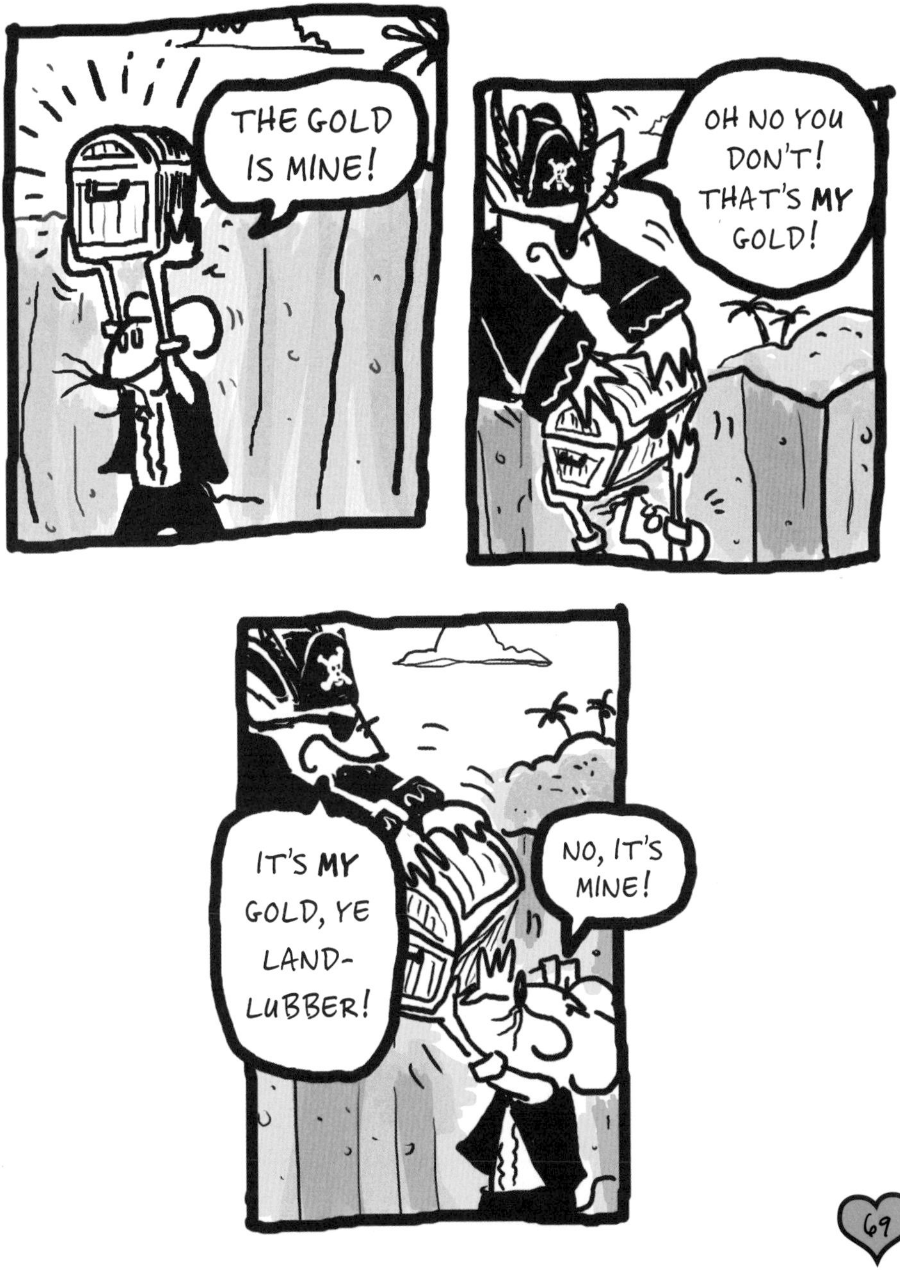
THE GOLD IS MINE!
OH NO YOU DON'T! THAT'S **MY** GOLD!
IT'S **MY** GOLD, YE LAND-LUBBER!
NO, IT'S MINE!

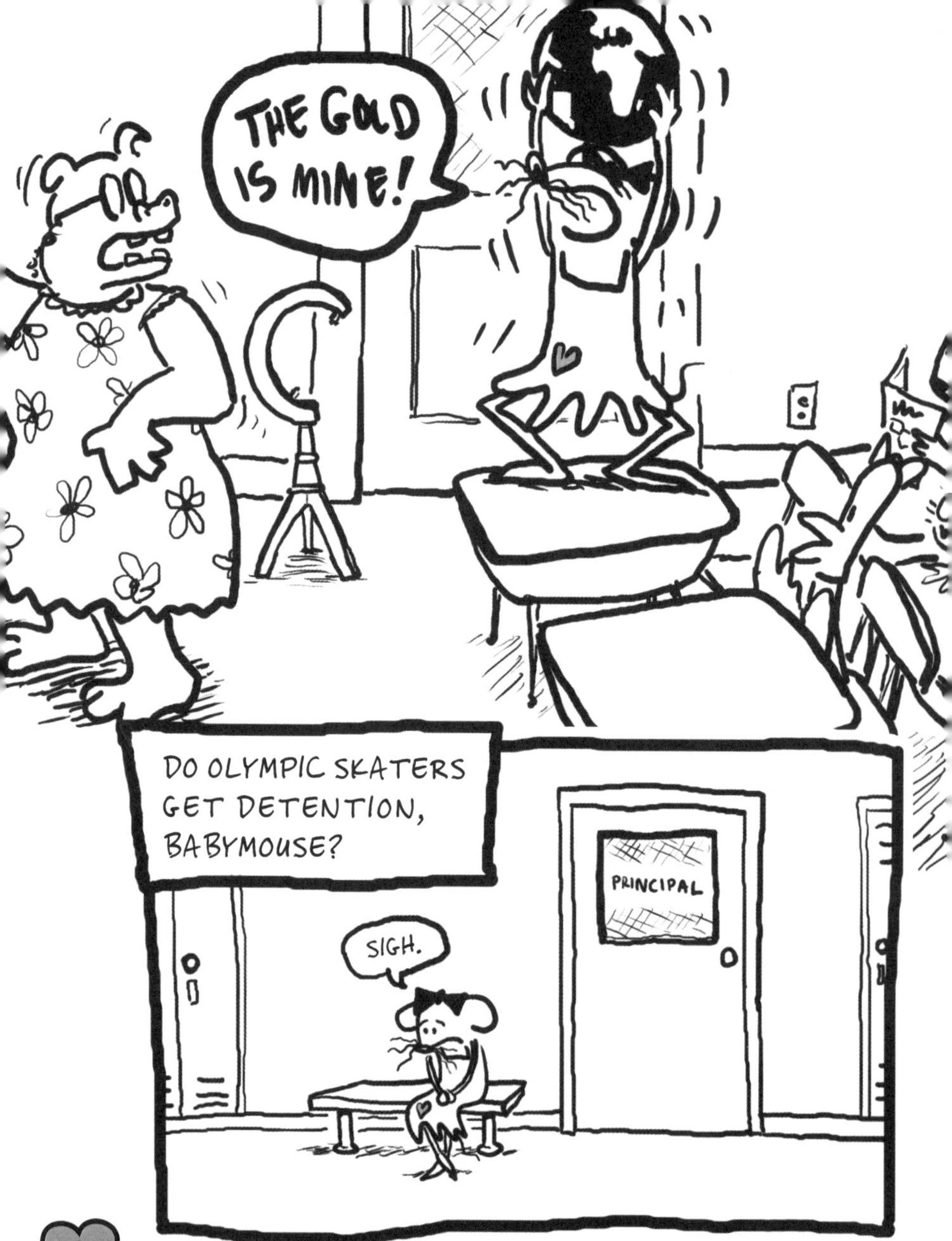
THE GOLD IS MINE!
DO OLYMPIC SKATERS GET DETENTION, BABYMOUSE?
PRINCIPAL
SIGH.

THE TRAINING OF A WINNER!

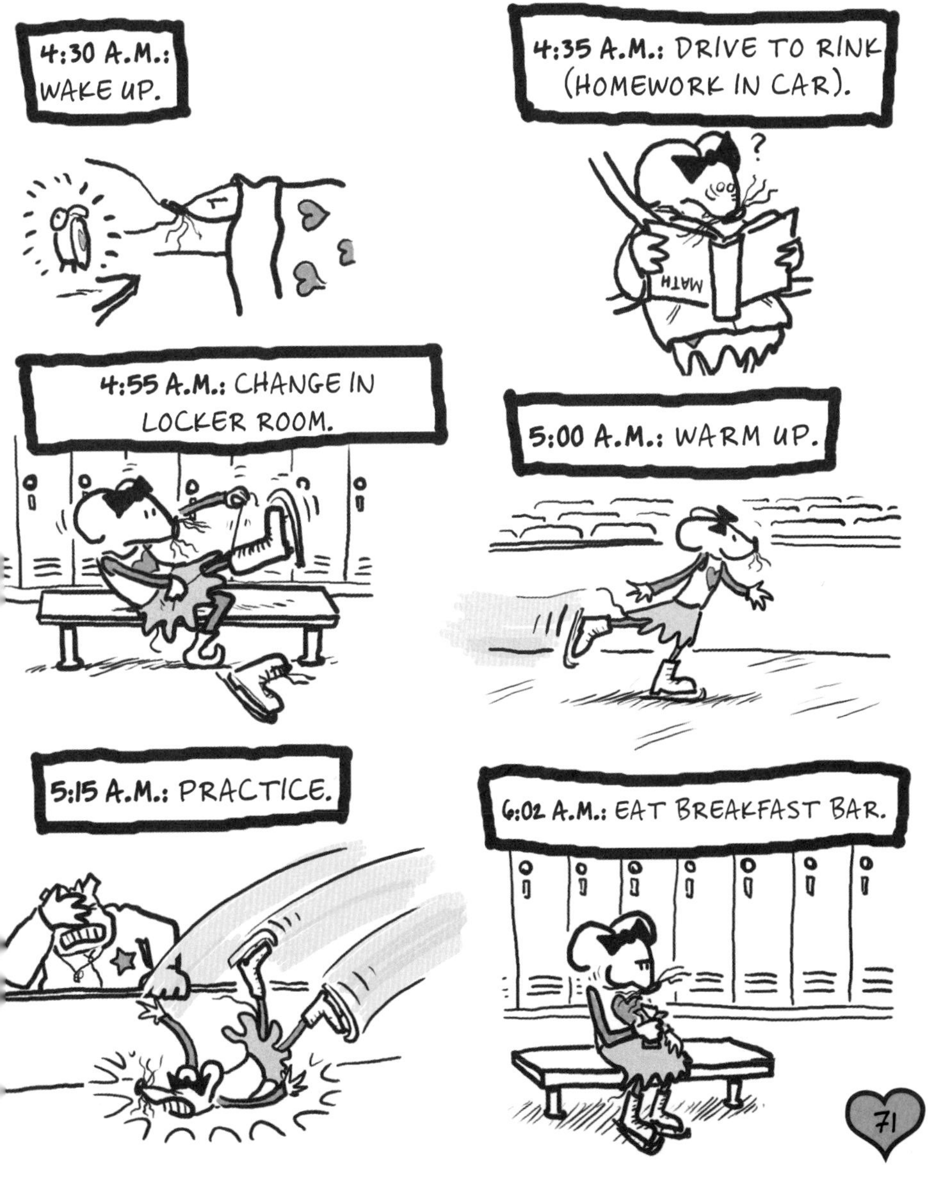
4:30 A.M.: WAKE UP.
4:35 A.M.: DRIVE TO RINK (HOMEWORK IN CAR).
?
MATH
4:55 A.M.: CHANGE IN LOCKER ROOM.
5:00 A.M.: WARM UP.
5:15 A.M.: PRACTICE.
6:02 A.M.: EAT BREAKFAST BAR.

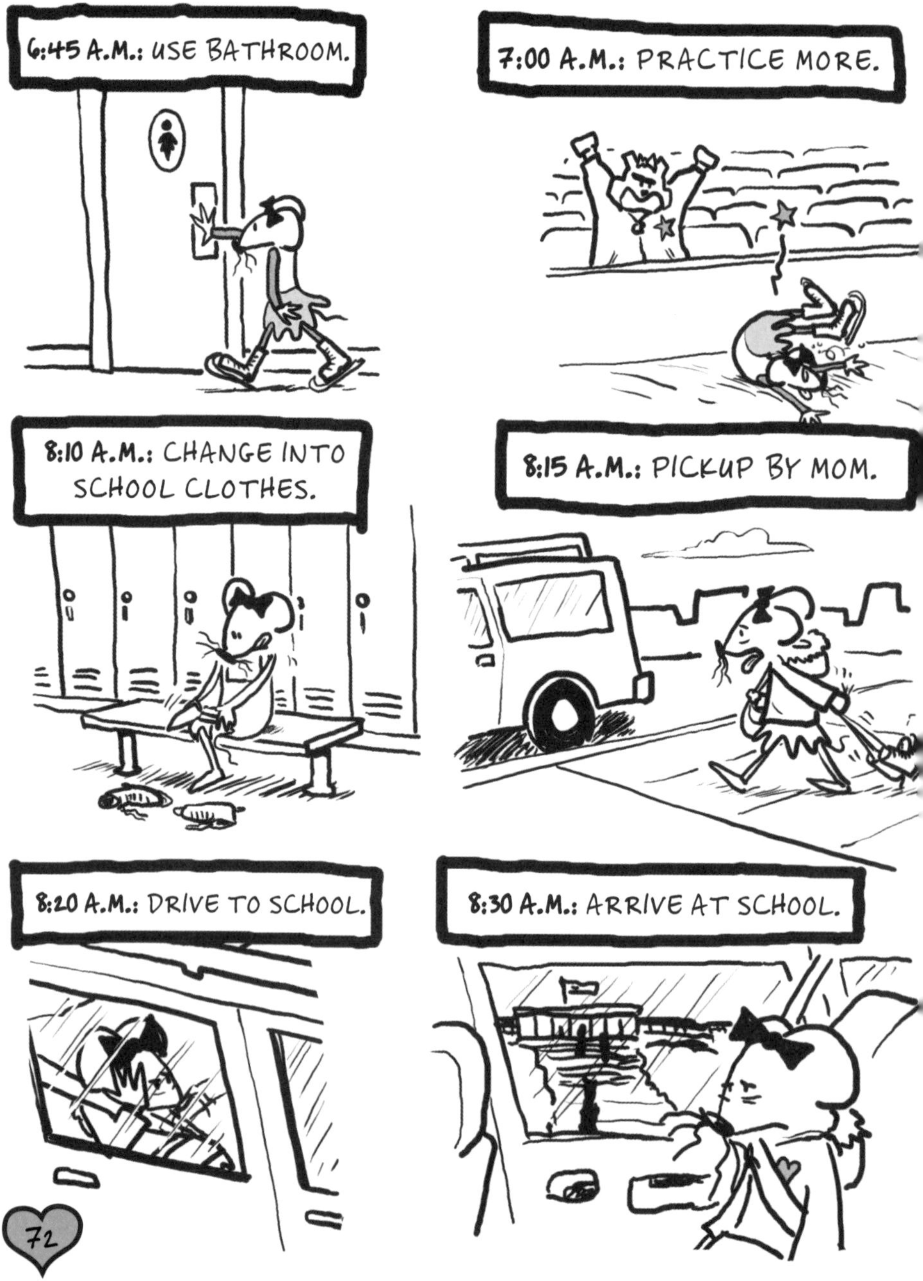
6:45 A.M.: USE BATHROOM.
7:00 A.M.: PRACTICE MORE.
8:10 A.M.: CHANGE INTO SCHOOL CLOTHES.
8:15 A.M.: PICKUP BY MOM.
8:20 A.M.: DRIVE TO SCHOOL.
8:30 A.M.: ARRIVE AT SCHOOL.

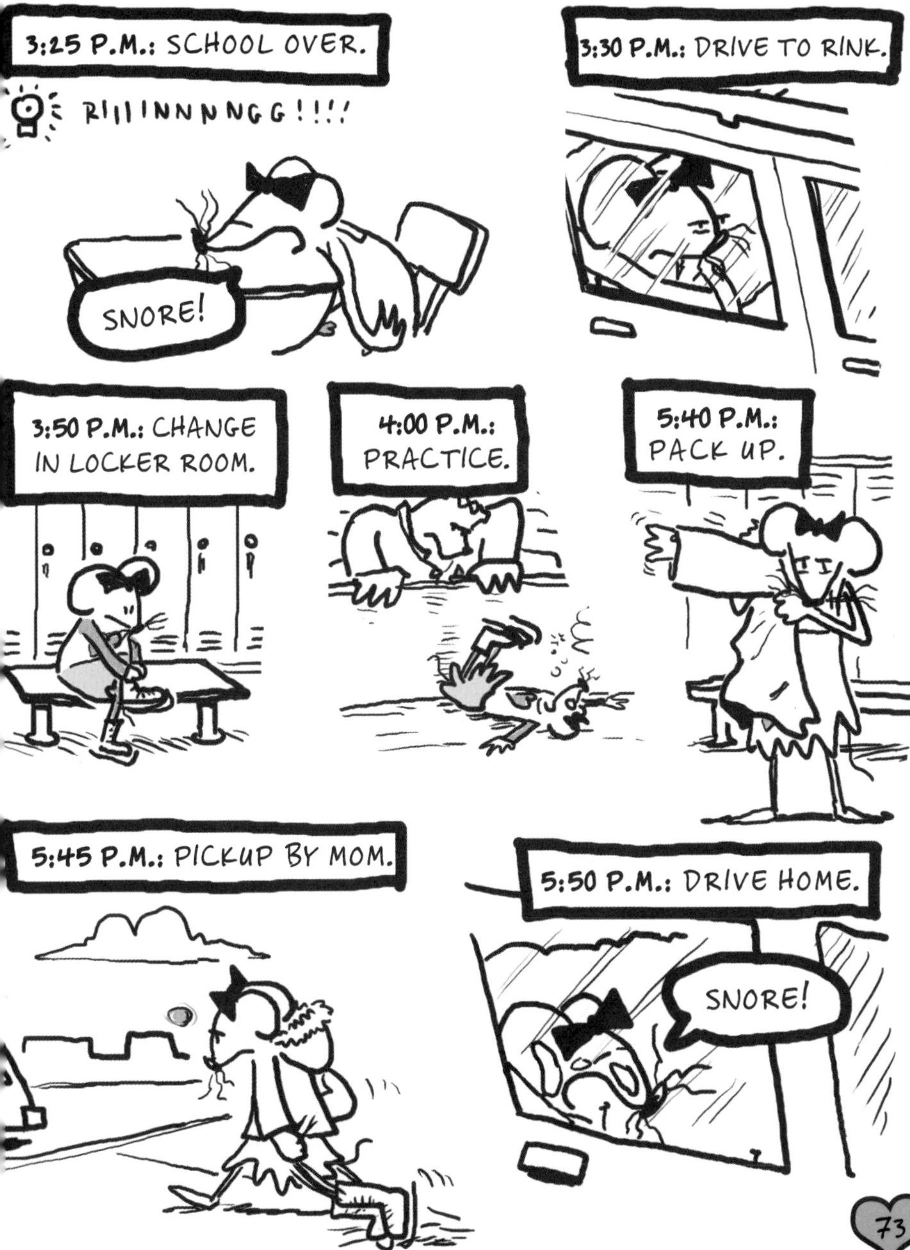
3:25 P.M.: SCHOOL OVER.
RIIIINNNNNGG!!!!
SNORE!
3:30 P.M.: DRIVE TO RINK.
3:50 P.M.: CHANGE IN LOCKER ROOM.
4:00 P.M.: PRACTICE.
5:40 P.M.: PACK UP.
5:45 P.M.: PICKUP BY MOM.
5:50 P.M.: DRIVE HOME.
SNORE!

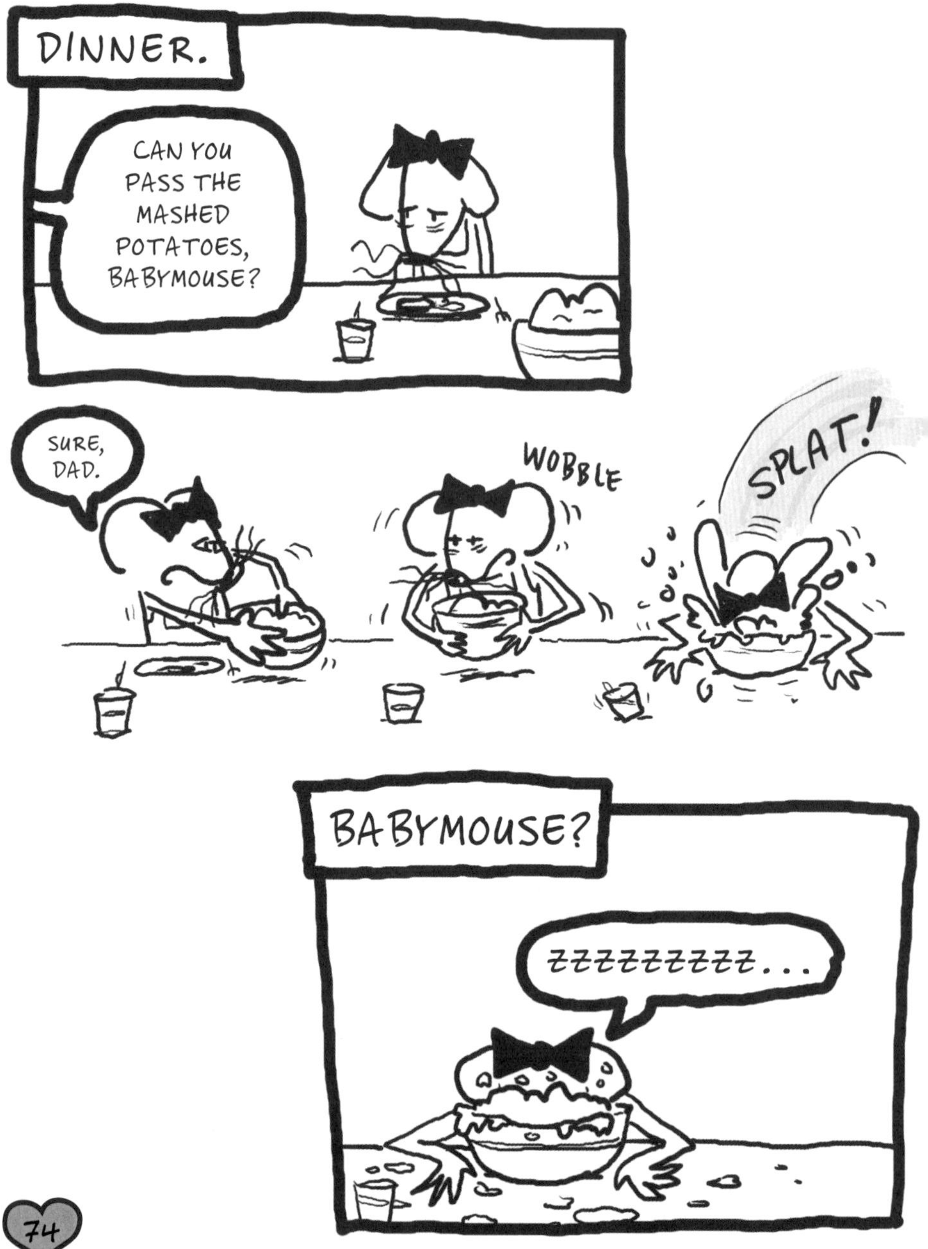
DINNER.
CAN YOU PASS THE MASHED POTATOES, BABYMOUSE?
SURE, DAD.
WOBBLE
SPLAT!
BABYMOUSE?
ZZZZZZZZZZ...

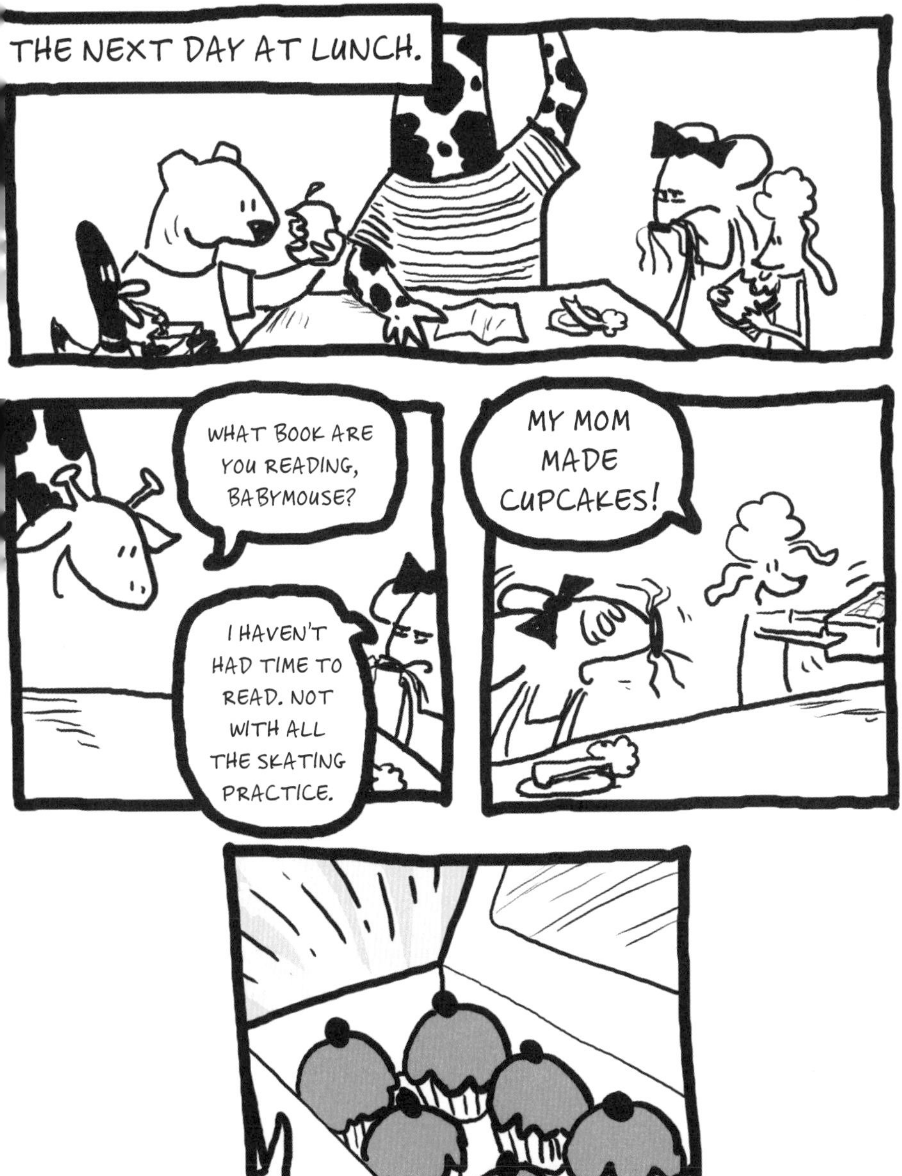
THE NEXT DAY AT LUNCH.
WHAT BOOK ARE YOU READING, BABYMOUSE?
I HAVEN'T HAD TIME TO READ. NOT WITH ALL THE SKATING PRACTICE.
MY MOM MADE CUPCAKES!

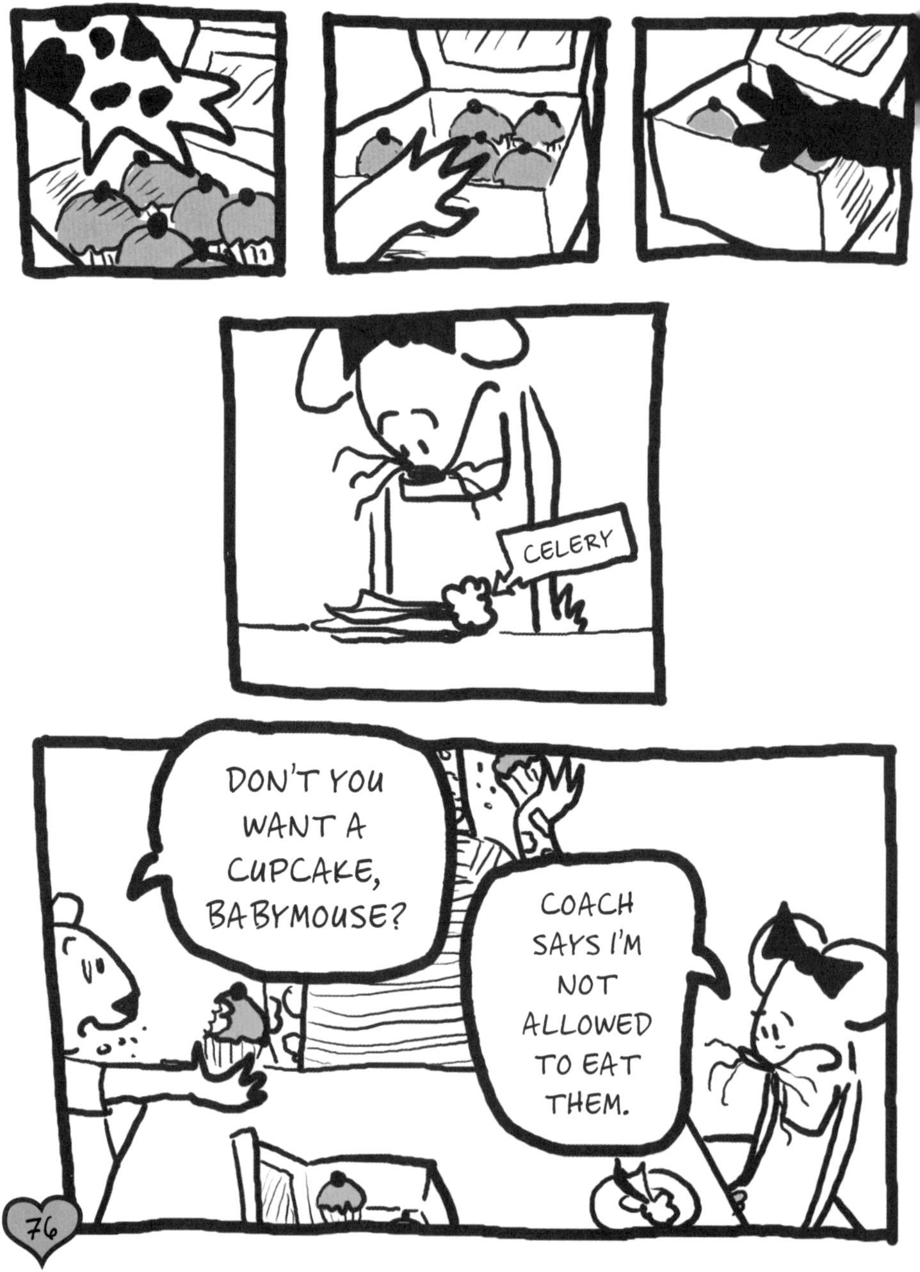
CELERY
DON'T YOU WANT A CUPCAKE, BABYMOUSE?
COACH SAYS I'M NOT ALLOWED TO EAT THEM.

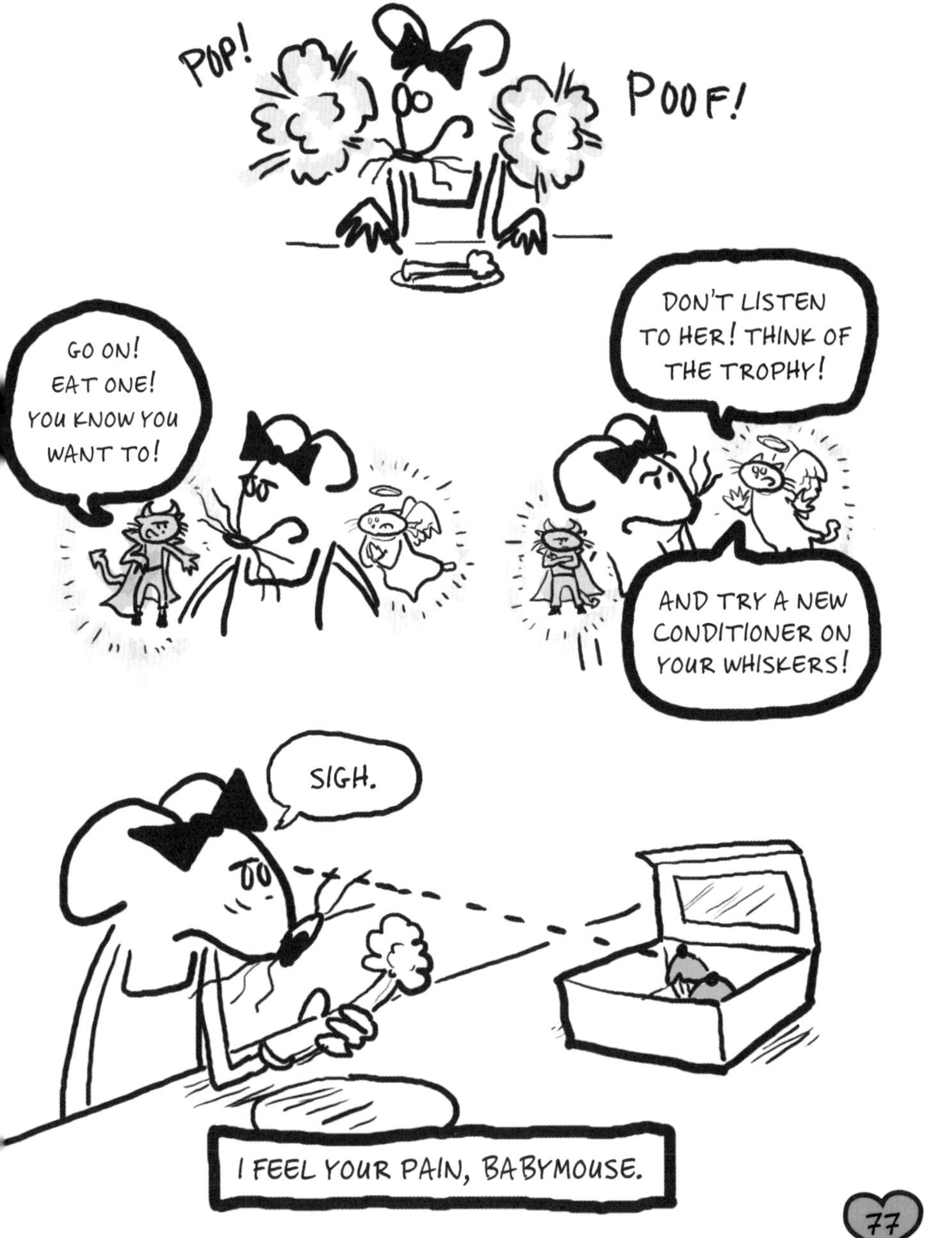

POP!
POOF!
GO ON! EAT ONE! YOU KNOW YOU WANT TO!
DON'T LISTEN TO HER! THINK OF THE TROPHY!
AND TRY A NEW CONDITIONER ON YOUR WHISKERS!
SIGH.
I FEEL YOUR PAIN, BABYMOUSE.

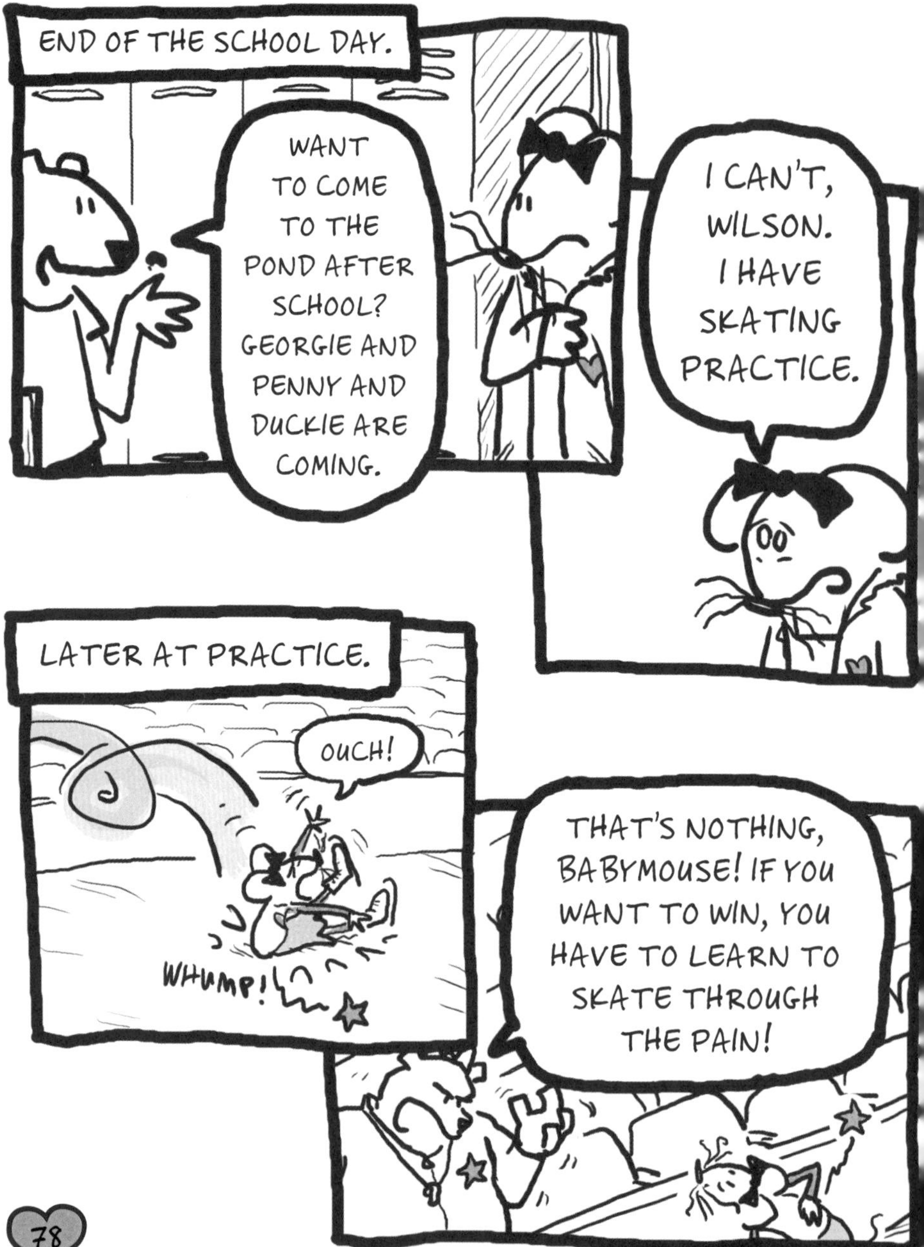
END OF THE SCHOOL DAY.
WANT TO COME TO THE POND AFTER SCHOOL? GEORGIE AND PENNY AND DUCKIE ARE COMING.
I CAN'T, WILSON. I HAVE SKATING PRACTICE.
LATER AT PRACTICE.
OUCH!
WHUMP!
THAT'S NOTHING, BABYMOUSE! IF YOU WANT TO WIN, YOU HAVE TO LEARN TO SKATE THROUGH THE PAIN!

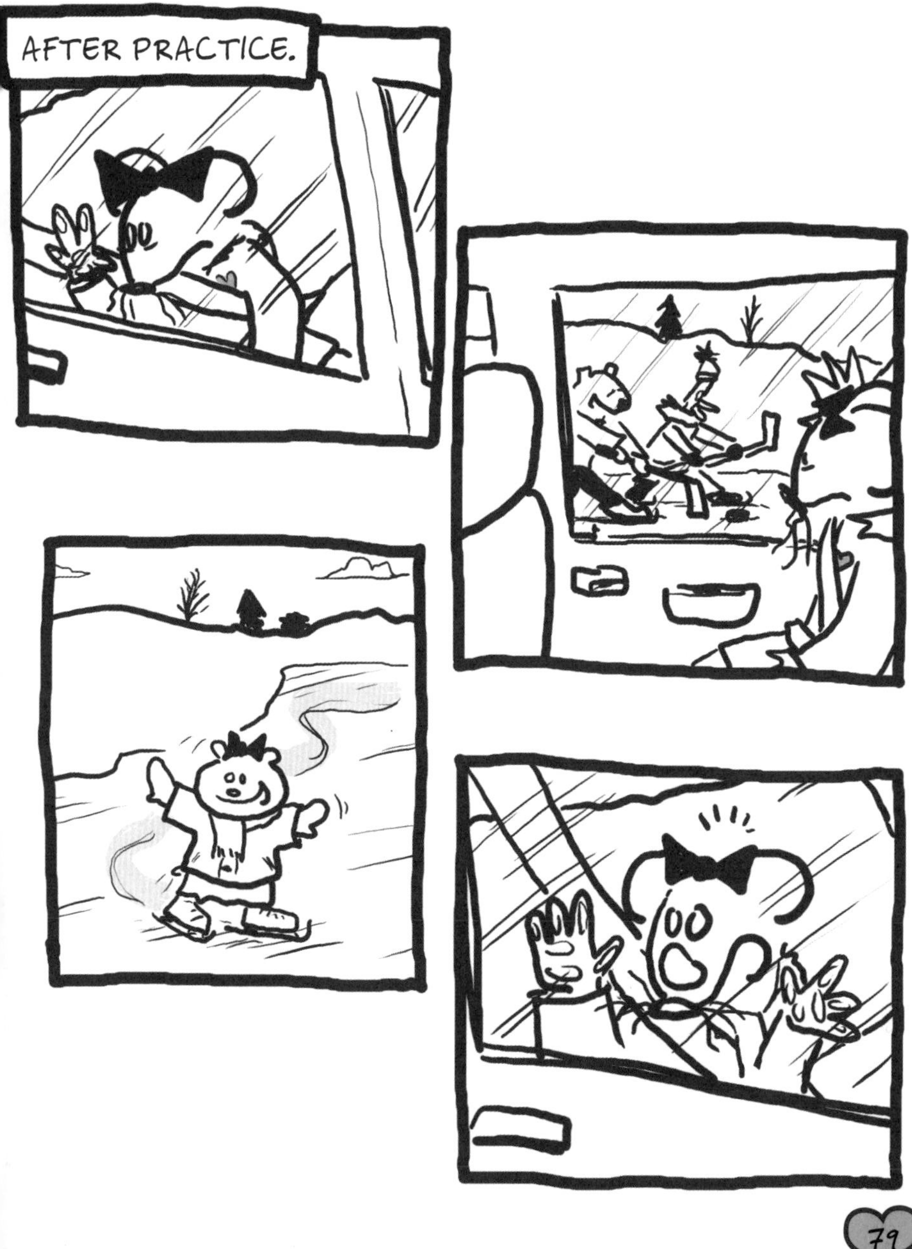
AFTER PRACTICE.

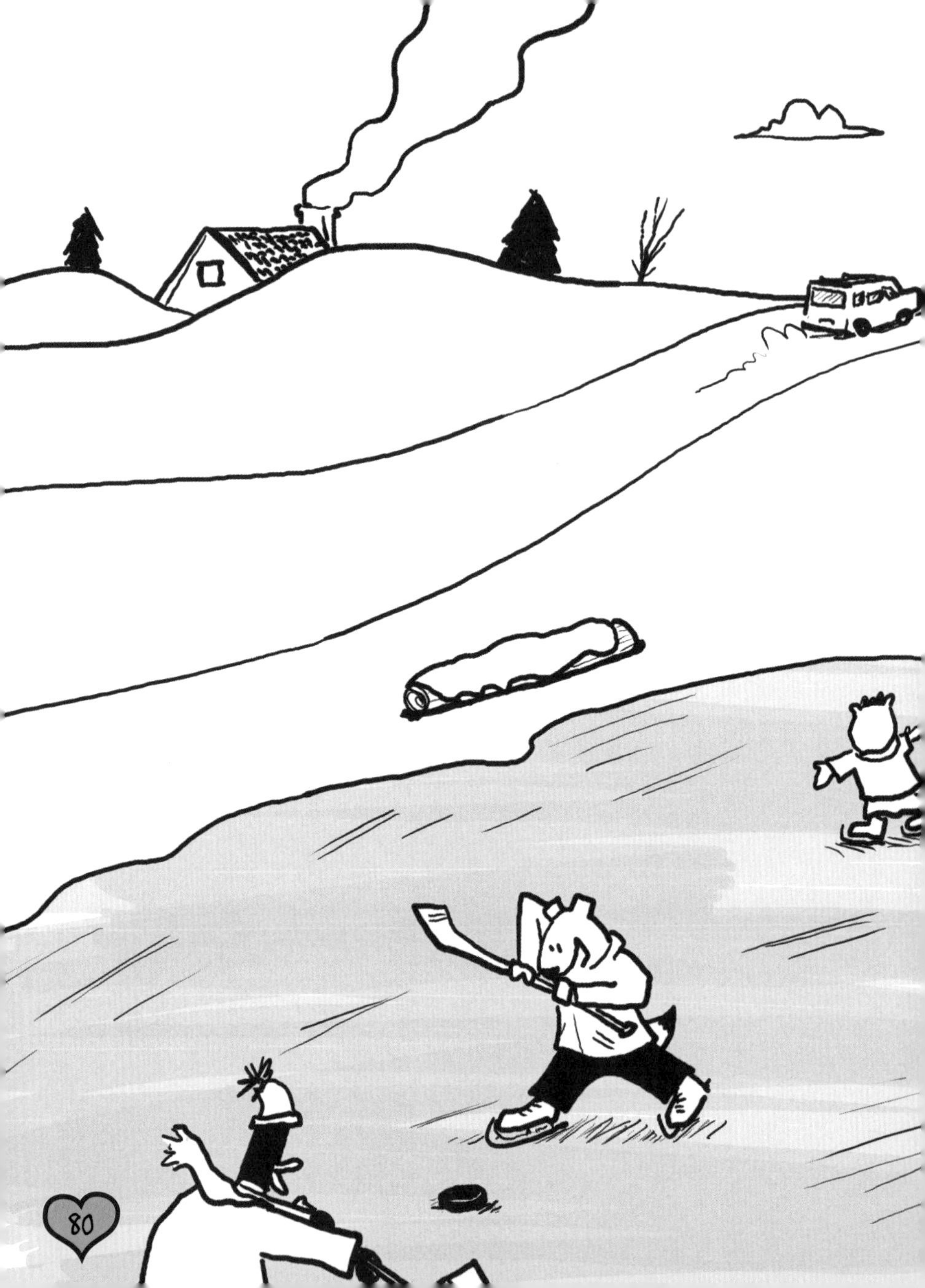

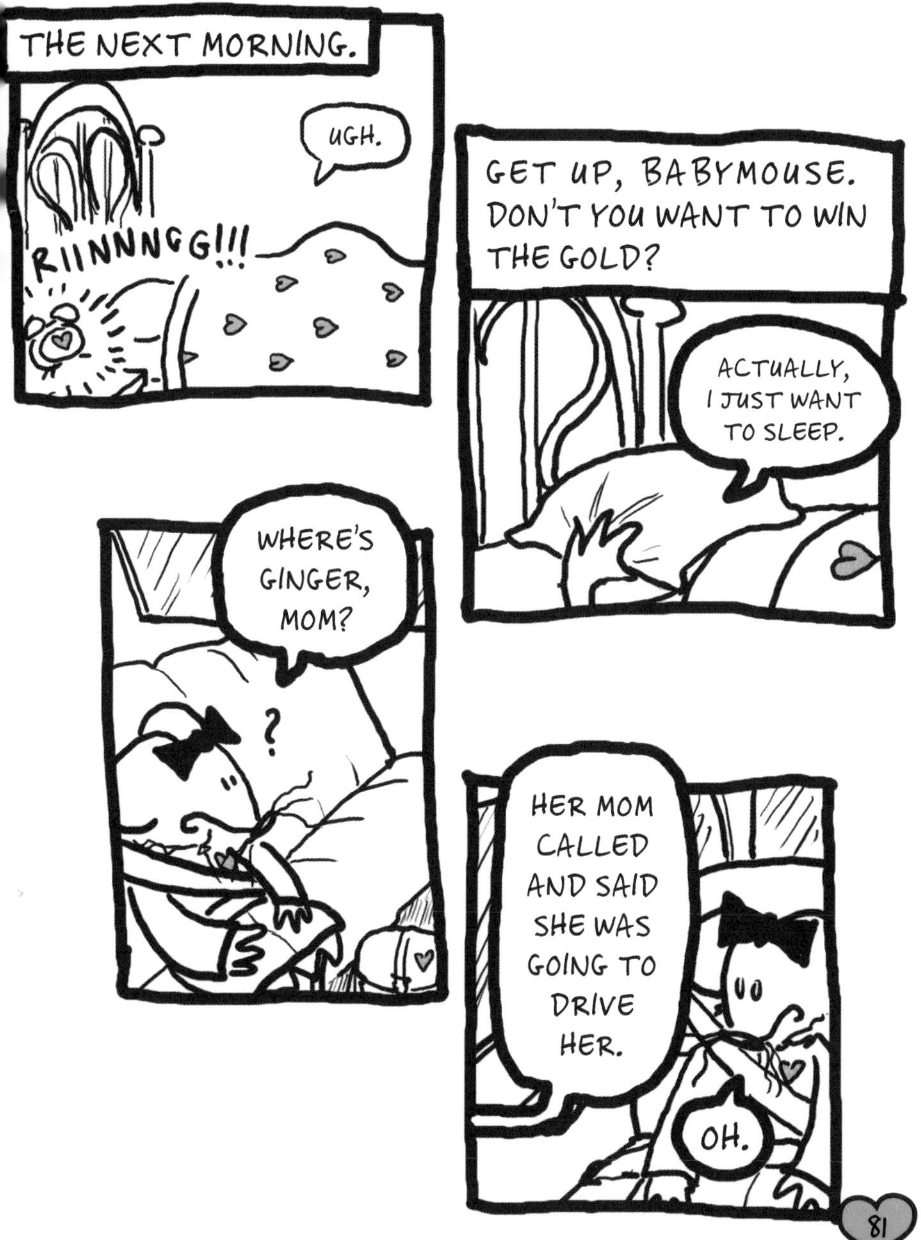
THE NEXT MORNING.
RIINNNGG!!!
UGH.
GET UP, BABYMOUSE. DON'T YOU WANT TO WIN THE GOLD?
ACTUALLY, I JUST WANT TO SLEEP.
WHERE'S GINGER, MOM?
?
HER MOM CALLED AND SAID SHE WAS GOING TO DRIVE HER.
OH.

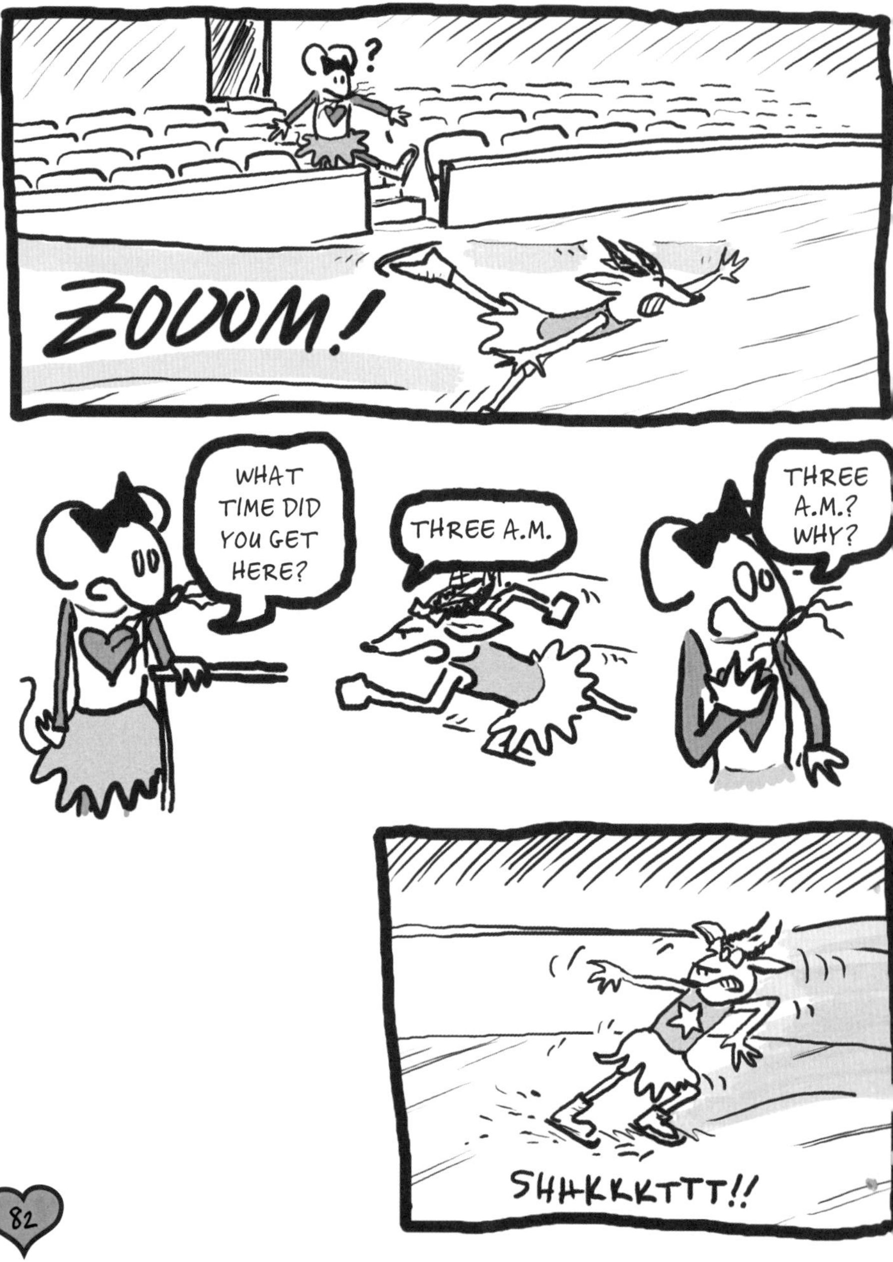
?
ZOOOM!
WHAT TIME DID YOU GET HERE?
THREE A.M.
THREE A.M.? WHY?
SHHKKKTTTT!!

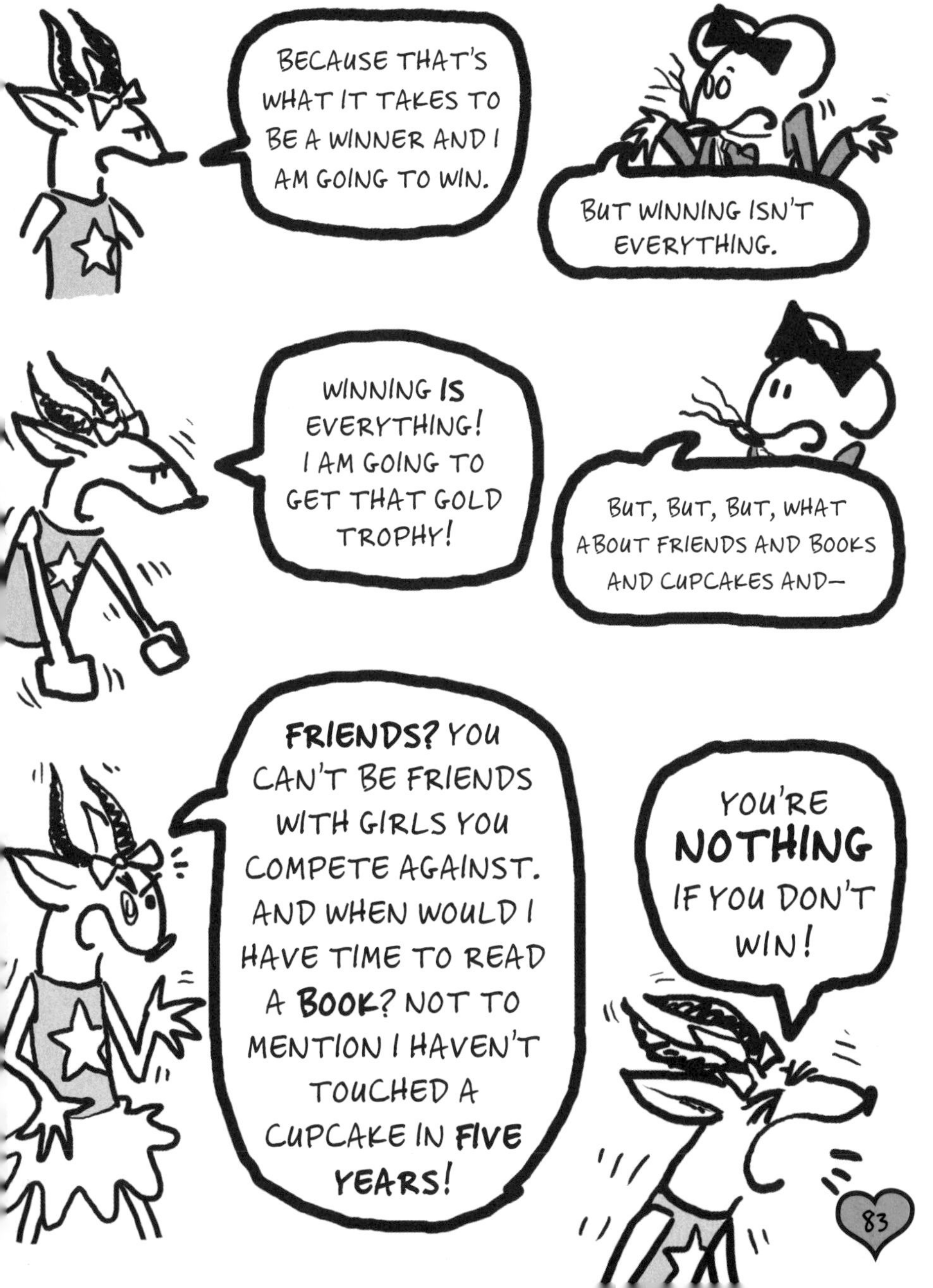
BECAUSE THAT'S WHAT IT TAKES TO BE A WINNER AND I AM GOING TO WIN.
BUT WINNING ISN'T EVERYTHING.
WINNING IS EVERYTHING! I AM GOING TO GET THAT GOLD TROPHY!
BUT, BUT, BUT, WHAT ABOUT FRIENDS AND BOOKS AND CUPCAKES AND—
FRIENDS? YOU CAN'T BE FRIENDS WITH GIRLS YOU COMPETE AGAINST. AND WHEN WOULD I HAVE TIME TO READ A BOOK? NOT TO MENTION I HAVEN'T TOUCHED A CUPCAKE IN FIVE YEARS!
YOU'RE NOTHING IF YOU DON'T WIN!

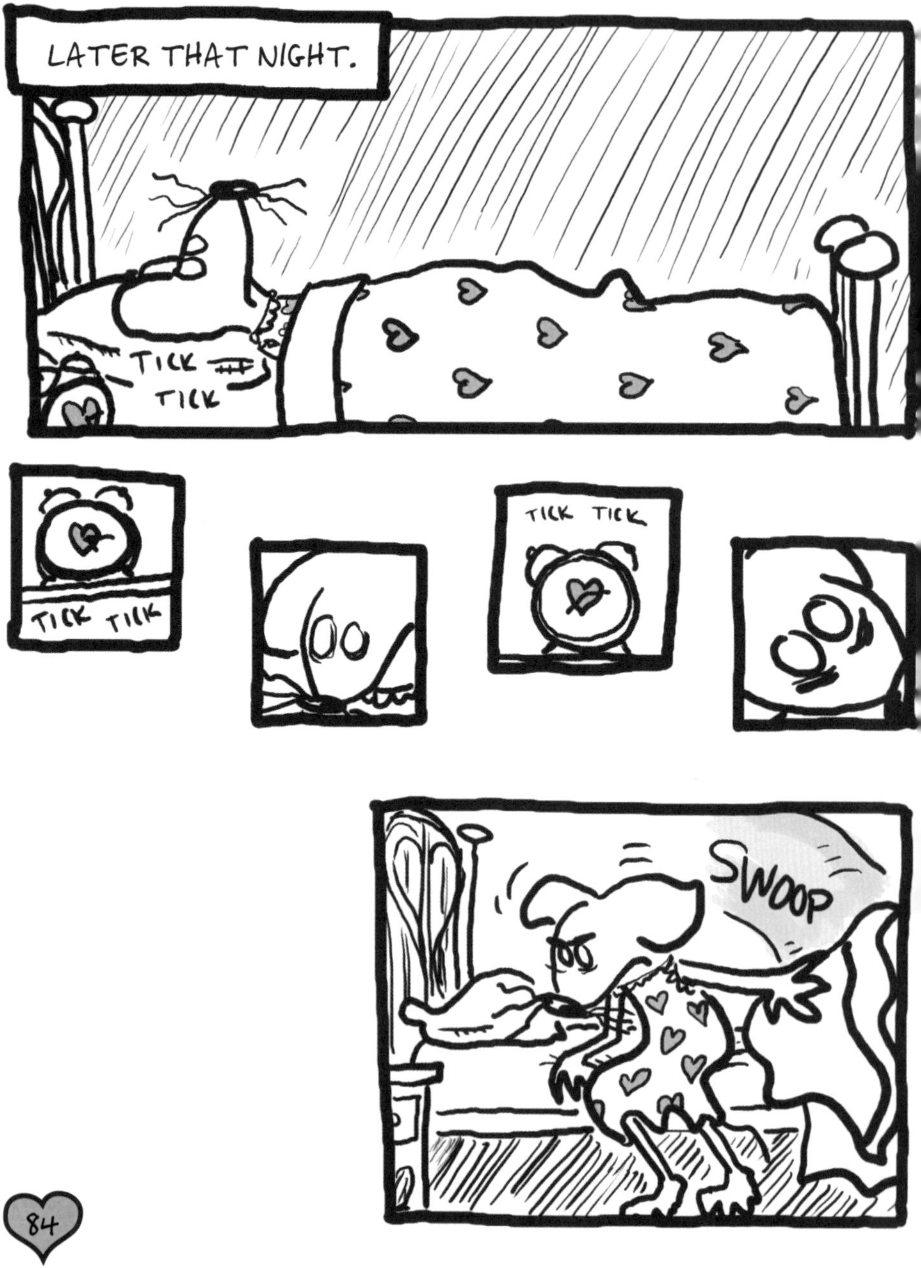
LATER THAT NIGHT.
TICK
TICK
TICK TICK
TICK TICK
SWOOP

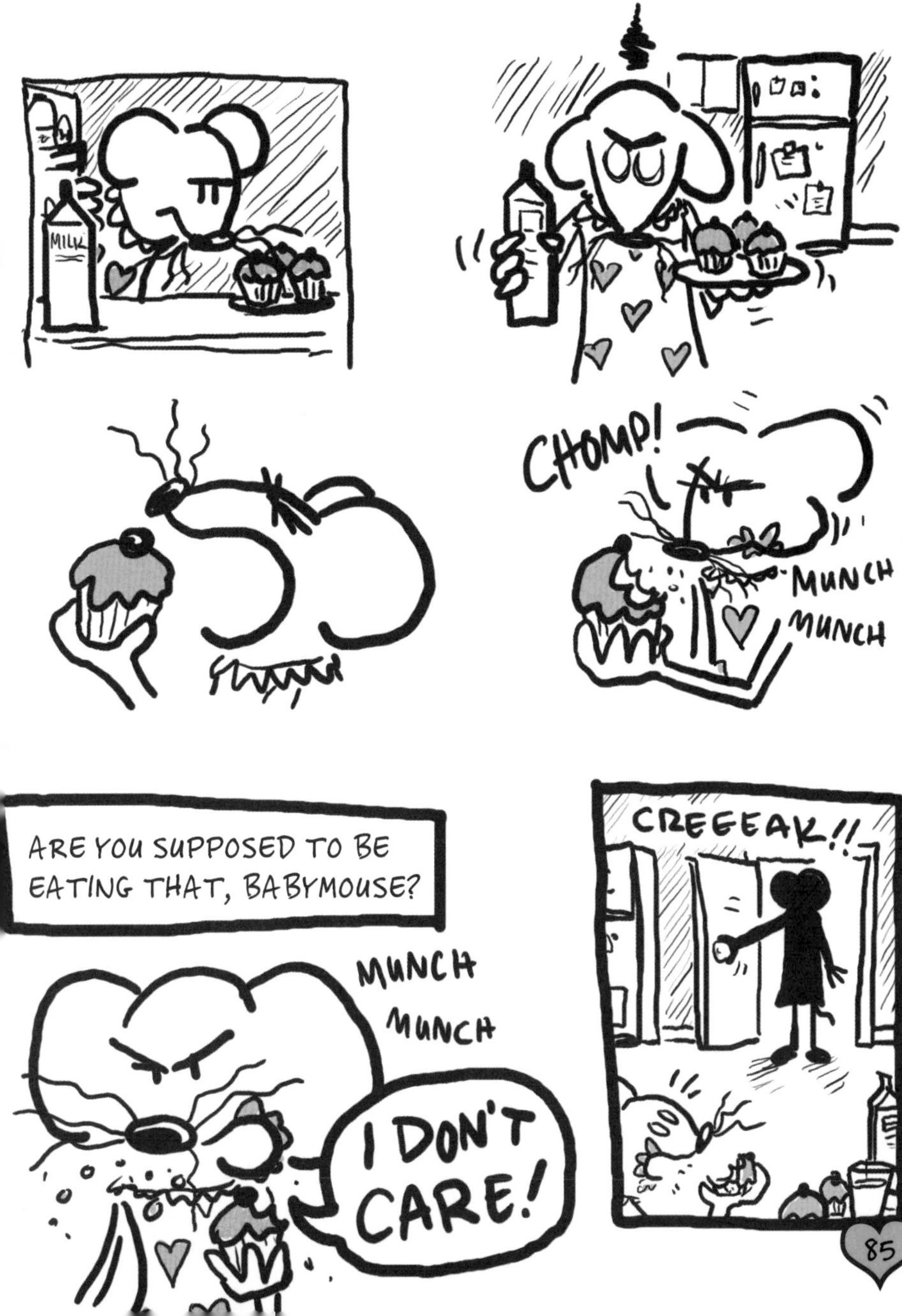
MILK
CHOMP!
MUNCH
MUNCH
ARE YOU SUPPOSED TO BE EATING THAT, BABYMOUSE?
MUNCH
MUNCH
I DON'T CARE!
CREEEAK!!

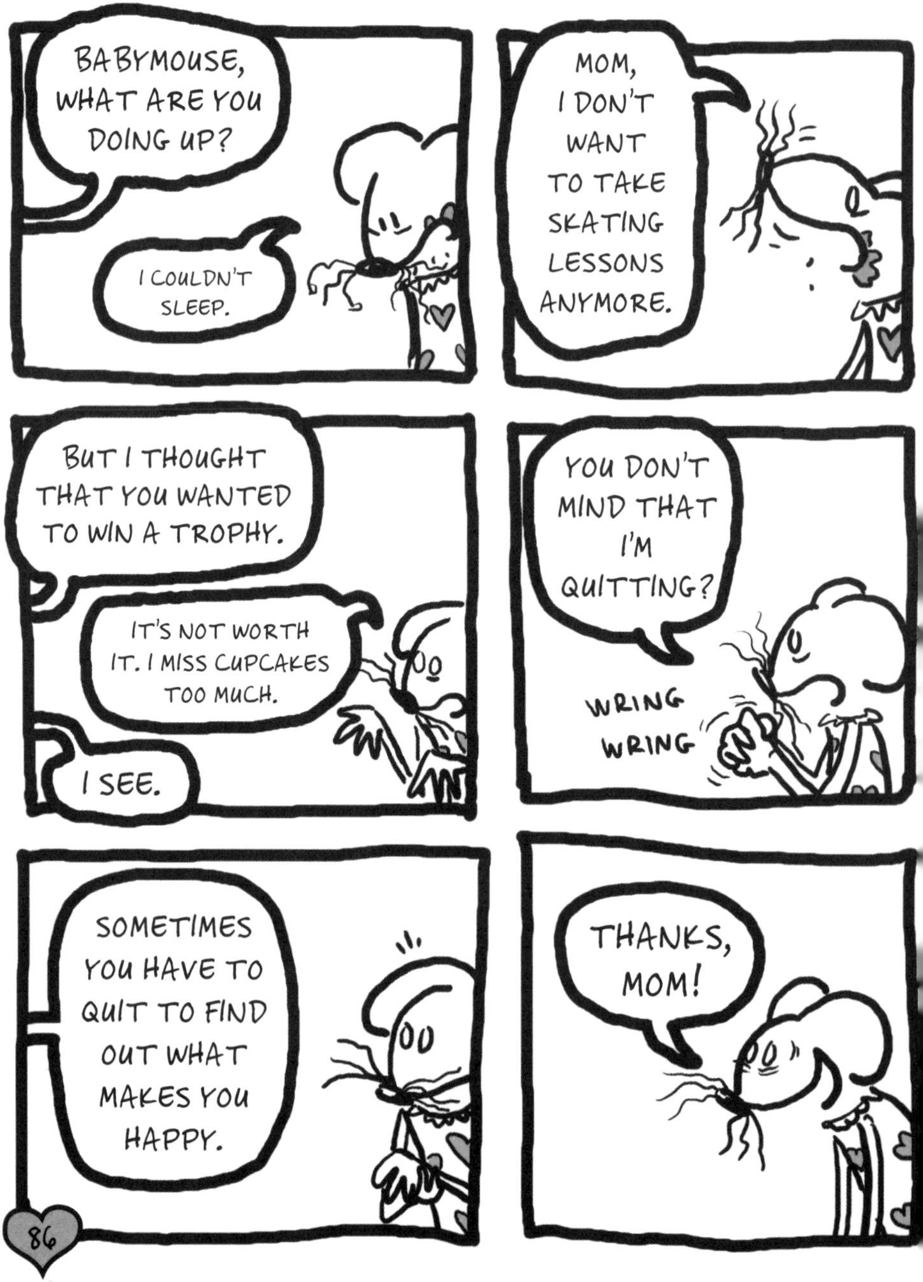
BABYMOUSE, WHAT ARE YOU DOING UP?
I COULDN'T SLEEP.
MOM, I DON'T WANT TO TAKE SKATING LESSONS ANYMORE.
BUT I THOUGHT THAT YOU WANTED TO WIN A TROPHY.
IT'S NOT WORTH IT. I MISS CUPCAKES TOO MUCH.
I SEE.
YOU DON'T MIND THAT I'M QUITTING?
WRING
WRING
SOMETIMES YOU HAVE TO QUIT TO FIND OUT WHAT MAKES YOU HAPPY.
THANKS, MOM!

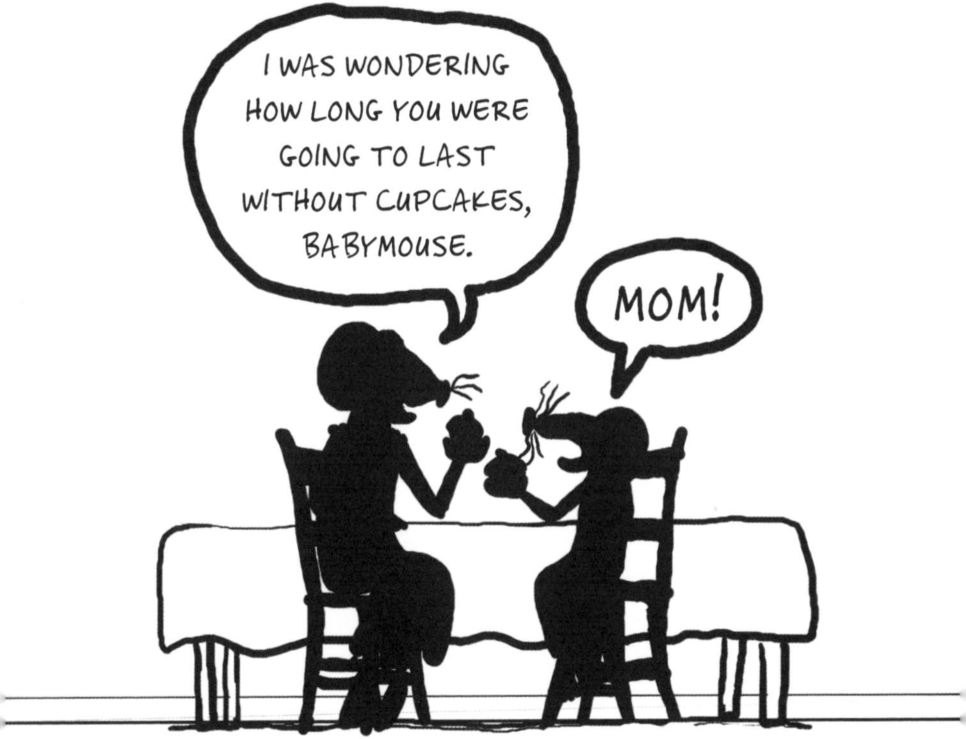
I WAS WONDERING HOW LONG YOU WERE GOING TO LAST WITHOUT CUPCAKES, BABYMOUSE.
MOM!

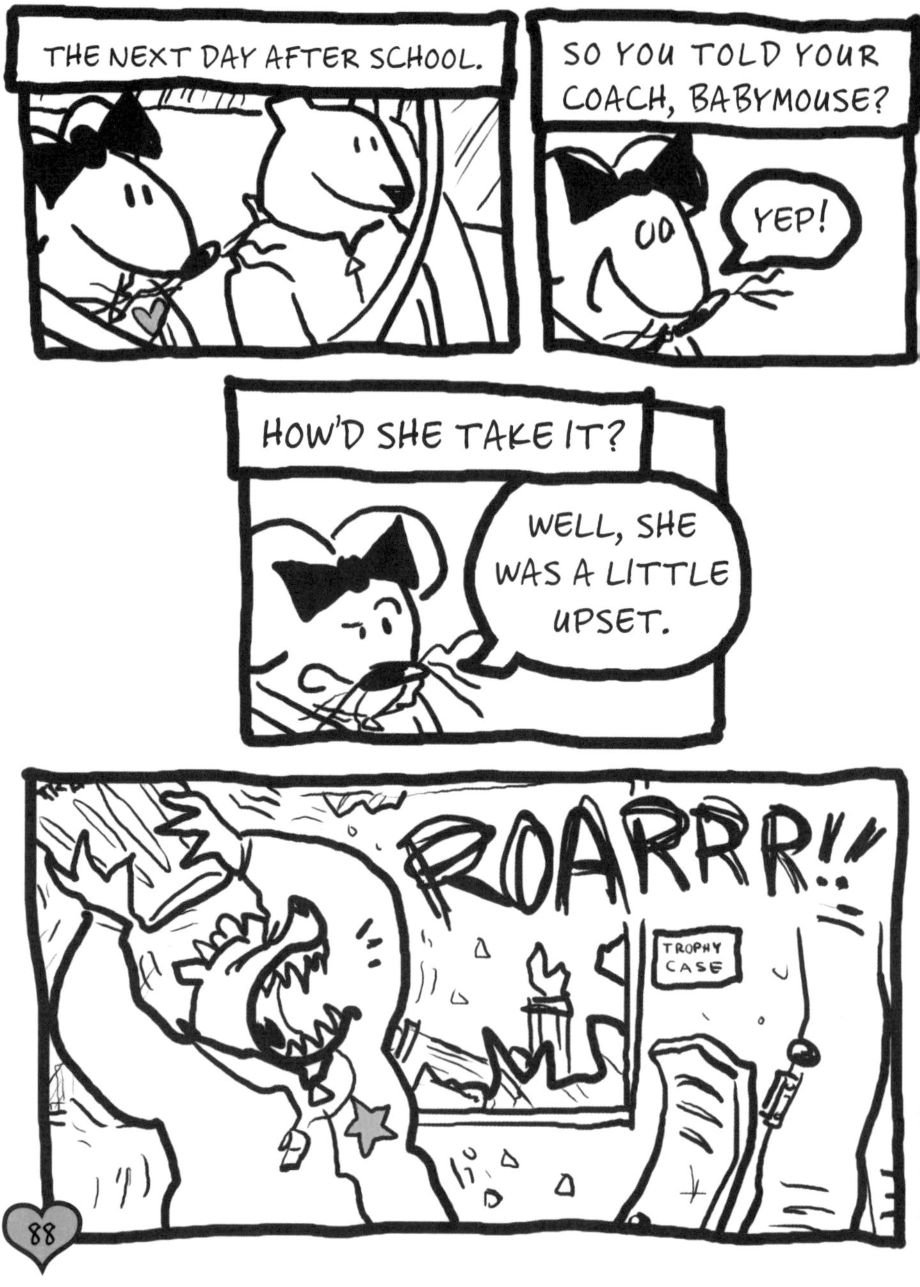
THE NEXT DAY AFTER SCHOOL.
SO YOU TOLD YOUR COACH, BABYMOUSE?
YEP!
HOW'D SHE TAKE IT?
WELL, SHE WAS A LITTLE UPSET.
ROARRR!!
TROPHY CASE

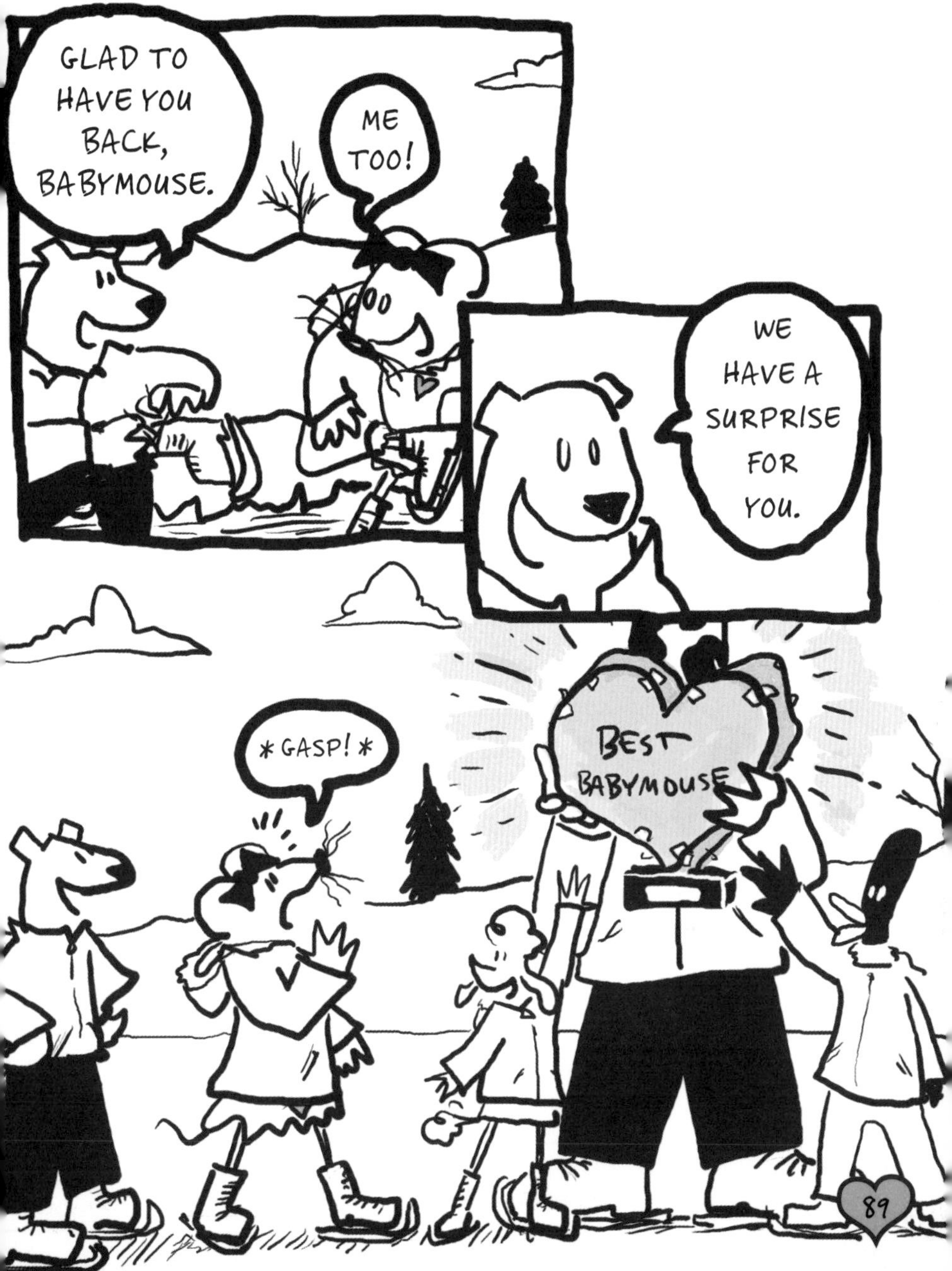
GLAD TO HAVE YOU BACK, BABYMOUSE.
ME TOO!
WE HAVE A SURPRISE FOR YOU.
GASP!
BEST BABYMOUSE

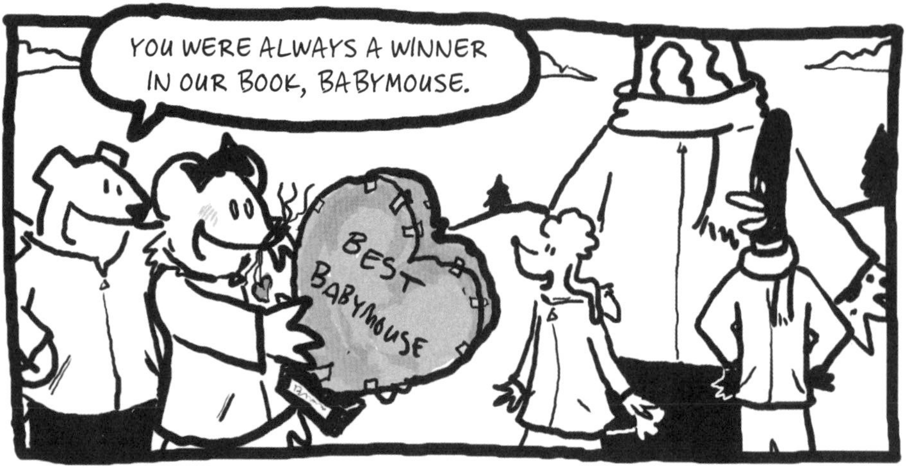
YOU WERE ALWAYS A WINNER IN OUR BOOK, BABYMOUSE.
BEST BABYMOUSE

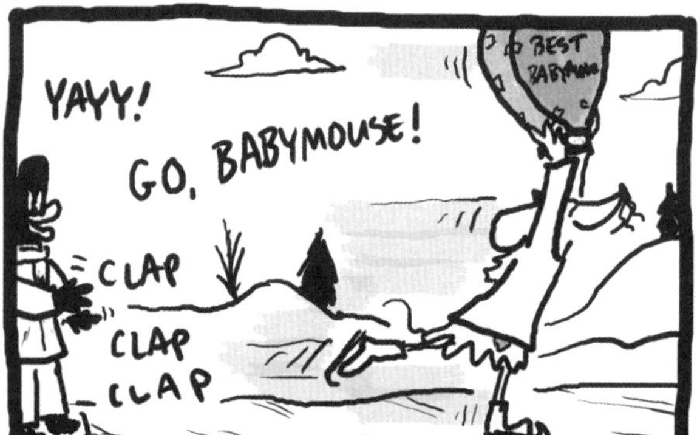
BEST BABYMOUSE
YAYY!
GO, BABYMOUSE!
CLAP
CLAP
CLAP

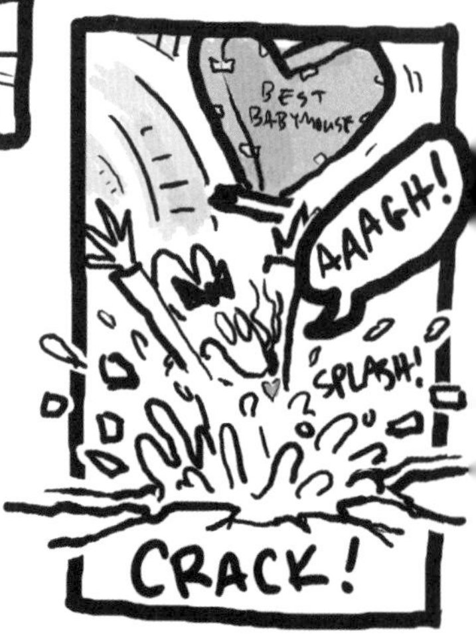
BEST BABYMOUSE
AAAGH!
SPLASH!
CRACK!

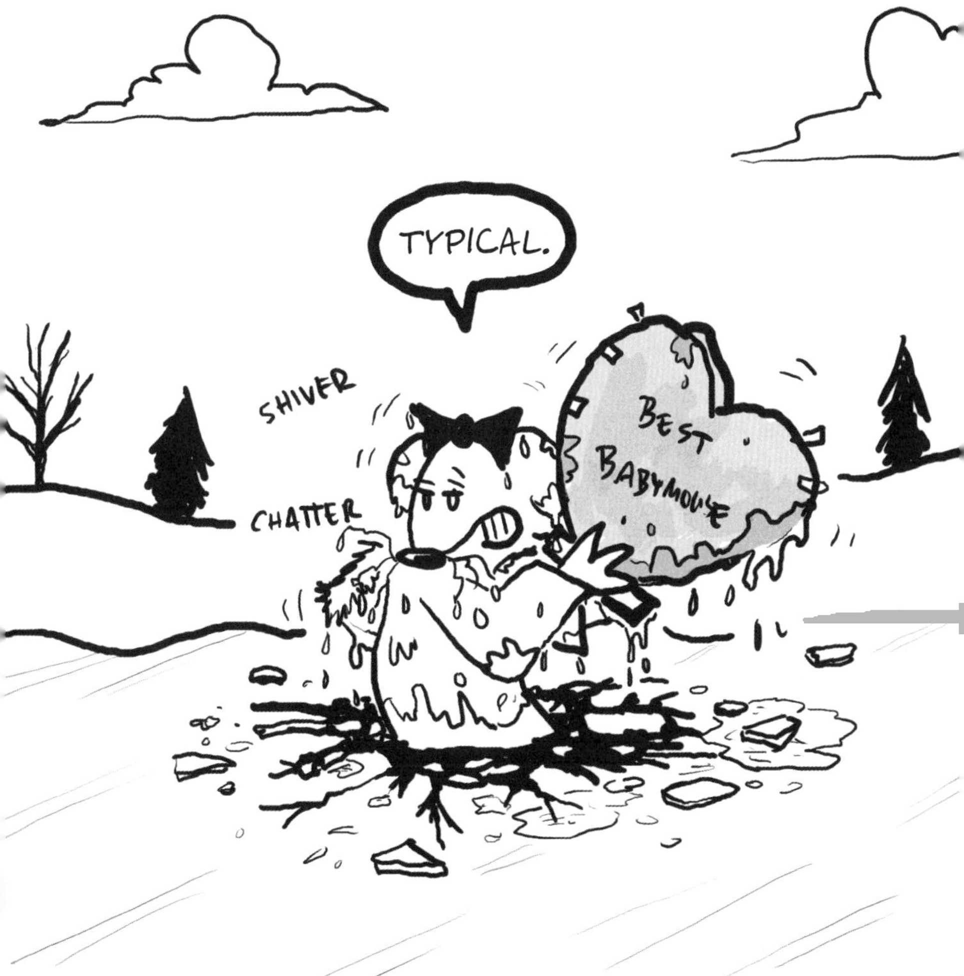
TYPICAL.
SHIVER
CHATTER
BEST BABYMOUSE

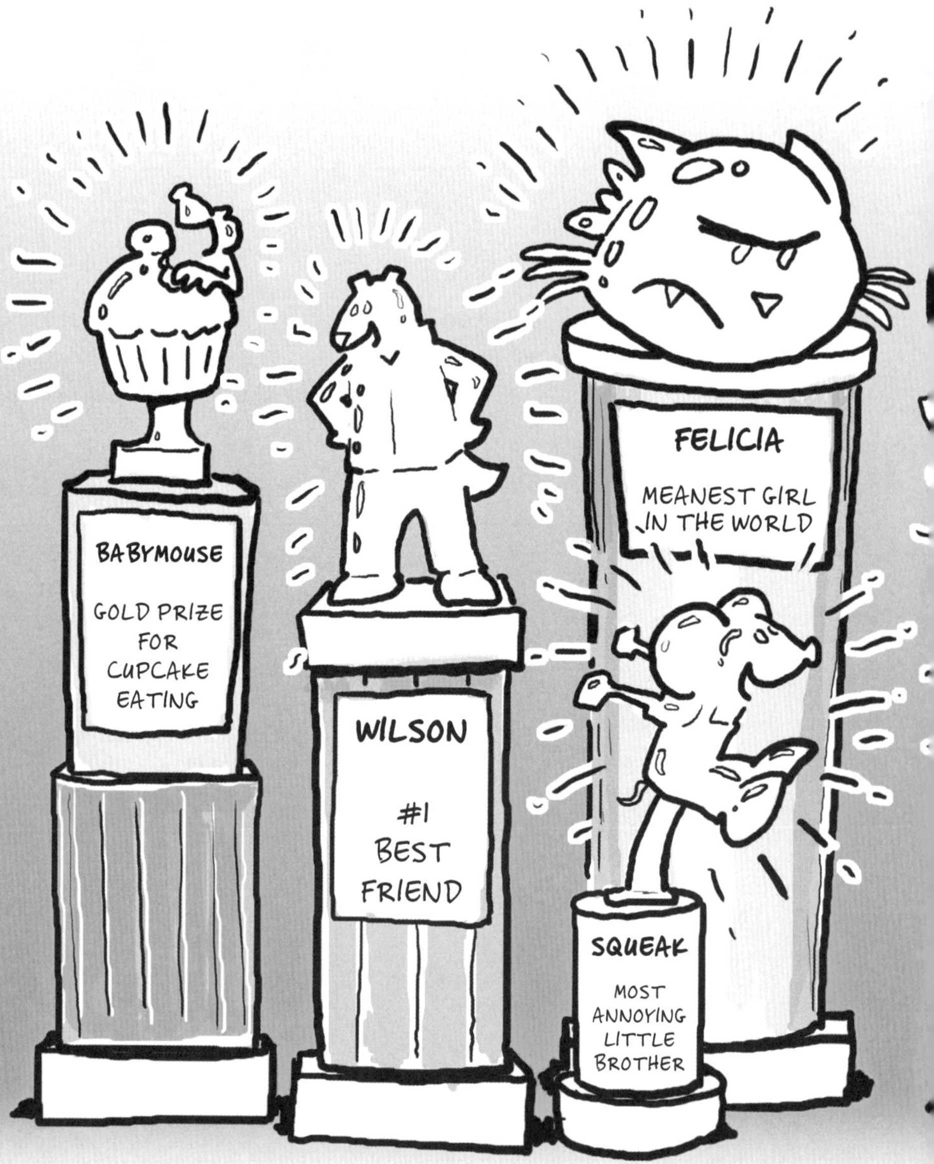
BABYMOUSE
GOLD PRIZE FOR CUPCAKE EATING
WILSON
#1 BEST FRIEND
FELICIA
MEANEST GIRL IN THE WORLD
SQUEAK
MOST ANNOYING LITTLE BROTHER

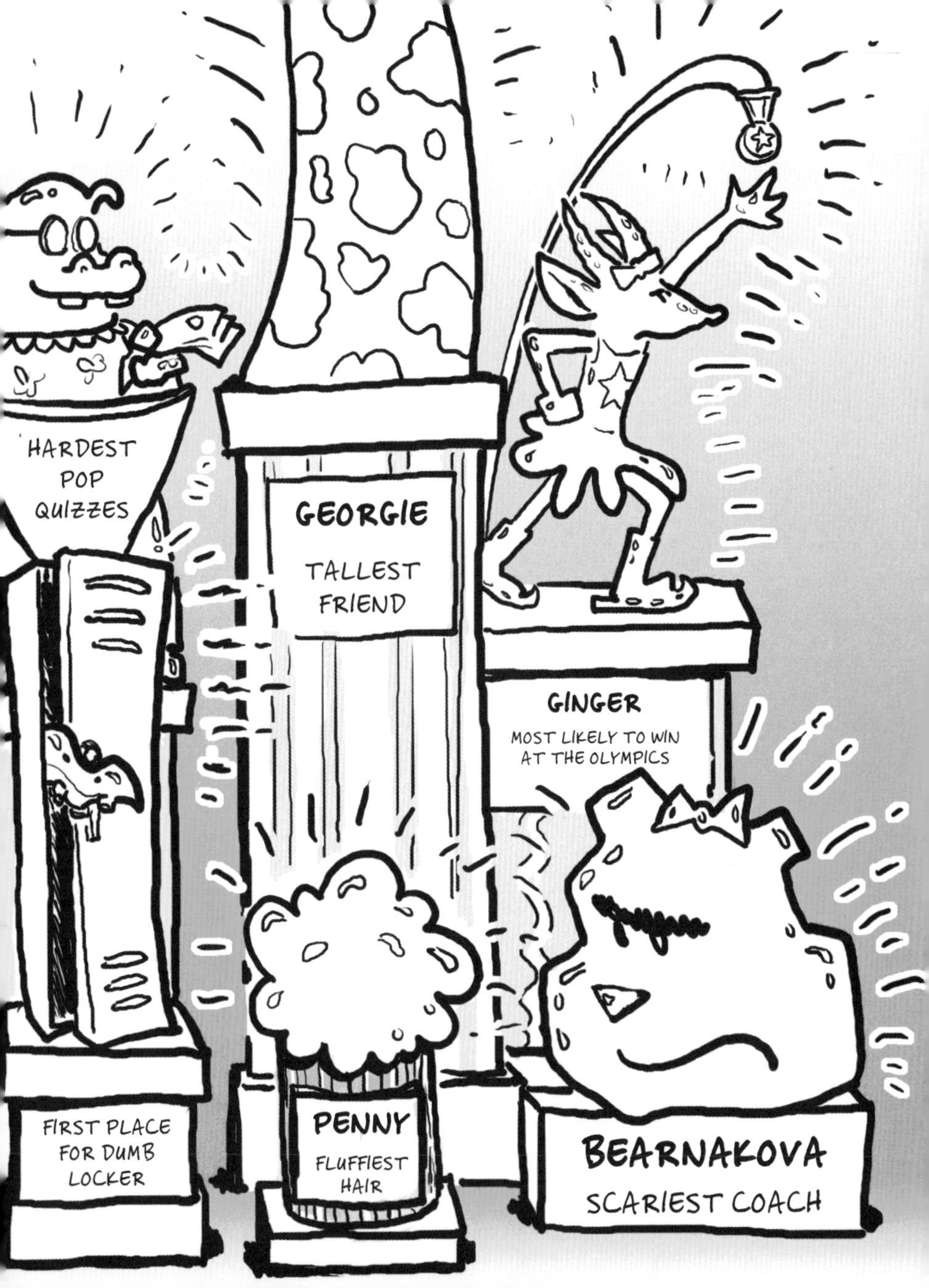
HARDEST POP QUIZZES
GEORGIE
TALLEST FRIEND
GINGER
MOST LIKELY TO WIN AT THE OLYMPICS
FIRST PLACE FOR DUMB LOCKER
PENNY
FLUFFIEST HAIR
BEARNAKOVA
SCARIEST COACH

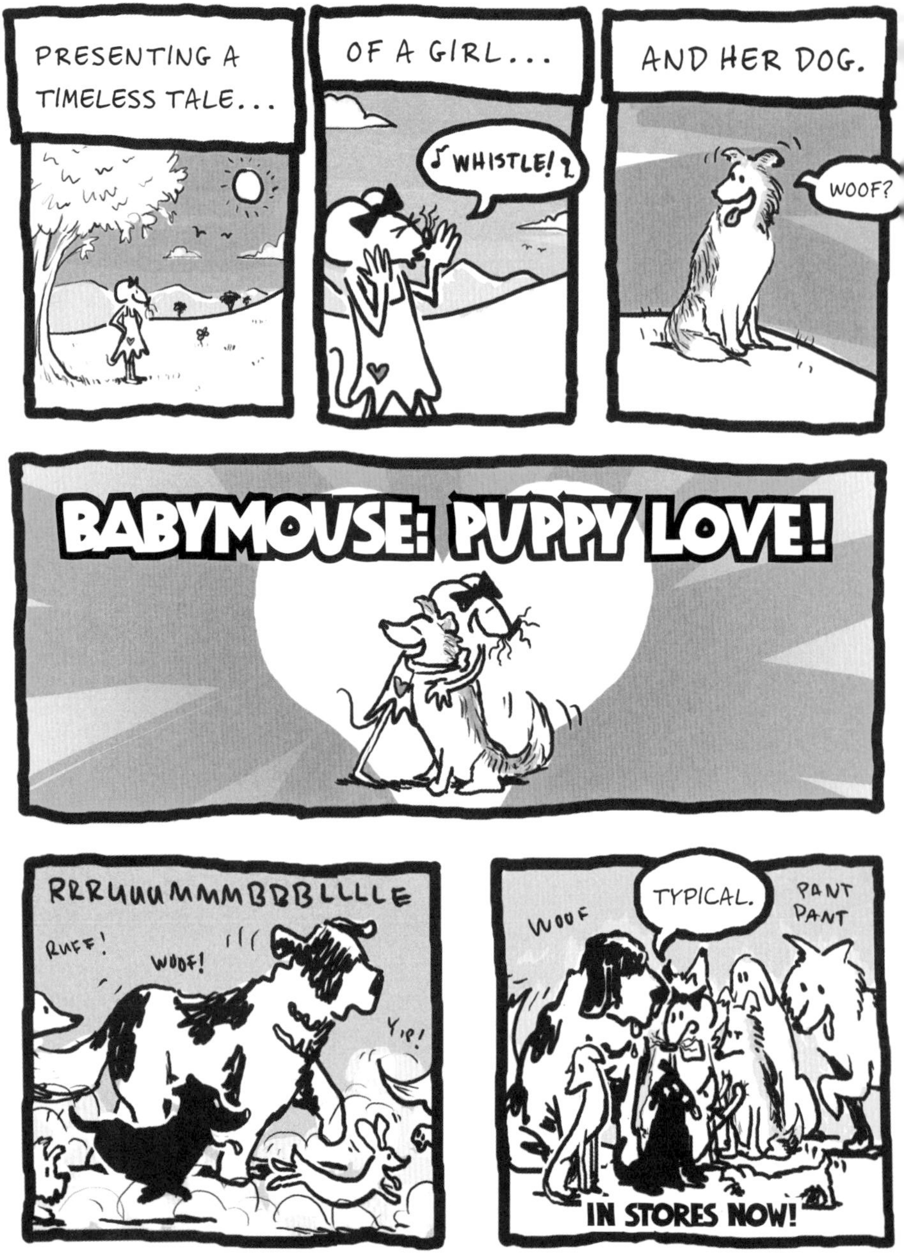
PRESENTING A TIMELESS TALE...
OF A GIRL...
WHISTLE!
AND HER DOG.
WOOF?
BABYMOUSE: PUPPY LOVE!
RRRUUUMMMBBBLLLLE
RUFF!
WOOF!
YIP!
WOOF
TYPICAL.
PANT PANT
IN STORES NOW!

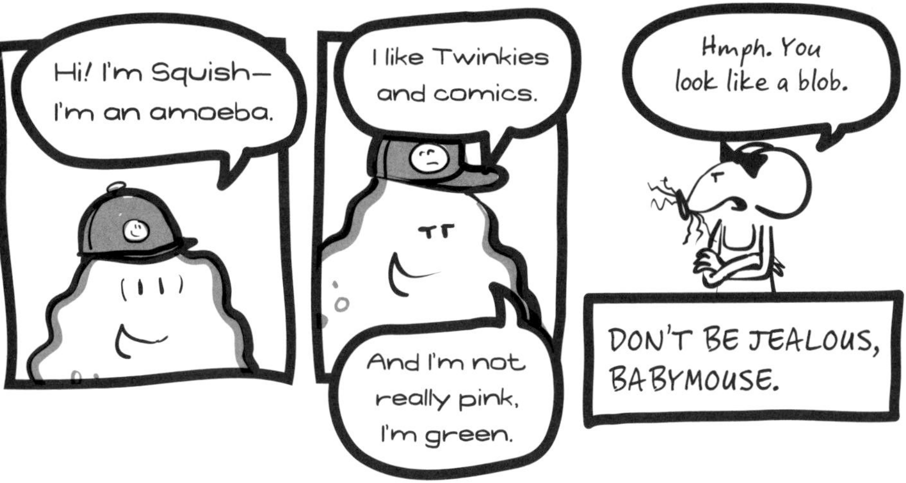
Hi! I'm Squish—
I'm an amoeba.
I like Twinkies
and comics.
And I'm not
really pink,
I'm green.
Hmph. You
look like a blob.
DON'T BE JEALOUS,
BABYMOUSE.

READ ABOUT
SQUISH'S AMAZING ADVENTURES IN:

#1 SQUISH: Super Amoeba

#2 SQUISH: Brave New Pond

#3 SQUISH: The Power of the Parasite

#4 SQUISH: Captain Disaster

#5 SQUISH: Game On!

AND COMING SOON:

#6 SQUISH: Fear the Amoeba

★ "IF EVER A NEW SERIES DESERVED TO GO VIRAL, THIS ONE DOES."
—*KIRKUS REVIEWS*, STARRED

If you like Babymouse,
you'll love these other great books
by Jennifer L. Holm!

THE BOSTON JANE TRILOGY

EIGHTH GRADE IS MAKING ME SICK

MIDDLE SCHOOL IS WORSE THAN MEATLOAF

OUR ONLY MAY AMELIA

PENNY FROM HEAVEN

TURTLE IN PARADISE

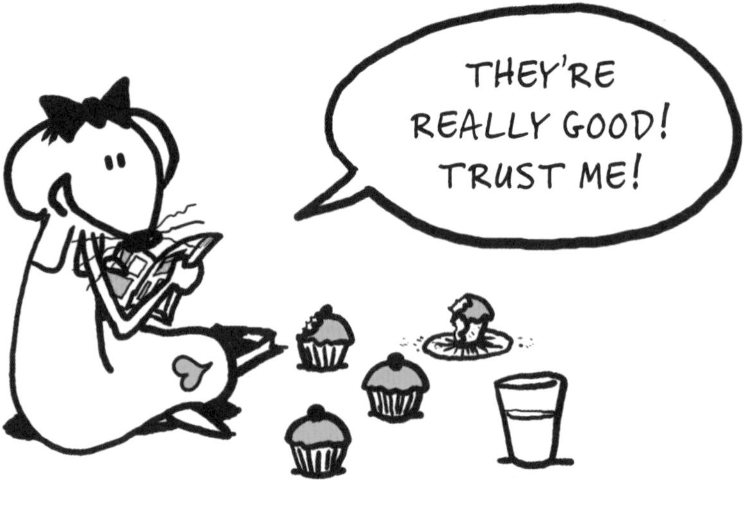
THEY'RE REALLY GOOD! TRUST ME!